WITHDRAWN

Algon

CAMPFIRE

KALYANI NAVYUG MEDIA PVT LTD
New Delhi

Jason and the Argonauts

Sitting around the Campfire, telling the story, were:

WORDSMITH **DAN WHITEHEAD**

ILLUSTRATOR **SANKHA BANERJEE**

COLOURIST **ANIL C K**

LETTERER **BHAVNATH CHAUDHARY**

EDITOR **ASWATHY SENAN**

PRODUCTION CONTROLLER **VISHAL SHARMA**

COVER ART **SANKHA BANERJEE**

DESIGNER **VIJAY SHARMA**

ART DIRECTOR **RAJESH NAGULAKONDA**

CAMPFIRE™

www.campfire.co.in

Published by Kalyani Navyug Media Pvt Ltd
101 C, Shiv House, Hari Nagar Ashram, New Delhi 110014, India

ISBN: 978-81-907515-1-3

Printed in India at Rave India

About the author

Born in 1973, Dan Whitehead was obsessed with films, comic books, and video games from a very young age. Since 1991 he has been writing for and about the entertainment industry, working with *Commodore Amiga* magazine, Guinness World Records, and *Movie Insider* magazine. He is currently working as the editor with *Megaton*, a video game magazine and website for children. His most treasured possession is a cinema programme for *King Kong*, signed by Ray Harryhausen who, in fact, worked on the animations in the 1963 film *Jason and the Argonauts*.

About the artist

A university topper in Visual Arts, Sankha Banerjee draws his inspiration from a variety of sources – from cave art to Pixar Studios, from Sukumar Ray to Satyajit Ray, and many others. He maintains an avid interest in photography, film, installation, illustration, and other visual art mediums which enable him to create vivid and wholesome artwork to stimulate young minds. *Legend: The Labours of Heracles*, *The Wind in the Willows*, and *Nelson Mandela* are a few titles that he has illustrated for Campfire Graphic Novels. Banerjee also actively participates in workshops organised for comic lovers, and finds interacting with kids in such spaces inspiring for his creative process.

Jason

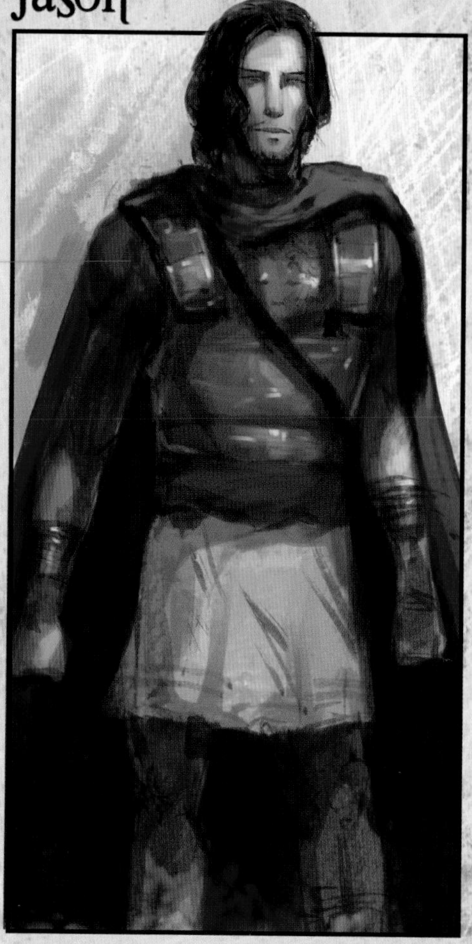

Medea

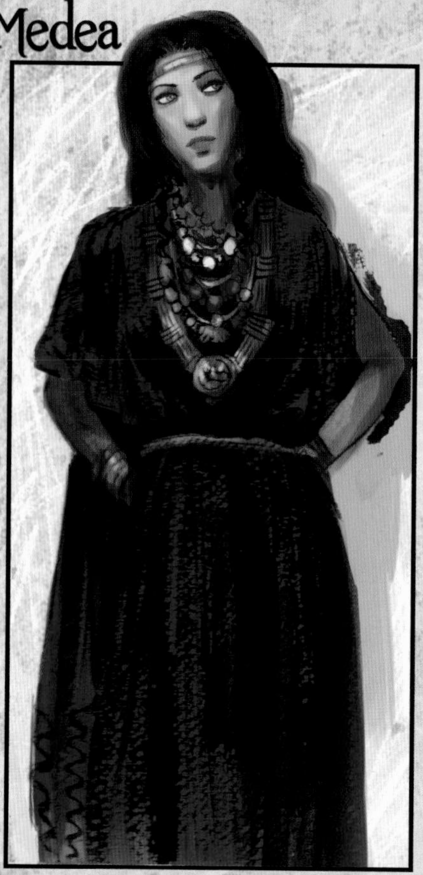

Pelias

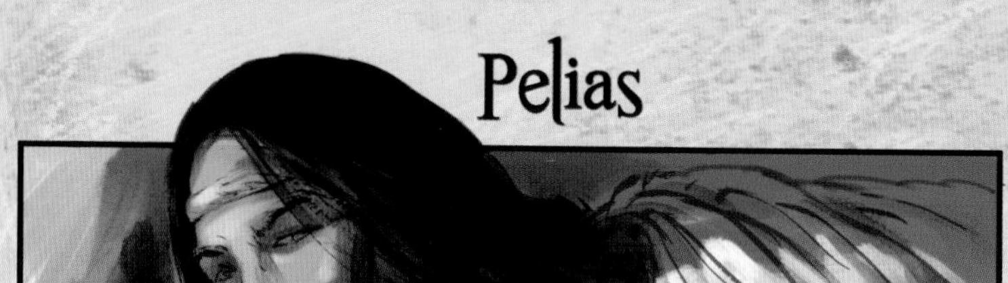

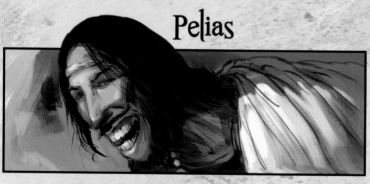

Acastus

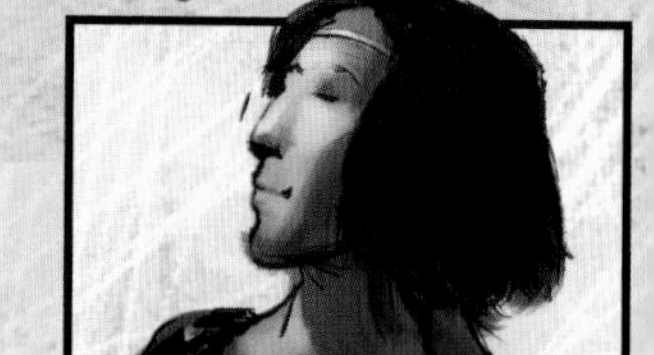

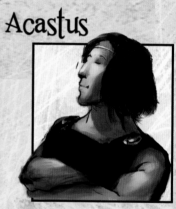

Hera

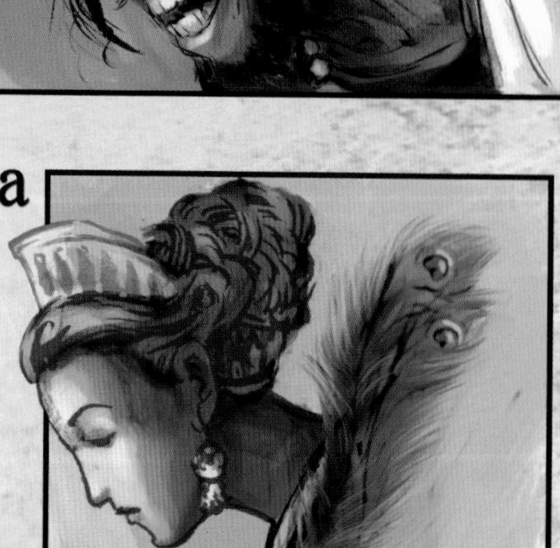

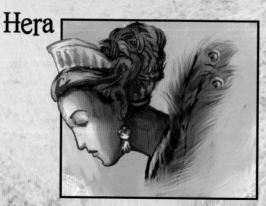

Orpheus

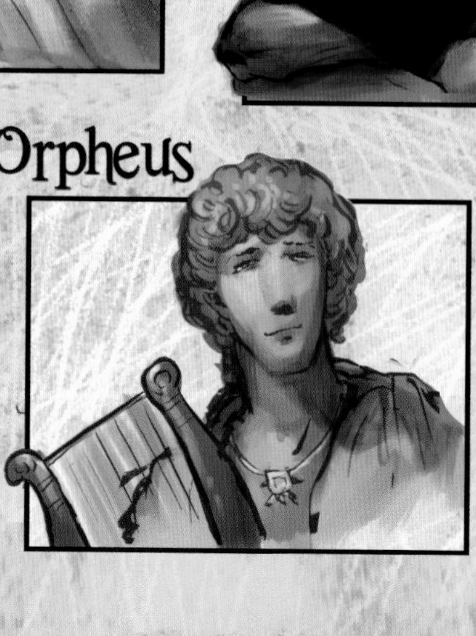

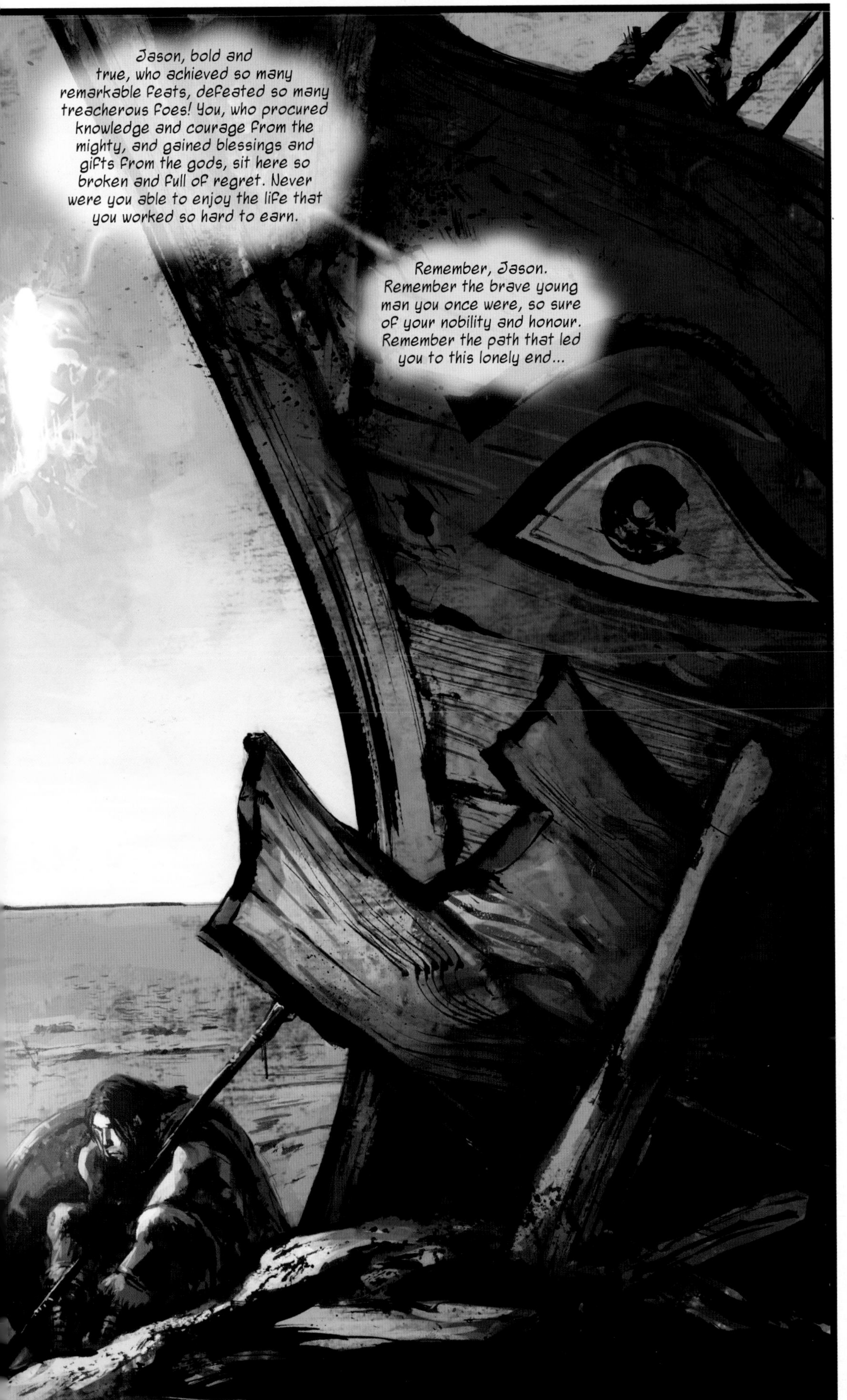
Jason, bold and true, who achieved so many remarkable feats, defeated so many treacherous foes! You, who procured knowledge and courage from the mighty, and gained blessings and gifts from the gods, sit here so broken and full of regret. Never were you able to enjoy the life that you worked so hard to earn.
Remember, Jason. Remember the brave young man you once were, so sure of your nobility and honour. Remember the path that led you to this lonely end...

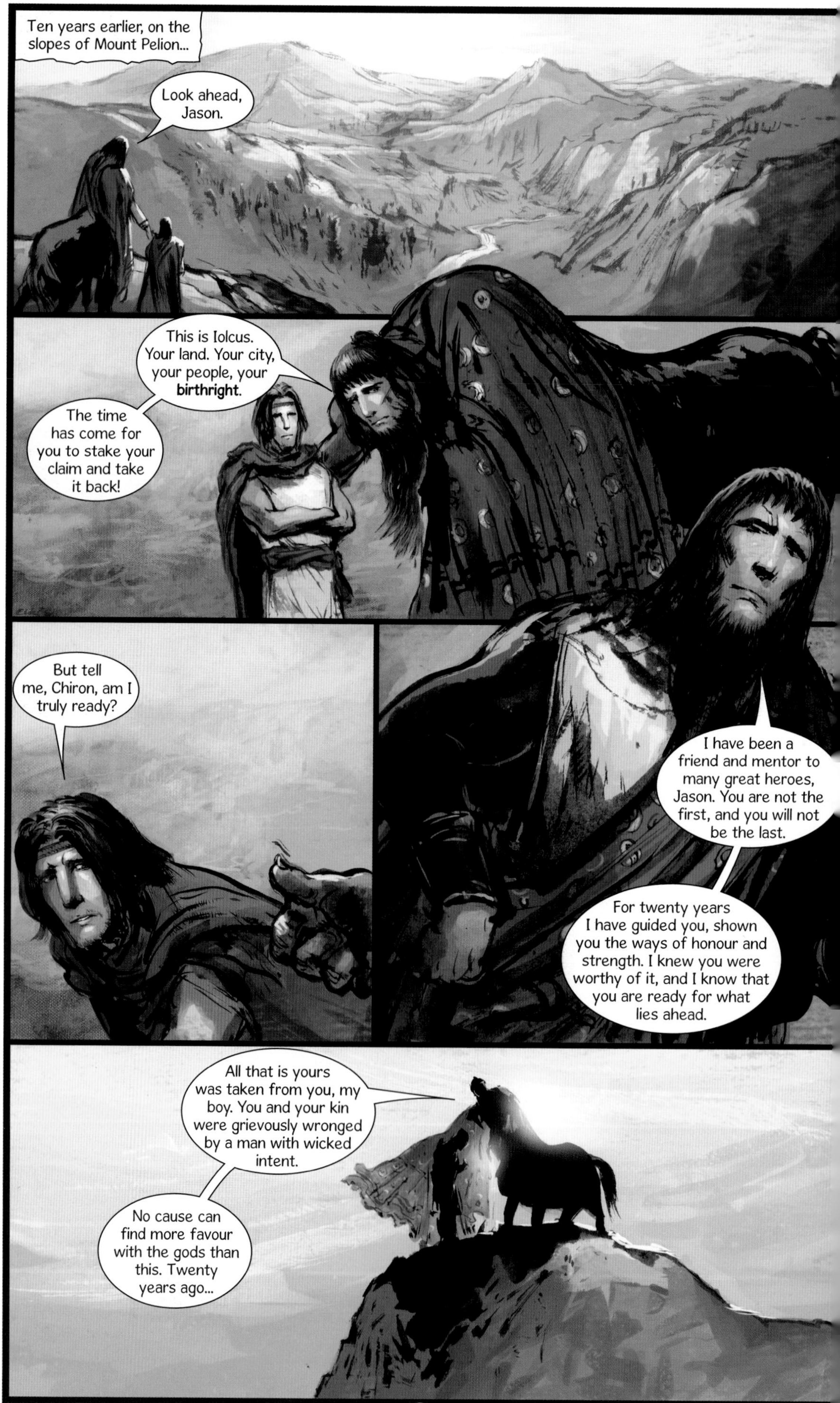

Ten years earlier, on the slopes of Mount Pelion...
Look ahead, Jason.
This is Iolcus. Your land. Your city, your people, your **birthright**.
The time has come for you to stake your claim and take it back!
But tell me, Chiron, am I truly ready?
I have been a friend and mentor to many great heroes, Jason. You are not the first, and you will not be the last.
For twenty years I have guided you, shown you the ways of honour and strength. I knew you were worthy of it, and I know that you are ready for what lies ahead.
All that is yours was taken from you, my boy. You and your kin were grievously wronged by a man with wicked intent.
No cause can find more favour with the gods than this. Twenty years ago...

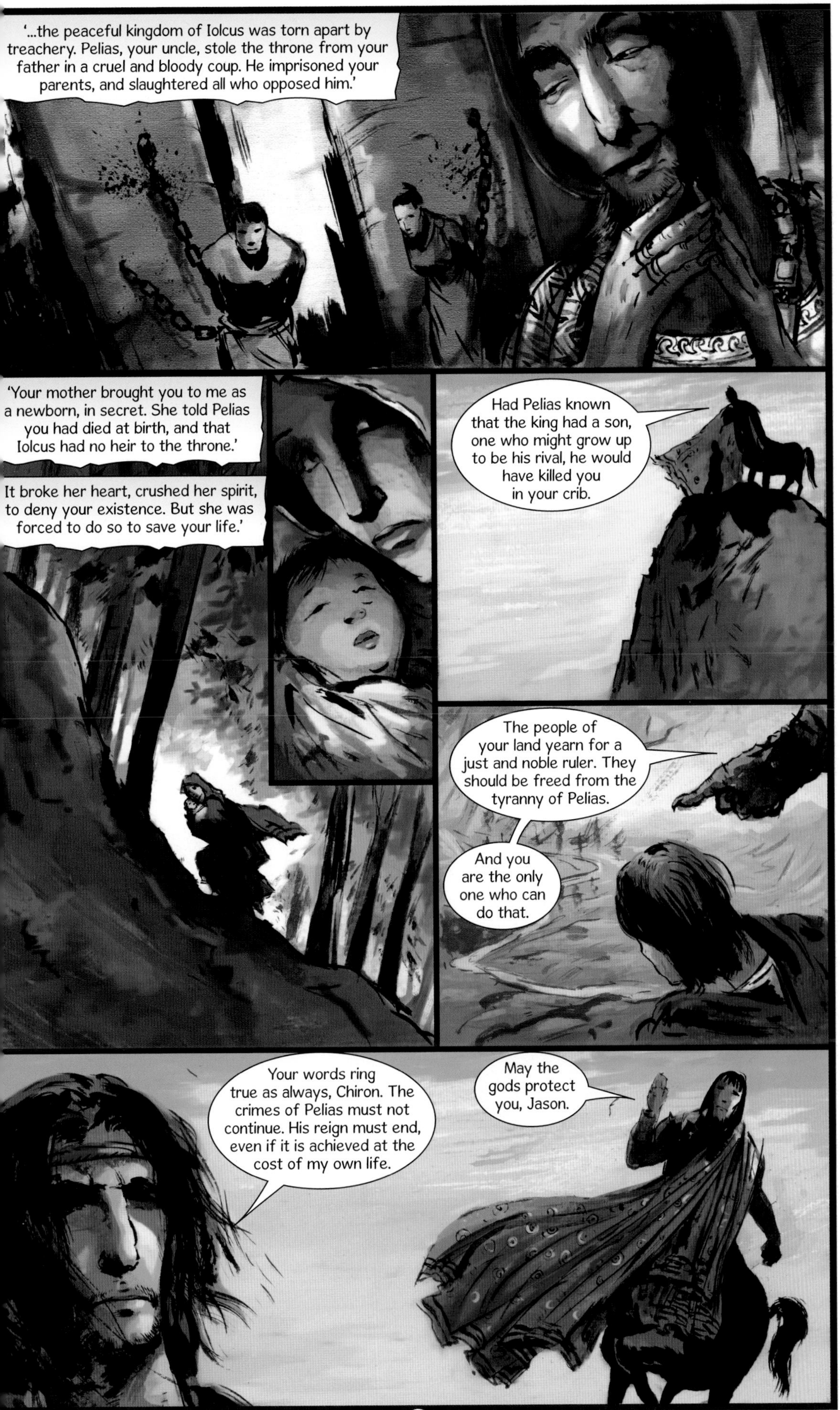
'...the peaceful kingdom of Iolcus was torn apart by treachery. Pelias, your uncle, stole the throne from your father in a cruel and bloody coup. He imprisoned your parents, and slaughtered all who opposed him.'
'Your mother brought you to me as a newborn, in secret. She told Pelias you had died at birth, and that Iolcus had no heir to the throne.'
It broke her heart, crushed her spirit, to deny your existence. But she was forced to do so to save your life.'
Had Pelias known that the king had a son, one who might grow up to be his rival, he would have killed you in your crib.
The people of your land yearn for a just and noble ruler. They should be freed from the tyranny of Pelias.
And you are the only one who can do that.
Your words ring true as always, Chiron. The crimes of Pelias must not continue. His reign must end, even if it is achieved at the cost of my own life.
May the gods protect you, Jason.

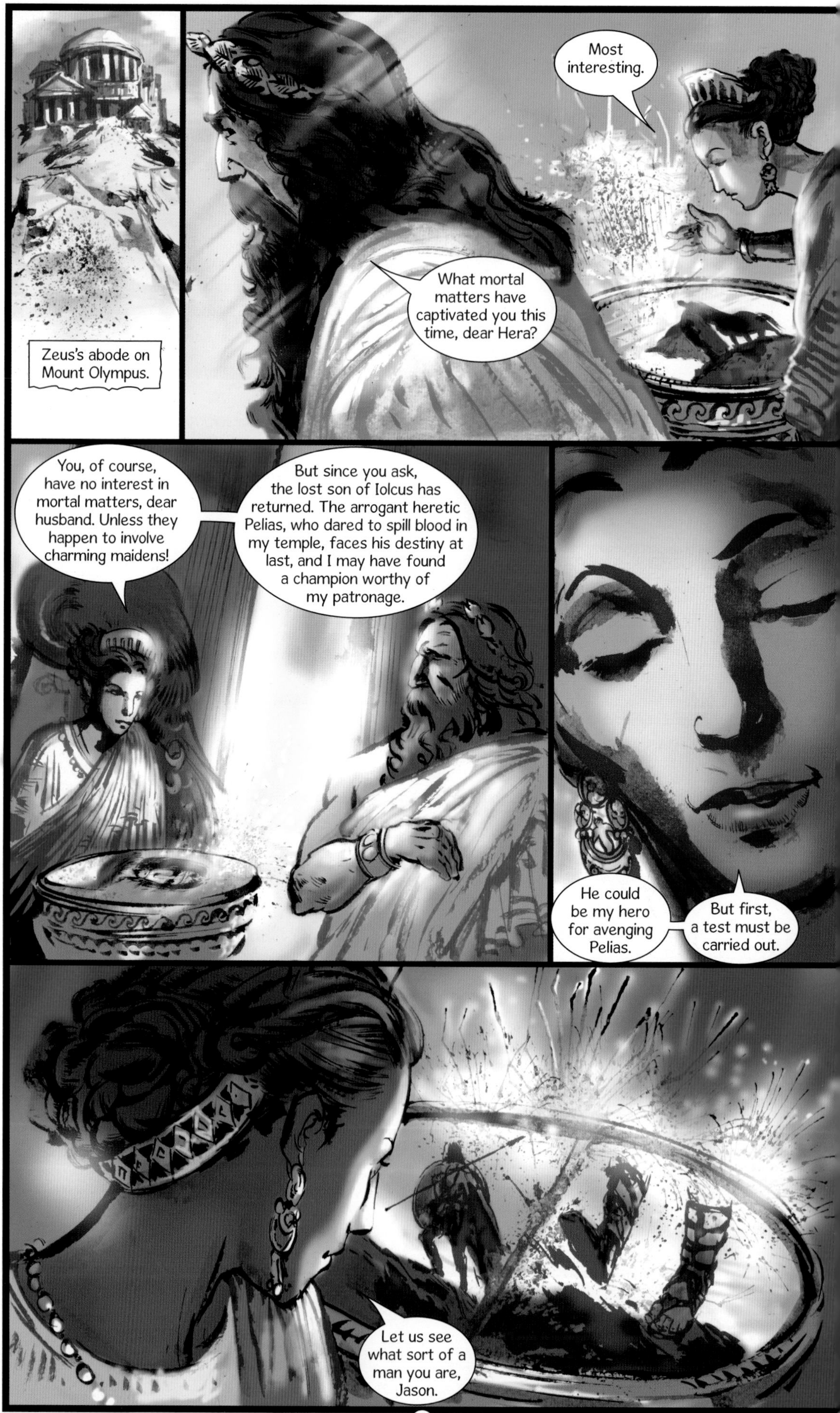
Zeus's abode on Mount Olympus.
Most interesting.
What mortal matters have captivated you this time, dear Hera?
You, of course, have no interest in mortal matters, dear husband. Unless they happen to involve charming maidens!
But since you ask, the lost son of Iolcus has returned. The arrogant heretic Pelias, who dared to spill blood in my temple, faces his destiny at last, and I may have found a champion worthy of my patronage.
He could be my hero for avenging Pelias.
But first, a test must be carried out.
Let us see what sort of a man you are, Jason.

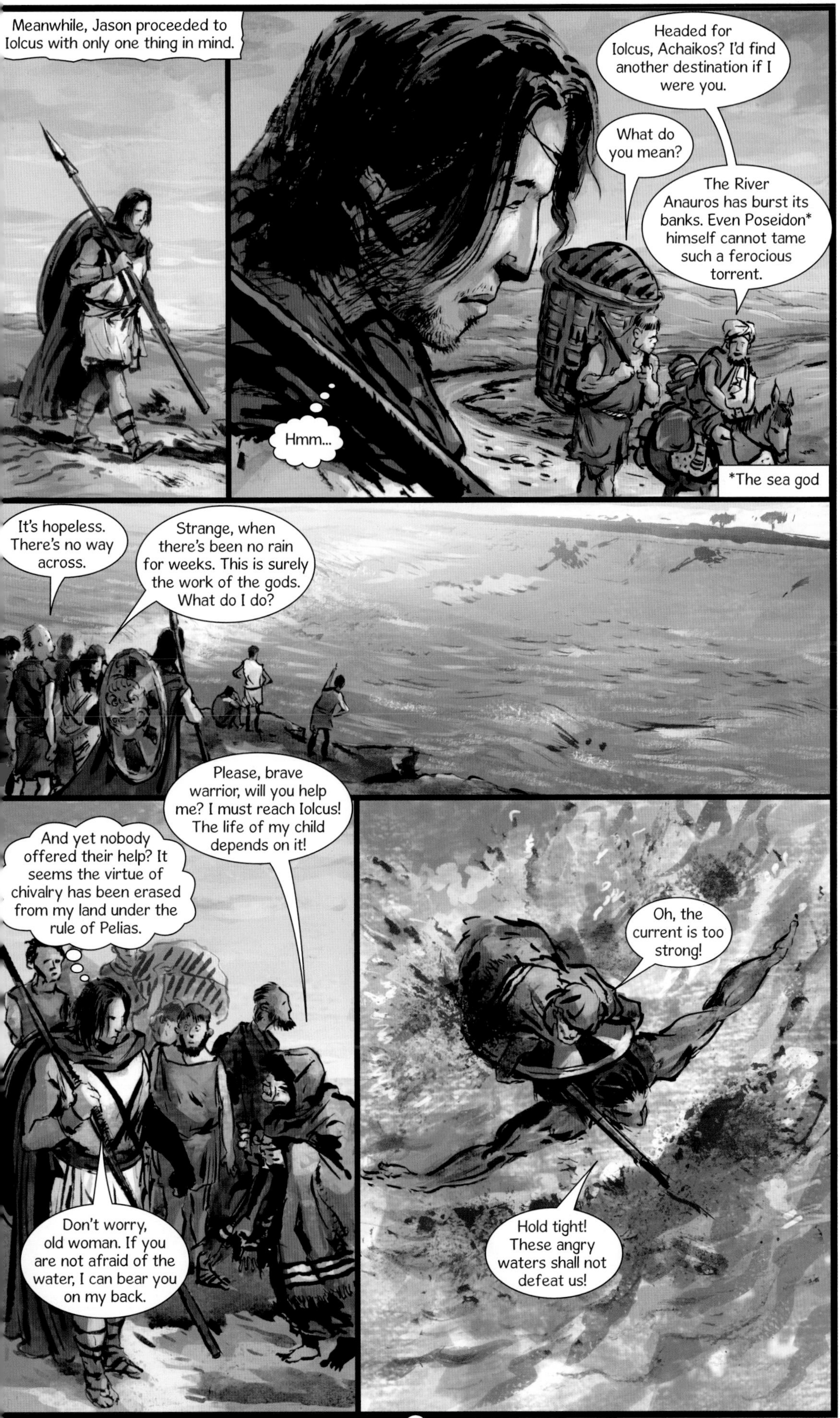

Meanwhile, Jason proceeded to Iolcus with only one thing in mind.
Headed for Iolcus, Achaikos? I'd find another destination if I were you.
What do you mean?
The River Anauros has burst its banks. Even Poseidon* himself cannot tame such a ferocious torrent.
Hmm...
*The sea god
It's hopeless. There's no way across.
Strange, when there's been no rain for weeks. This is surely the work of the gods. What do I do?
Please, brave warrior, will you help me? I must reach Iolcus! The life of my child depends on it!
And yet nobody offered their help? It seems the virtue of chivalry has been erased from my land under the rule of Pelias.
Don't worry, old woman. If you are not afraid of the water, I can bear you on my back.
Oh, the current is too strong!
Hold tight! These angry waters shall not defeat us!

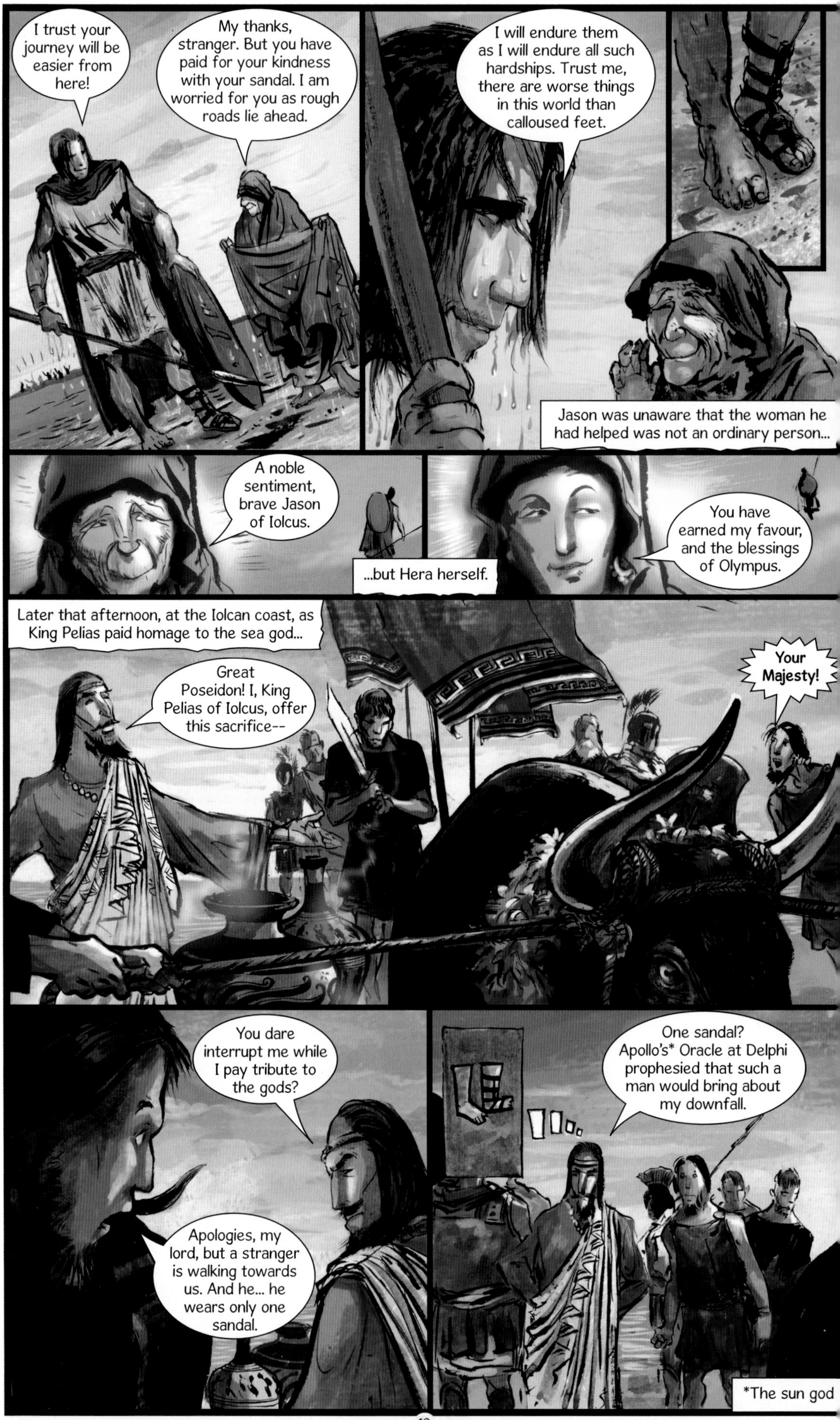
I trust your journey will be easier from here!
My thanks, stranger. But you have paid for your kindness with your sandal. I am worried for you as rough roads lie ahead.
I will endure them as I will endure all such hardships. Trust me, there are worse things in this world than calloused feet.
Jason was unaware that the woman he had helped was not an ordinary person...
A noble sentiment, brave Jason of Iolcus.
...but Hera herself.
You have earned my favour, and the blessings of Olympus.
Later that afternoon, at the Iolcan coast, as King Pelias paid homage to the sea god...
Great Poseidon! I, King Pelias of Iolcus, offer this sacrifice--
Your Majesty!
You dare interrupt me while I pay tribute to the gods?
Apologies, my lord, but a stranger is walking towards us. And he... he wears only one sandal.
One sandal? Apollo's* Oracle at Delphi prophesied that such a man would bring about my downfall.
*The sun god

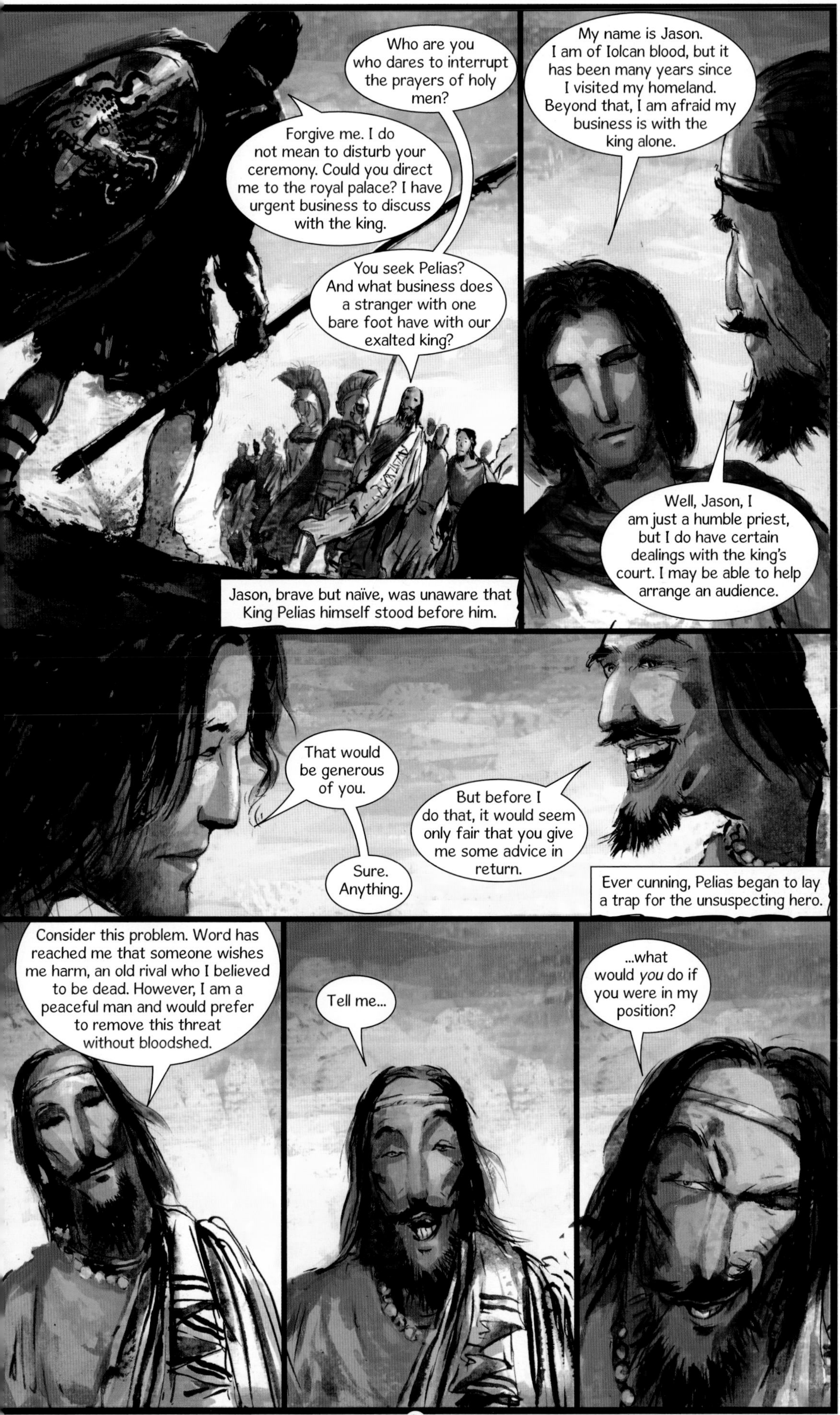
Who are you who dares to interrupt the prayers of holy men?
Forgive me. I do not mean to disturb your ceremony. Could you direct me to the royal palace? I have urgent business to discuss with the king.
You seek Pelias? And what business does a stranger with one bare foot have with our exalted king?
Jason, brave but naïve, was unaware that King Pelias himself stood before him.
My name is Jason. I am of Iolcan blood, but it has been many years since I visited my homeland. Beyond that, I am afraid my business is with the king alone.
Well, Jason, I am just a humble priest, but I do have certain dealings with the king's court. I may be able to help arrange an audience.
That would be generous of you.
But before I do that, it would seem only fair that you give me some advice in return.
Sure. Anything.
Ever cunning, Pelias began to lay a trap for the unsuspecting hero.
Consider this problem. Word has reached me that someone wishes me harm, an old rival who I believed to be dead. However, I am a peaceful man and would prefer to remove this threat without bloodshed.
Tell me...
...what would *you* do if you were in my position?

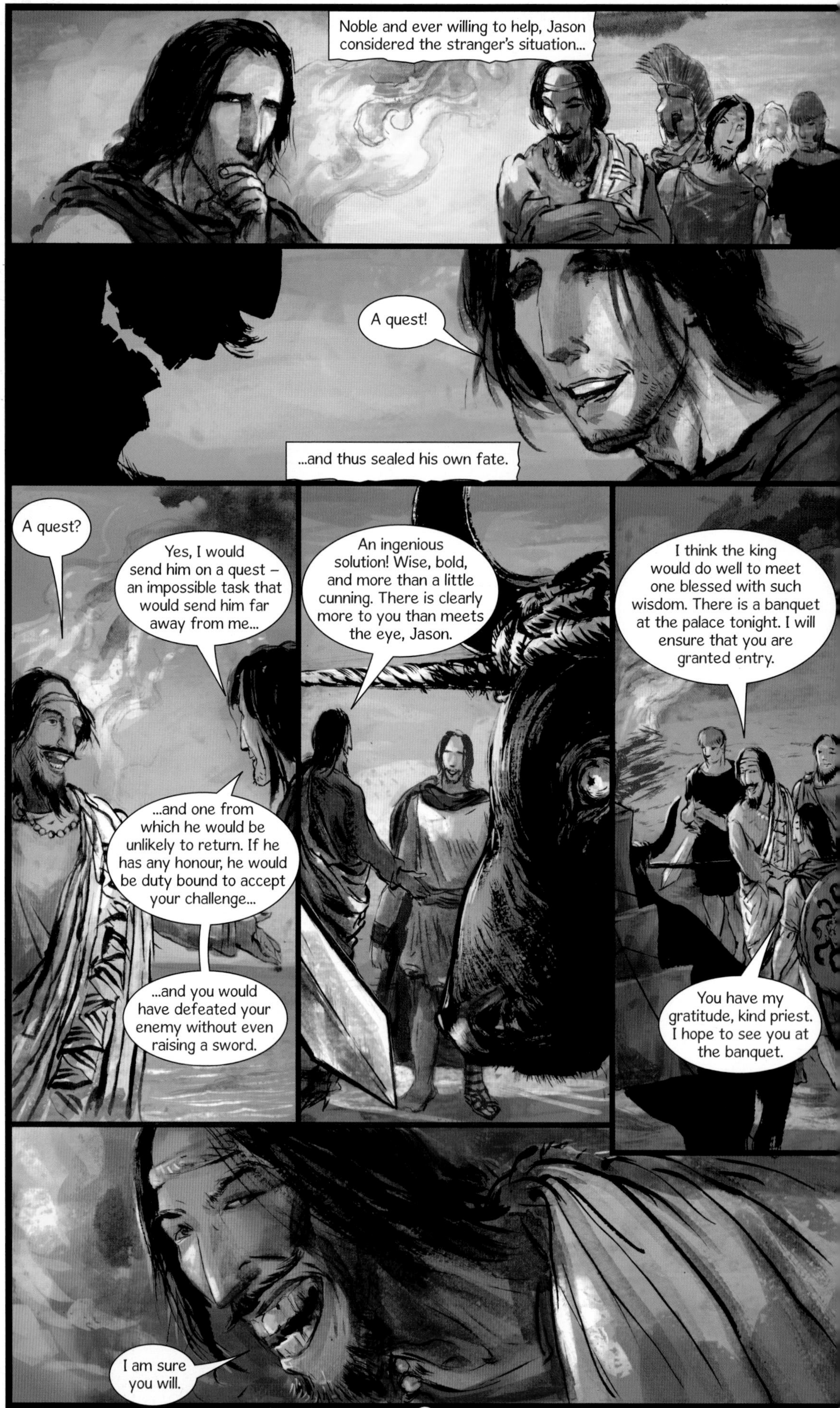

Noble and ever willing to help, Jason considered the stranger's situation...
A quest!
...and thus sealed his own fate.
A quest?
Yes, I would send him on a quest – an impossible task that would send him far away from me...
...and one from which he would be unlikely to return. If he has any honour, he would be duty bound to accept your challenge...
...and you would have defeated your enemy without even raising a sword.
An ingenious solution! Wise, bold, and more than a little cunning. There is clearly more to you than meets the eye, Jason.
I think the king would do well to meet one blessed with such wisdom. There is a banquet at the palace tonight. I will ensure that you are granted entry.
You have my gratitude, kind priest. I hope to see you at the banquet.
I am sure you will.

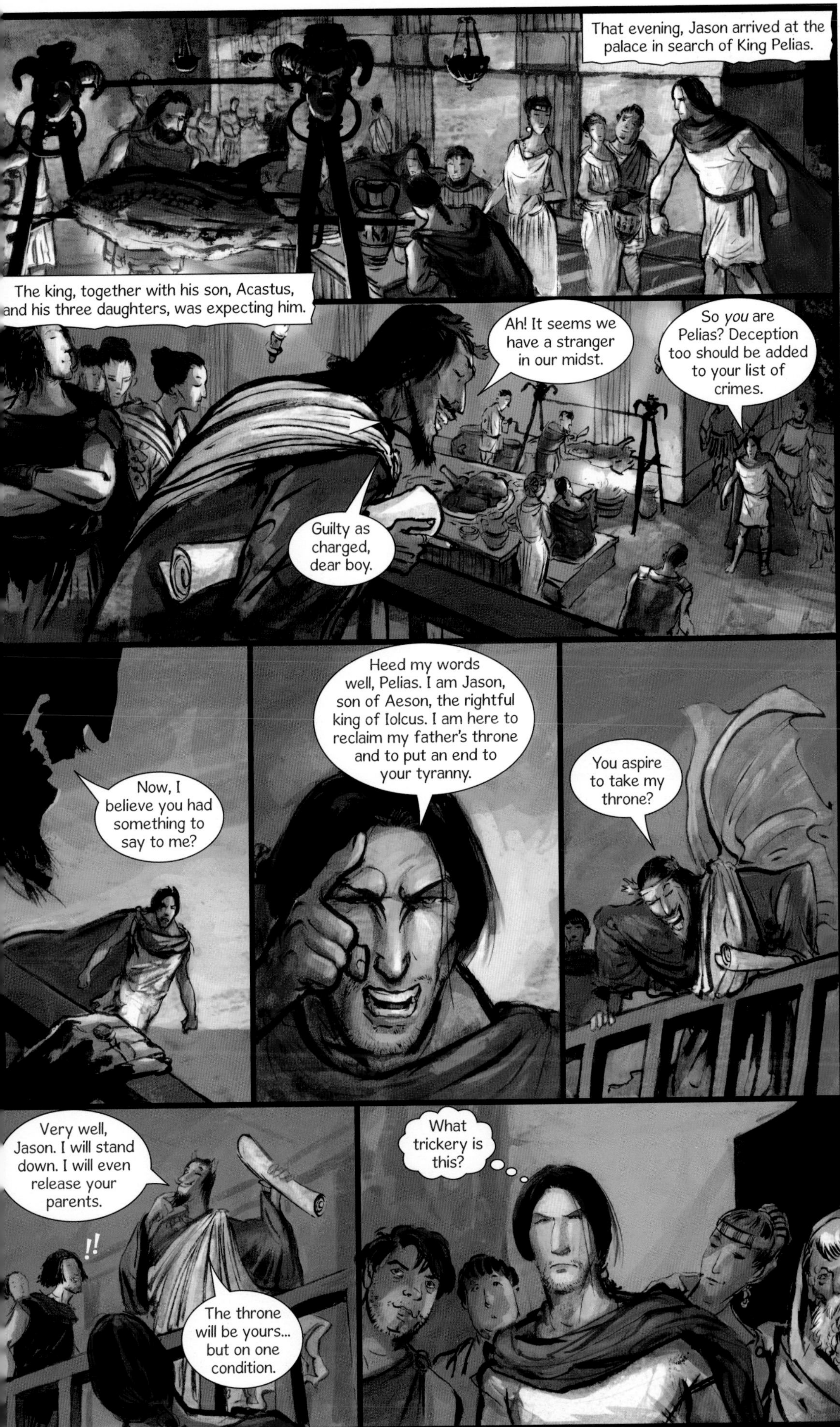
That evening, Jason arrived at the palace in search of King Pelias.
The king, together with his son, Acastus, and his three daughters, was expecting him.
Ah! It seems we have a stranger in our midst.
So *you* are Pelias? Deception too should be added to your list of crimes.
Guilty as charged, dear boy.
Now, I believe you had something to say to me?
Heed my words well, Pelias. I am Jason, son of Aeson, the rightful king of Iolcus. I am here to reclaim my father's throne and to put an end to your tyranny.
You aspire to take my throne?
Very well, Jason. I will stand down. I will even release your parents.
!!
The throne will be yours... but on one condition.
What trickery is this?

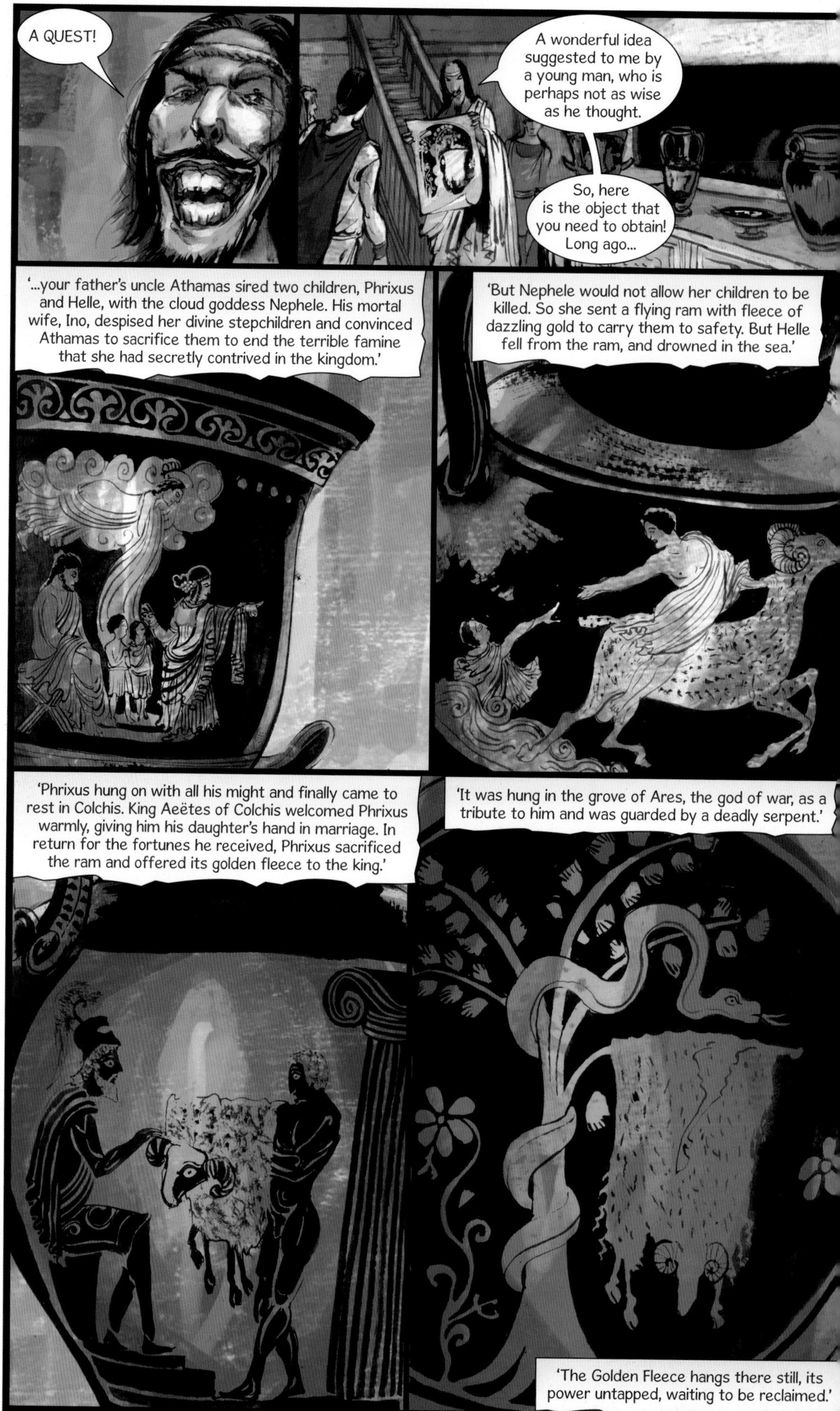
A QUEST!
A wonderful idea suggested to me by a young man, who is perhaps not as wise as he thought.
So, here is the object that you need to obtain! Long ago...
'...your father's uncle Athamas sired two children, Phrixus and Helle, with the cloud goddess Nephele. His mortal wife, Ino, despised her divine stepchildren and convinced Athamas to sacrifice them to end the terrible famine that she had secretly contrived in the kingdom.'
'But Nephele would not allow her children to be killed. So she sent a flying ram with fleece of dazzling gold to carry them to safety. But Helle fell from the ram, and drowned in the sea.'
'Phrixus hung on with all his might and finally came to rest in Colchis. King Aeëtes of Colchis welcomed Phrixus warmly, giving him his daughter's hand in marriage. In return for the fortunes he received, Phrixus sacrificed the ram and offered its golden fleece to the king.'
'It was hung in the grove of Ares, the god of war, as a tribute to him and was guarded by a deadly serpent.'
'The Golden Fleece hangs there still, its power untapped, waiting to be reclaimed.'

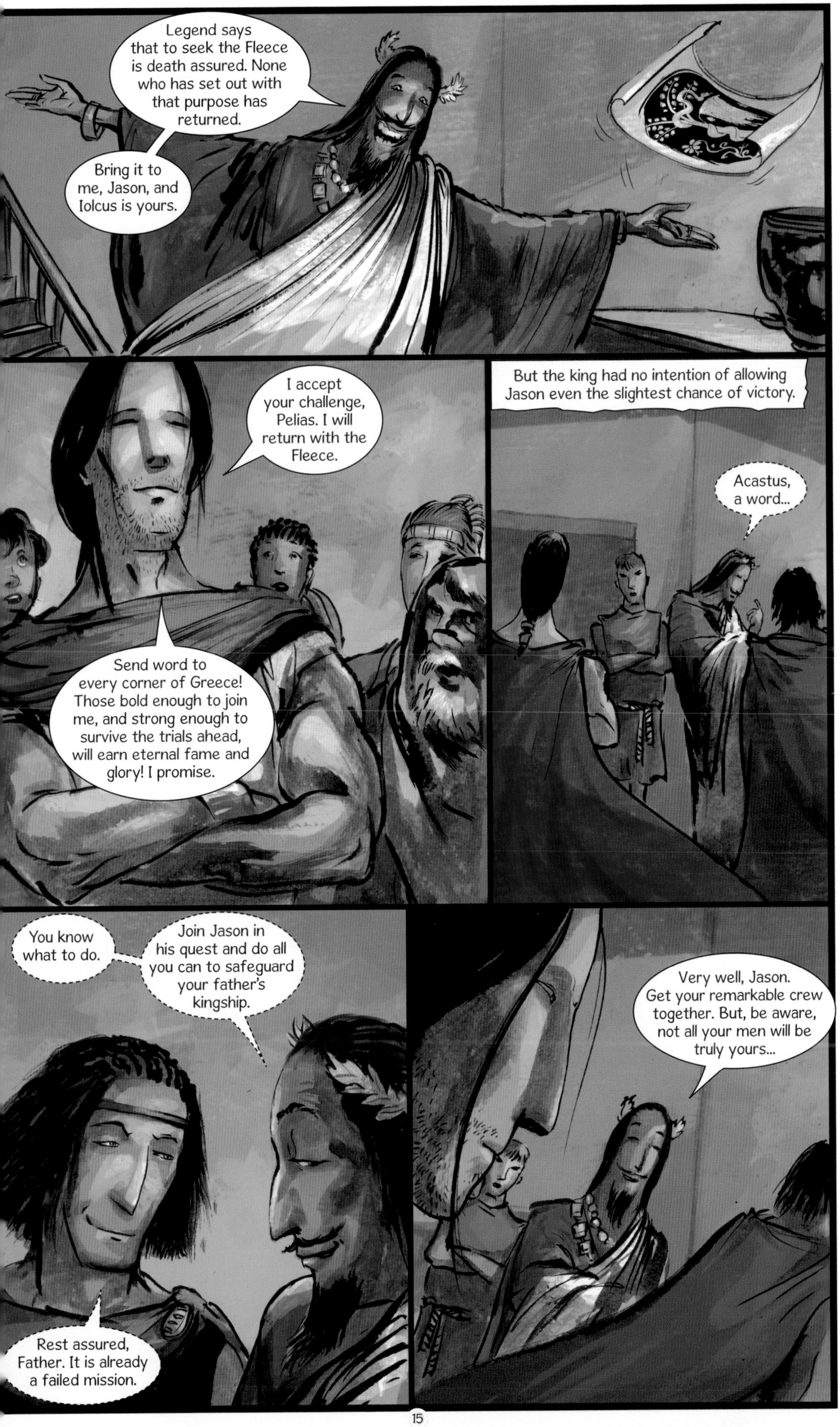
Legend says that to seek the Fleece is death assured. None who has set out with that purpose has returned.
Bring it to me, Jason, and Iolcus is yours.
I accept your challenge, Pelias. I will return with the Fleece.
Send word to every corner of Greece! Those bold enough to join me, and strong enough to survive the trials ahead, will earn eternal fame and glory! I promise.
But the king had no intention of allowing Jason even the slightest chance of victory.
Acastus, a word...
You know what to do.
Join Jason in his quest and do all you can to safeguard your father's kingship.
Rest assured, Father. It is already a failed mission.
Very well, Jason. Get your remarkable crew together. But, be aware, not all your men will be truly yours...

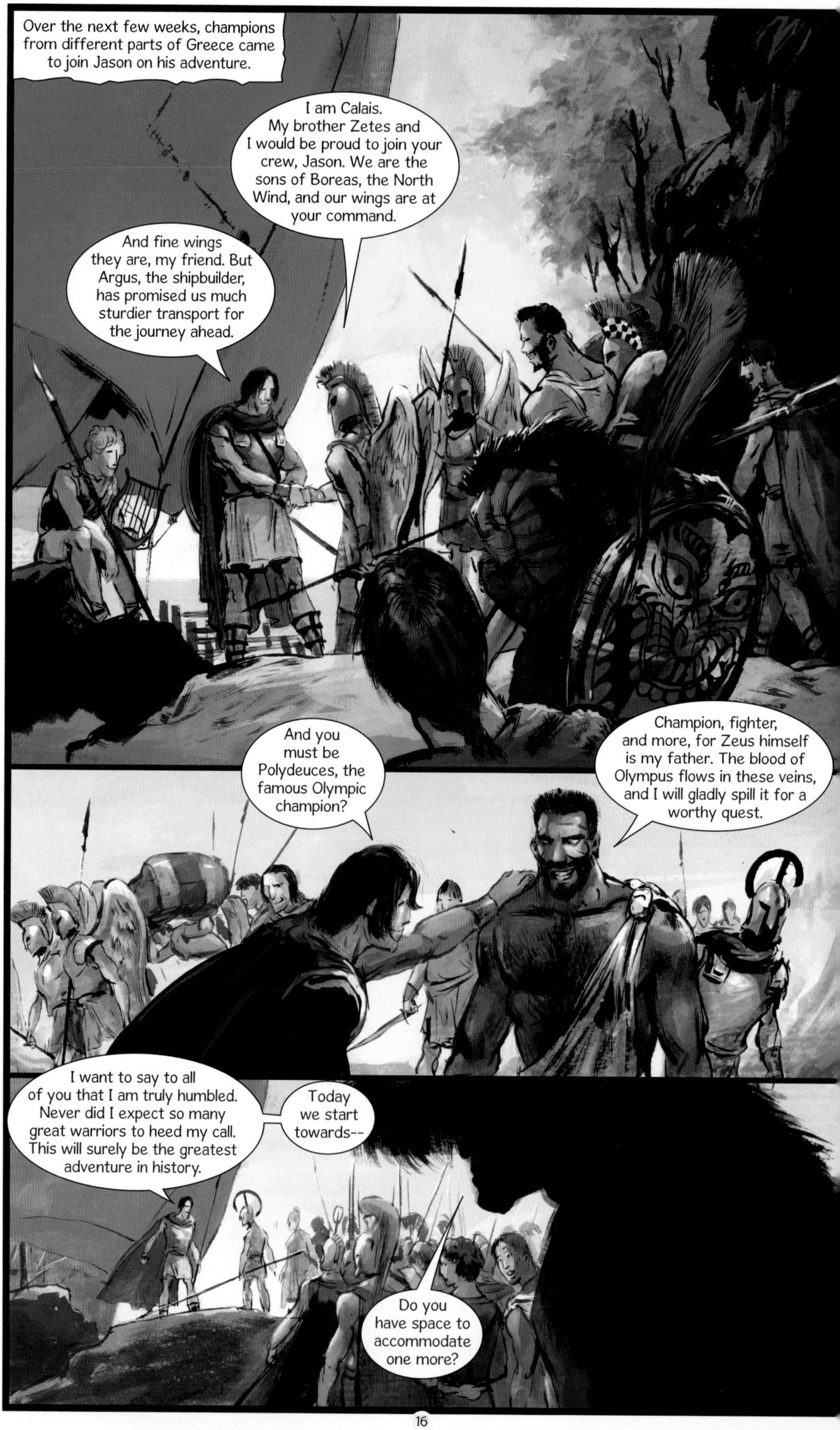
Over the next few weeks, champions from different parts of Greece came to join Jason on his adventure.
I am Calais. My brother Zetes and I would be proud to join your crew, Jason. We are the sons of Boreas, the North Wind, and our wings are at your command.
And fine wings they are, my friend. But Argus, the shipbuilder, has promised us much sturdier transport for the journey ahead.
And you must be Polydeuces, the famous Olympic champion?
Champion, fighter, and more, for Zeus himself is my father. The blood of Olympus flows in these veins, and I will gladly spill it for a worthy quest.
I want to say to all of you that I am truly humbled. Never did I expect so many great warriors to heed my call. This will surely be the greatest adventure in history.
Today we start towards--
Do you have space to accommodate one more?

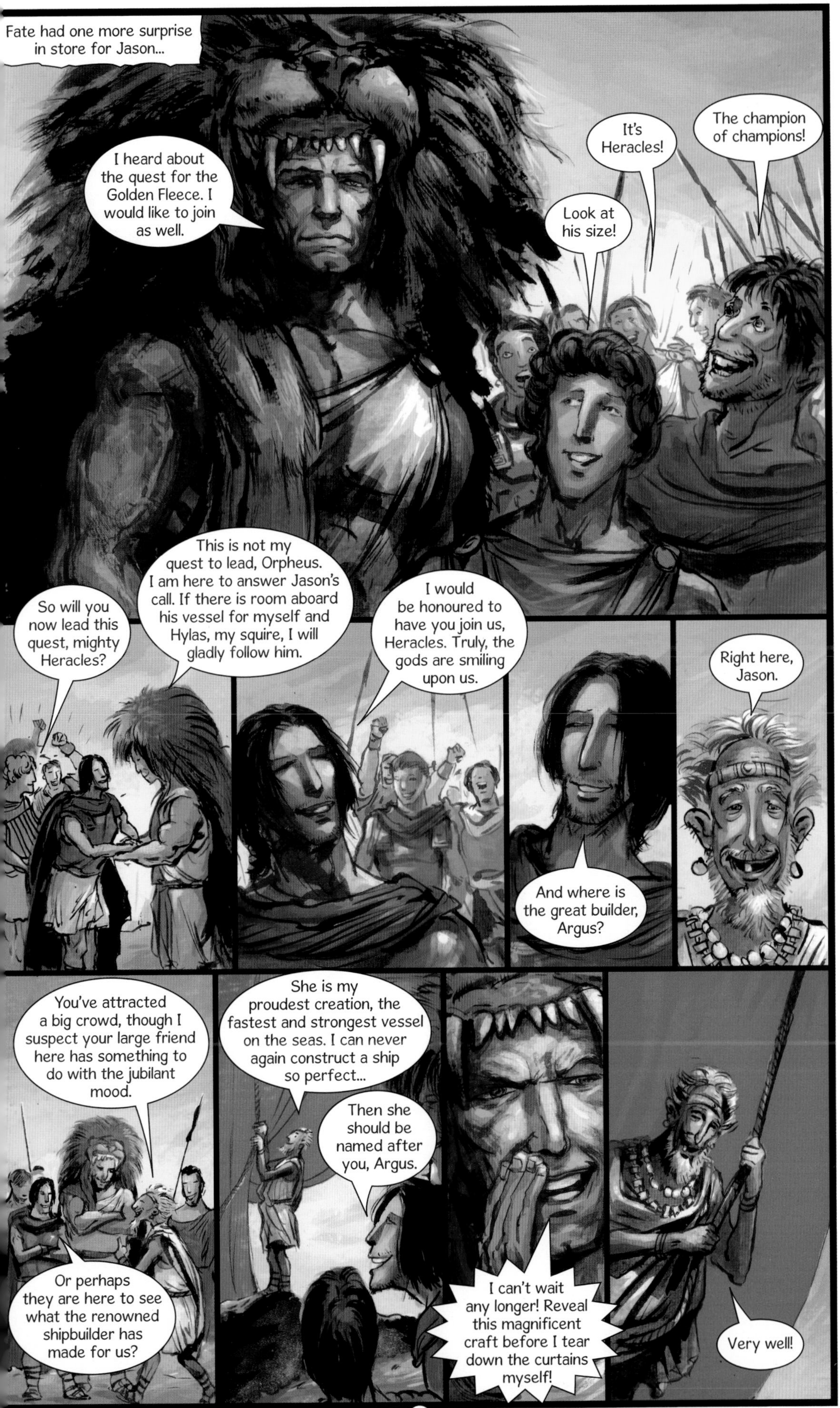

Fate had one more surprise in store for Jason...
I heard about the quest for the Golden Fleece. I would like to join as well.
It's Heracles!
The champion of champions!
Look at his size!
So will you now lead this quest, mighty Heracles?
This is not my quest to lead, Orpheus. I am here to answer Jason's call. If there is room aboard his vessel for myself and Hylas, my squire, I will gladly follow him.
I would be honoured to have you join us, Heracles. Truly, the gods are smiling upon us.
And where is the great builder, Argus?
Right here, Jason.
You've attracted a big crowd, though I suspect your large friend here has something to do with the jubilant mood.
Or perhaps they are here to see what the renowned shipbuilder has made for us?
She is my proudest creation, the fastest and strongest vessel on the seas. I can never again construct a ship so perfect...
Then she should be named after you, Argus.
I can't wait any longer! Reveal this magnificent craft before I tear down the curtains myself!
Very well!

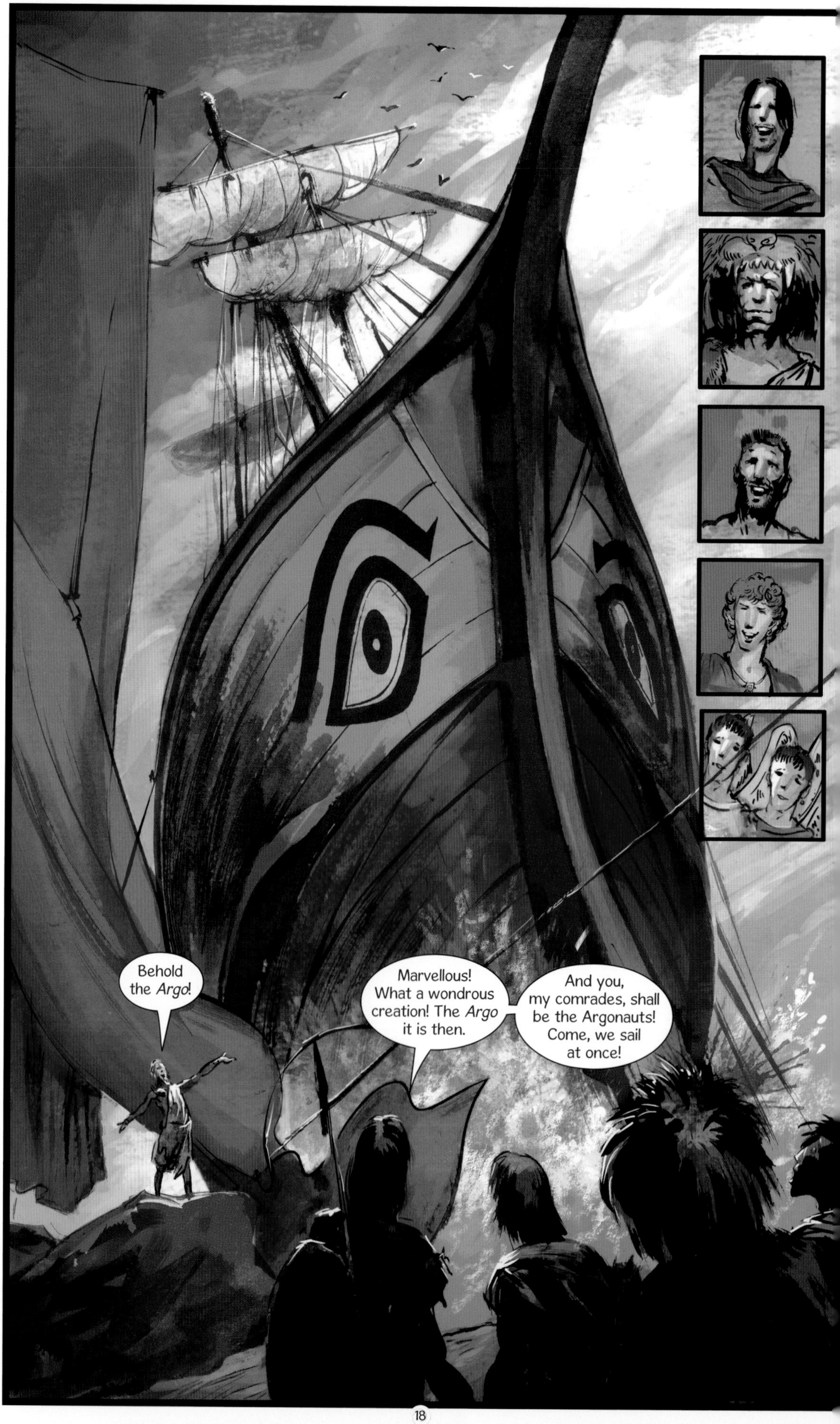
Behold the *Argo*!
Marvellous! What a wondrous creation! The *Argo* it is then.
And you, my comrades, shall be the Argonauts! Come, we sail at once!

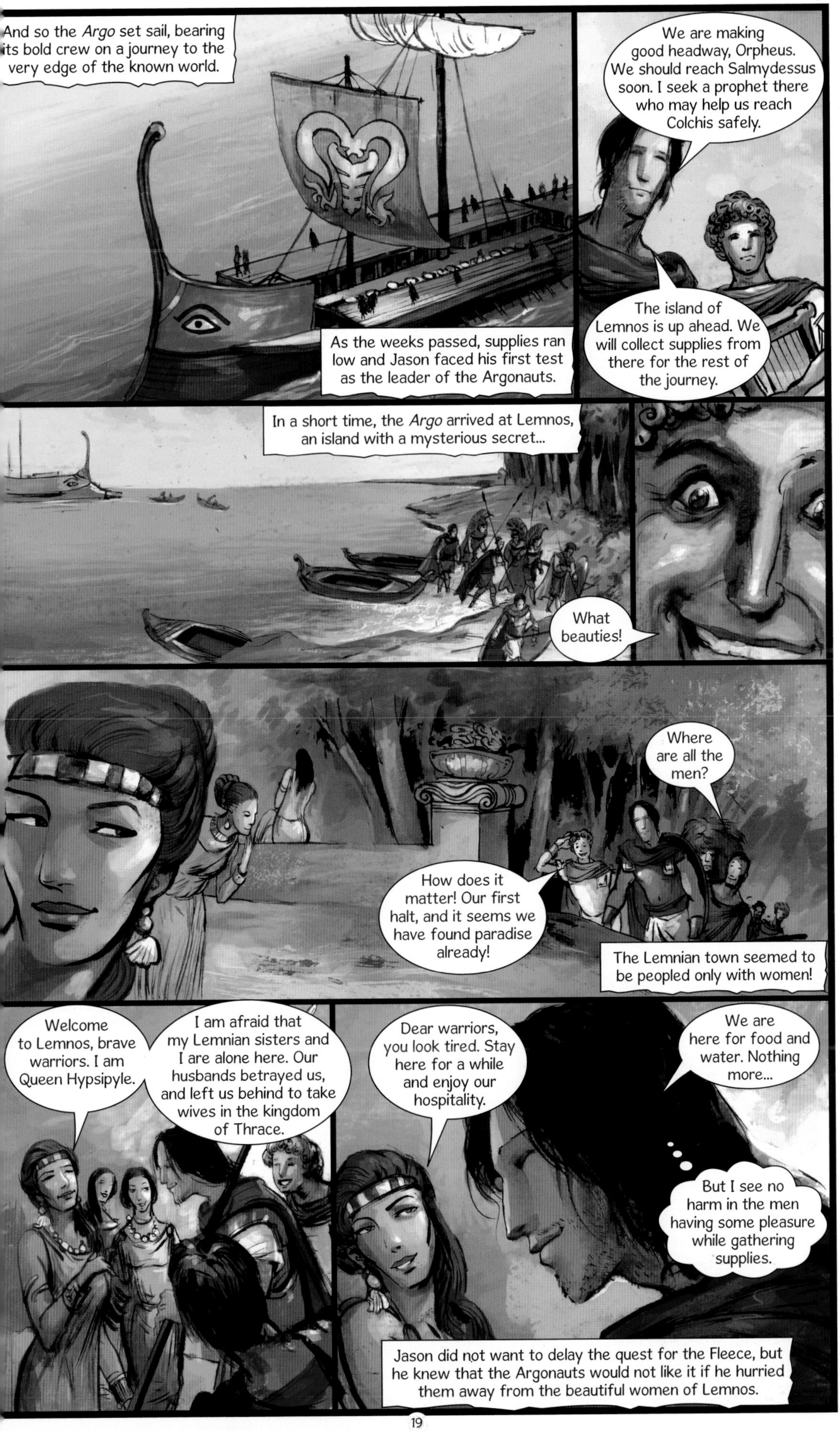
And so the Argo set sail, bearing its bold crew on a journey to the very edge of the known world.
As the weeks passed, supplies ran low and Jason faced his first test as the leader of the Argonauts.
We are making good headway, Orpheus. We should reach Salmydessus soon. I seek a prophet there who may help us reach Colchis safely.
The island of Lemnos is up ahead. We will collect supplies from there for the rest of the journey.
In a short time, the Argo arrived at Lemnos, an island with a mysterious secret...
What beauties!
Where are all the men?
How does it matter! Our first halt, and it seems we have found paradise already!
The Lemnian town seemed to be peopled only with women!
Welcome to Lemnos, brave warriors. I am Queen Hypsipyle.
I am afraid that my Lemnian sisters and I are alone here. Our husbands betrayed us, and left us behind to take wives in the kingdom of Thrace.
Dear warriors, you look tired. Stay here for a while and enjoy our hospitality.
We are here for food and water. Nothing more...
But I see no harm in the men having some pleasure while gathering supplies.
Jason did not want to delay the quest for the Fleece, but he knew that the Argonauts would not like it if he hurried them away from the beautiful women of Lemnos.

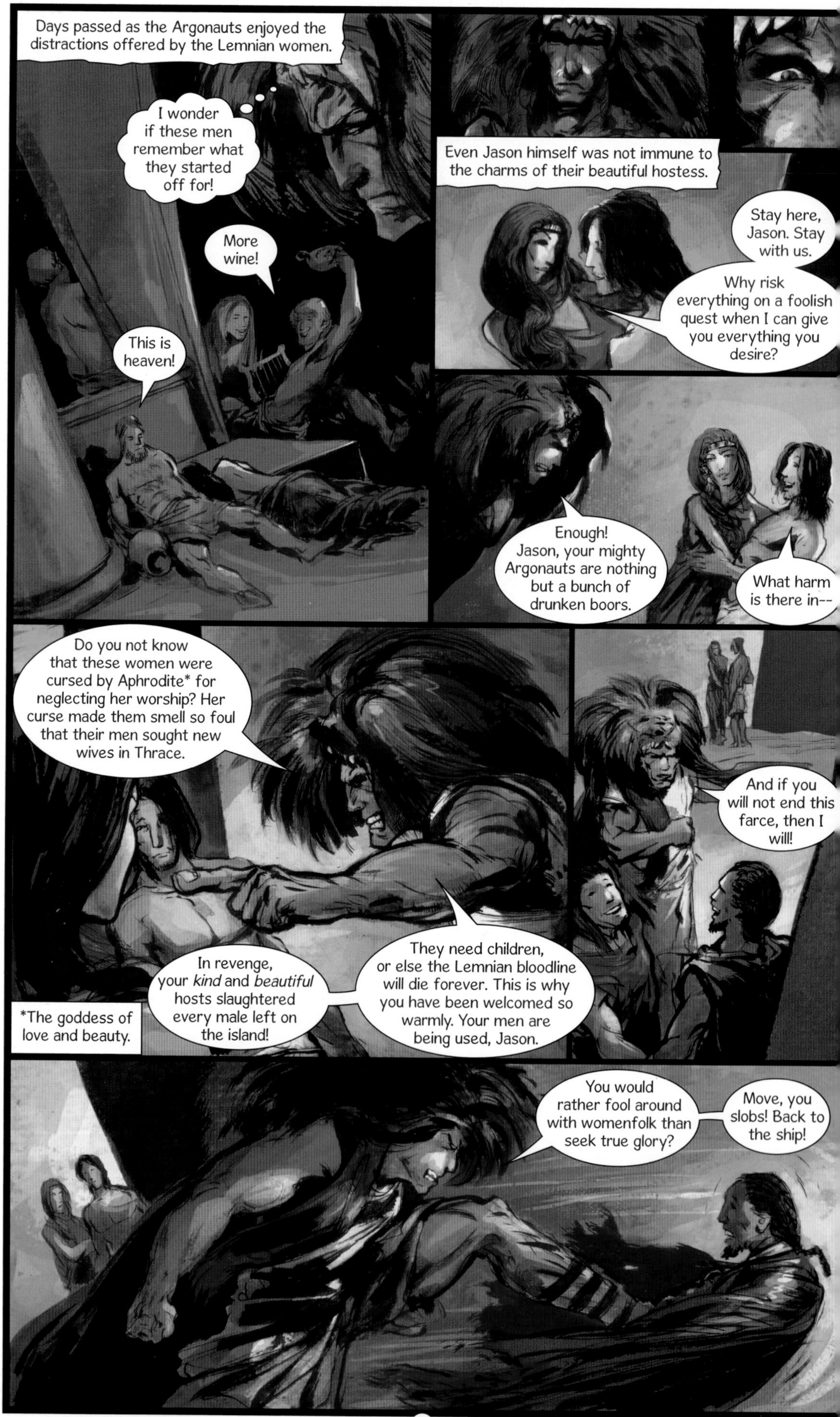

Days passed as the Argonauts enjoyed the distractions offered by the Lemnian women.
I wonder if these men remember what they started off for!
More wine!
This is heaven!
Even Jason himself was not immune to the charms of their beautiful hostess.
Stay here, Jason. Stay with us.
Why risk everything on a foolish quest when I can give you everything you desire?
Enough! Jason, your mighty Argonauts are nothing but a bunch of drunken boors.
What harm is there in--
Do you not know that these women were cursed by Aphrodite* for neglecting her worship? Her curse made them smell so foul that their men sought new wives in Thrace.
In revenge, your *kind* and *beautiful* hosts slaughtered every male left on the island!
They need children, or else the Lemnian bloodline will die forever. This is why you have been welcomed so warmly. Your men are being used, Jason.
*The goddess of love and beauty.
And if you will not end this farce, then I will!
You would rather fool around with womenfolk than seek true glory?
Move, you slobs! Back to the ship!

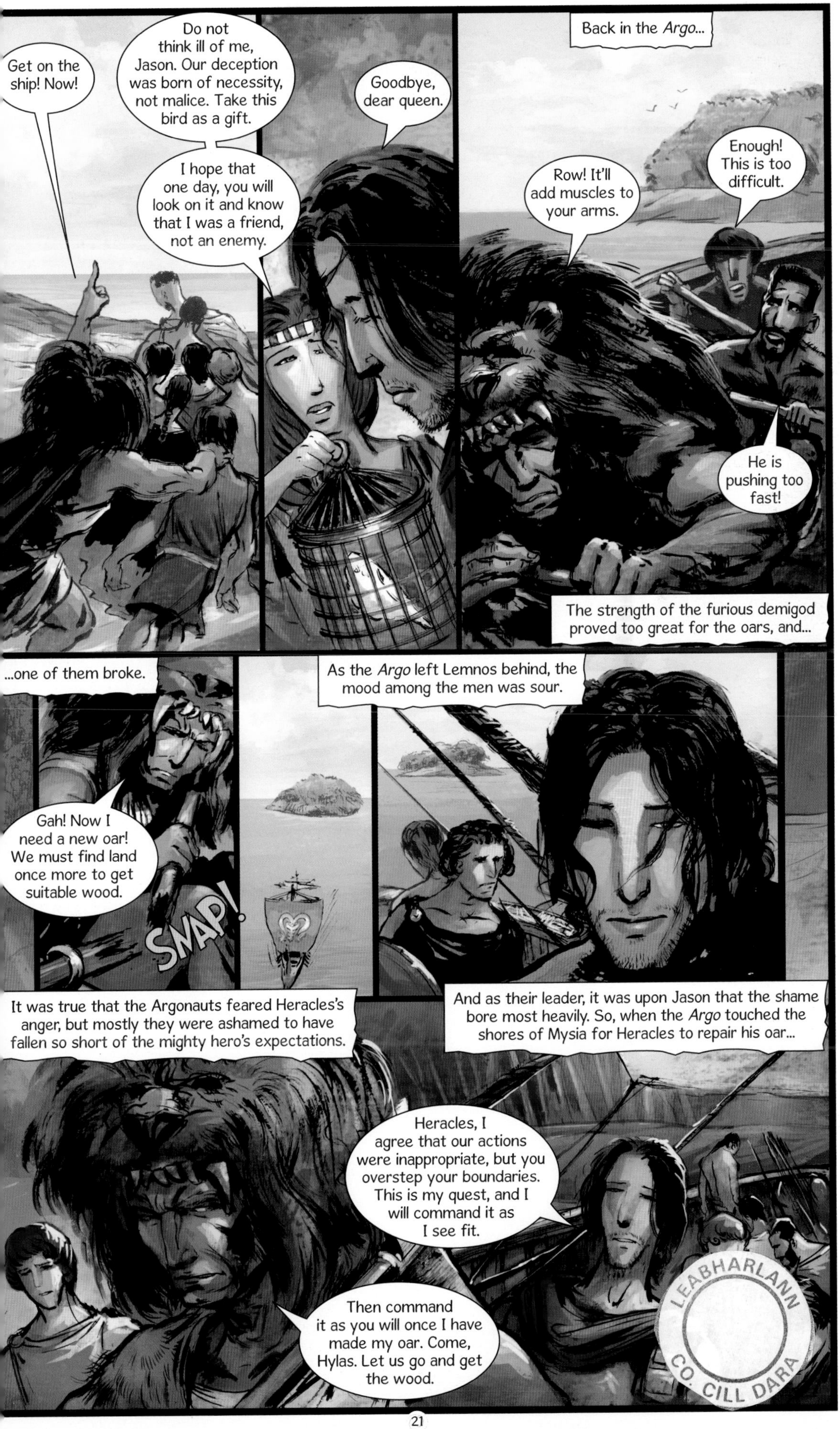
Get on the ship! Now!
Do not think ill of me, Jason. Our deception was born of necessity, not malice. Take this bird as a gift.
I hope that one day, you will look on it and know that I was a friend, not an enemy.
Goodbye, dear queen.
Back in the *Argo*...
Row! It'll add muscles to your arms.
Enough! This is too difficult.
He is pushing too fast!
The strength of the furious demigod proved too great for the oars, and...
...one of them broke.
Gah! Now I need a new oar! We must find land once more to get suitable wood.
SNAP!
As the *Argo* left Lemnos behind, the mood among the men was sour.
It was true that the Argonauts feared Heracles's anger, but mostly they were ashamed to have fallen so short of the mighty hero's expectations.
And as their leader, it was upon Jason that the shame bore most heavily. So, when the *Argo* touched the shores of Mysia for Heracles to repair his oar...
Heracles, I agree that our actions were inappropriate, but you overstep your boundaries. This is my quest, and I will command it as I see fit.
Then command it as you will once I have made my oar. Come, Hylas. Let us go and get the wood.

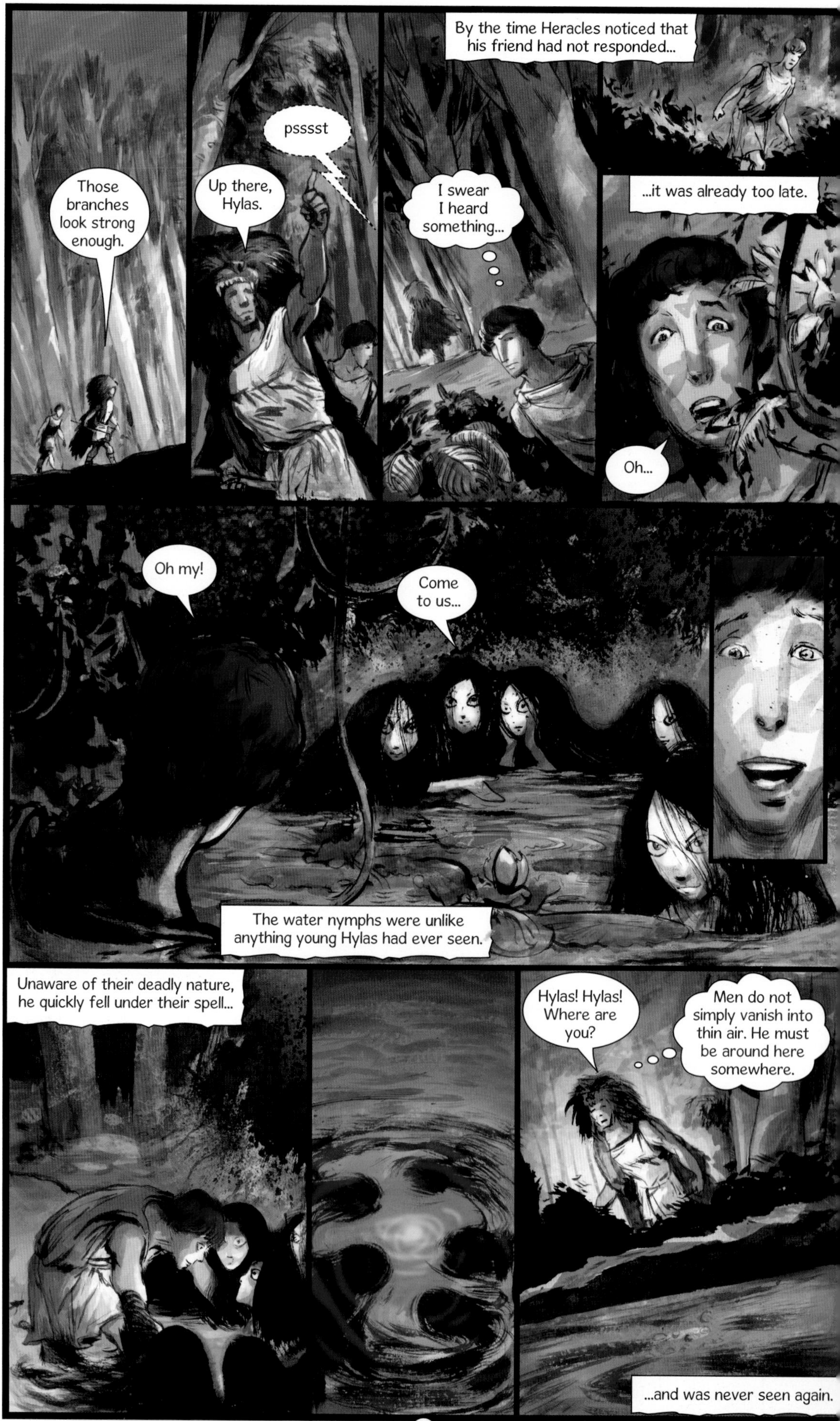
Those branches look strong enough.
psssst
Up there, Hylas.
By the time Heracles noticed that his friend had not responded...
I swear I heard something...
...it was already too late.
Oh...
Oh my!
Come to us...
The water nymphs were unlike anything young Hylas had ever seen.
Unaware of their deadly nature, he quickly fell under their spell...
Hylas! Hylas! Where are you?
Men do not simply vanish into thin air. He must be around here somewhere.
...and was never seen again.

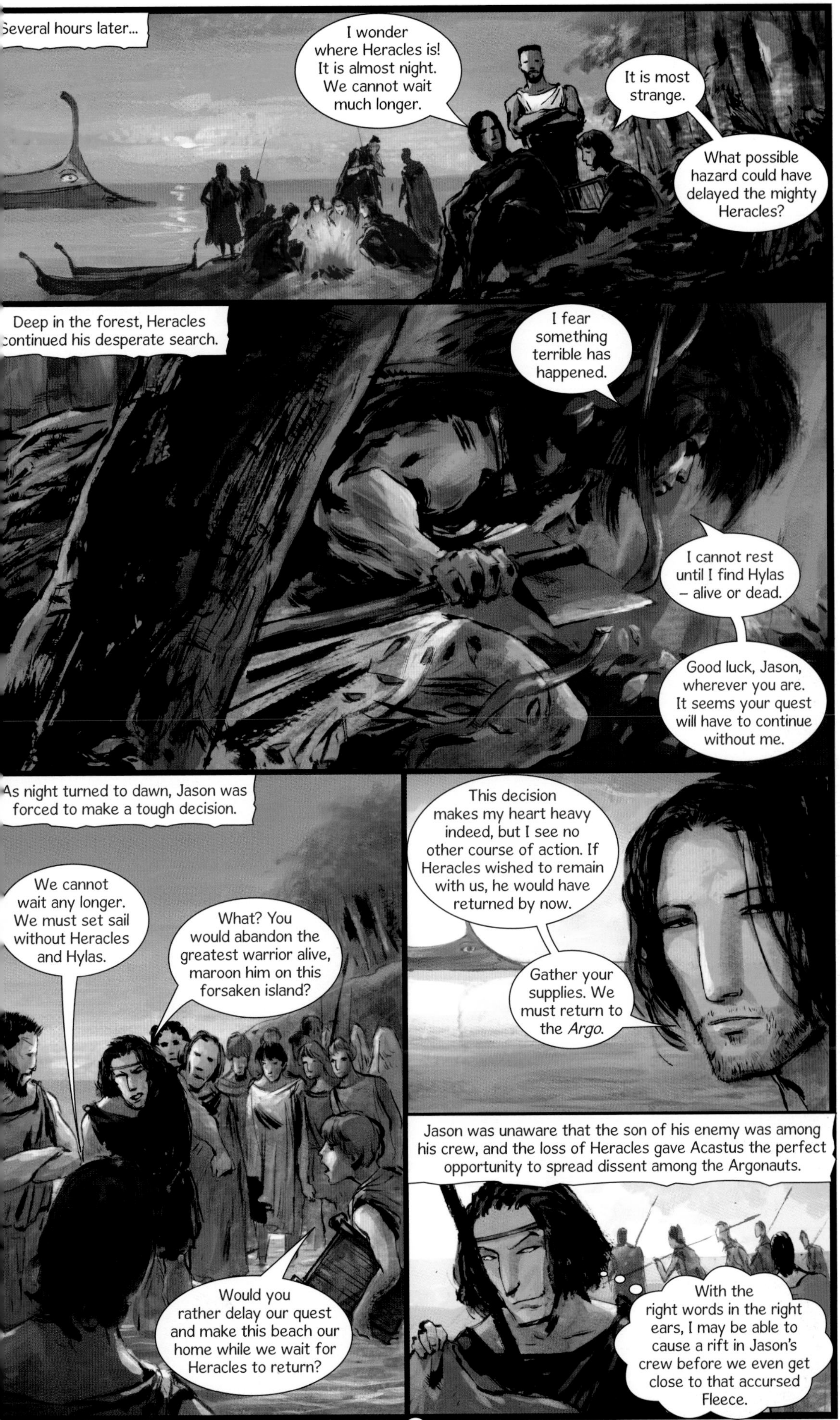
Several hours later...
I wonder where Heracles is! It is almost night. We cannot wait much longer.
It is most strange.
What possible hazard could have delayed the mighty Heracles?
Deep in the forest, Heracles continued his desperate search.
I fear something terrible has happened.
I cannot rest until I find Hylas – alive or dead.
Good luck, Jason, wherever you are. It seems your quest will have to continue without me.
As night turned to dawn, Jason was forced to make a tough decision.
We cannot wait any longer. We must set sail without Heracles and Hylas.
What? You would abandon the greatest warrior alive, maroon him on this forsaken island?
Would you rather delay our quest and make this beach our home while we wait for Heracles to return?
This decision makes my heart heavy indeed, but I see no other course of action. If Heracles wished to remain with us, he would have returned by now.
Gather your supplies. We must return to the *Argo*.
Jason was unaware that the son of his enemy was among his crew, and the loss of Heracles gave Acastus the perfect opportunity to spread dissent among the Argonauts.
With the right words in the right ears, I may be able to cause a rift in Jason's crew before we even get close to that accursed Fleece.

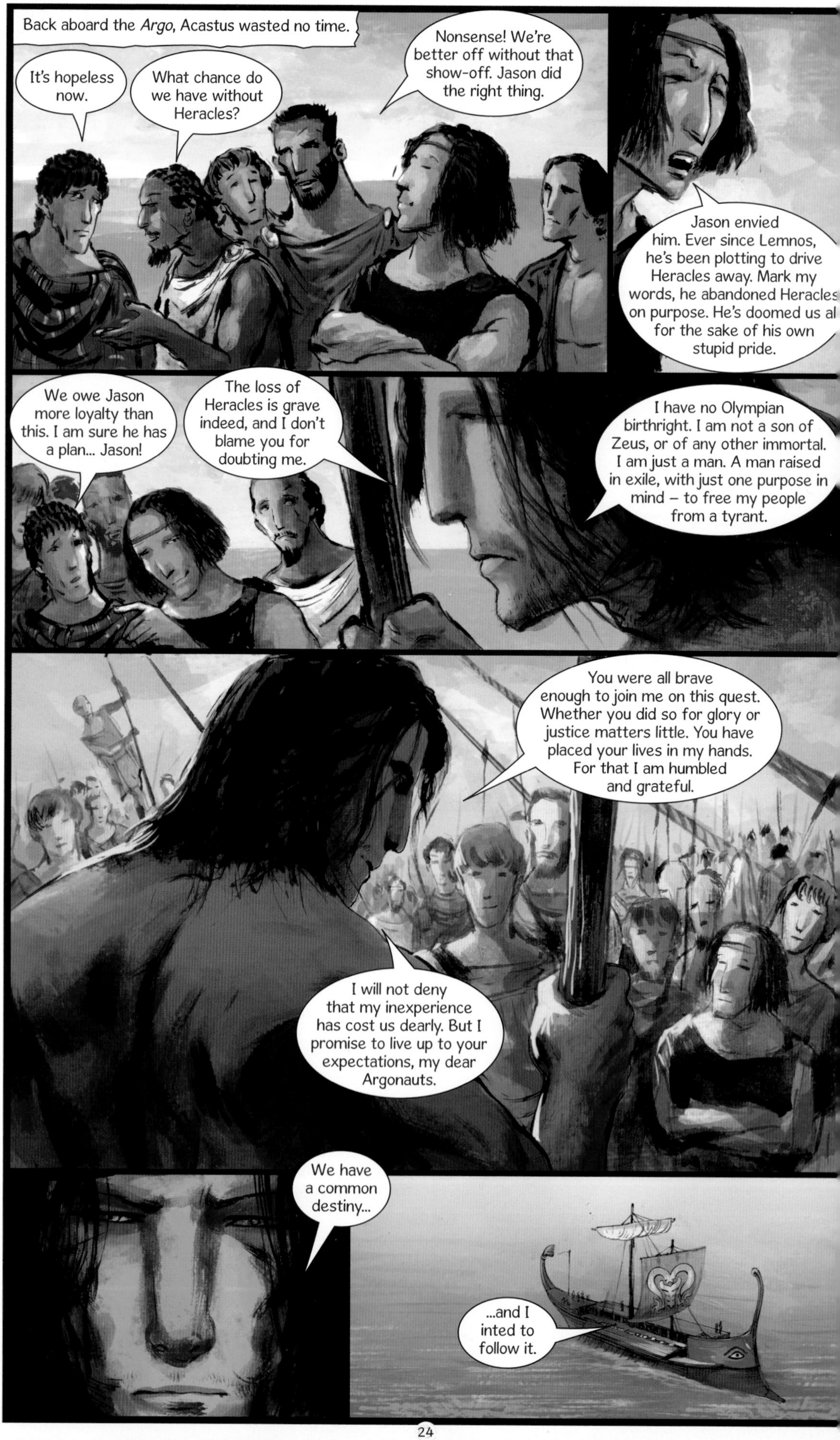
Back aboard the *Argo*, Acastus wasted no time.
It's hopeless now.
What chance do we have without Heracles?
Nonsense! We're better off without that show-off. Jason did the right thing.
Jason envied him. Ever since Lemnos, he's been plotting to drive Heracles away. Mark my words, he abandoned Heracles on purpose. He's doomed us all for the sake of his own stupid pride.
We owe Jason more loyalty than this. I am sure he has a plan... Jason!
The loss of Heracles is grave indeed, and I don't blame you for doubting me.
I have no Olympian birthright. I am not a son of Zeus, or of any other immortal. I am just a man. A man raised in exile, with just one purpose in mind – to free my people from a tyrant.
You were all brave enough to join me on this quest. Whether you did so for glory or justice matters little. You have placed your lives in my hands. For that I am humbled and grateful.
I will not deny that my inexperience has cost us dearly. But I promise to live up to your expectations, my dear Argonauts.
We have a common destiny...
...and I inted to follow it.

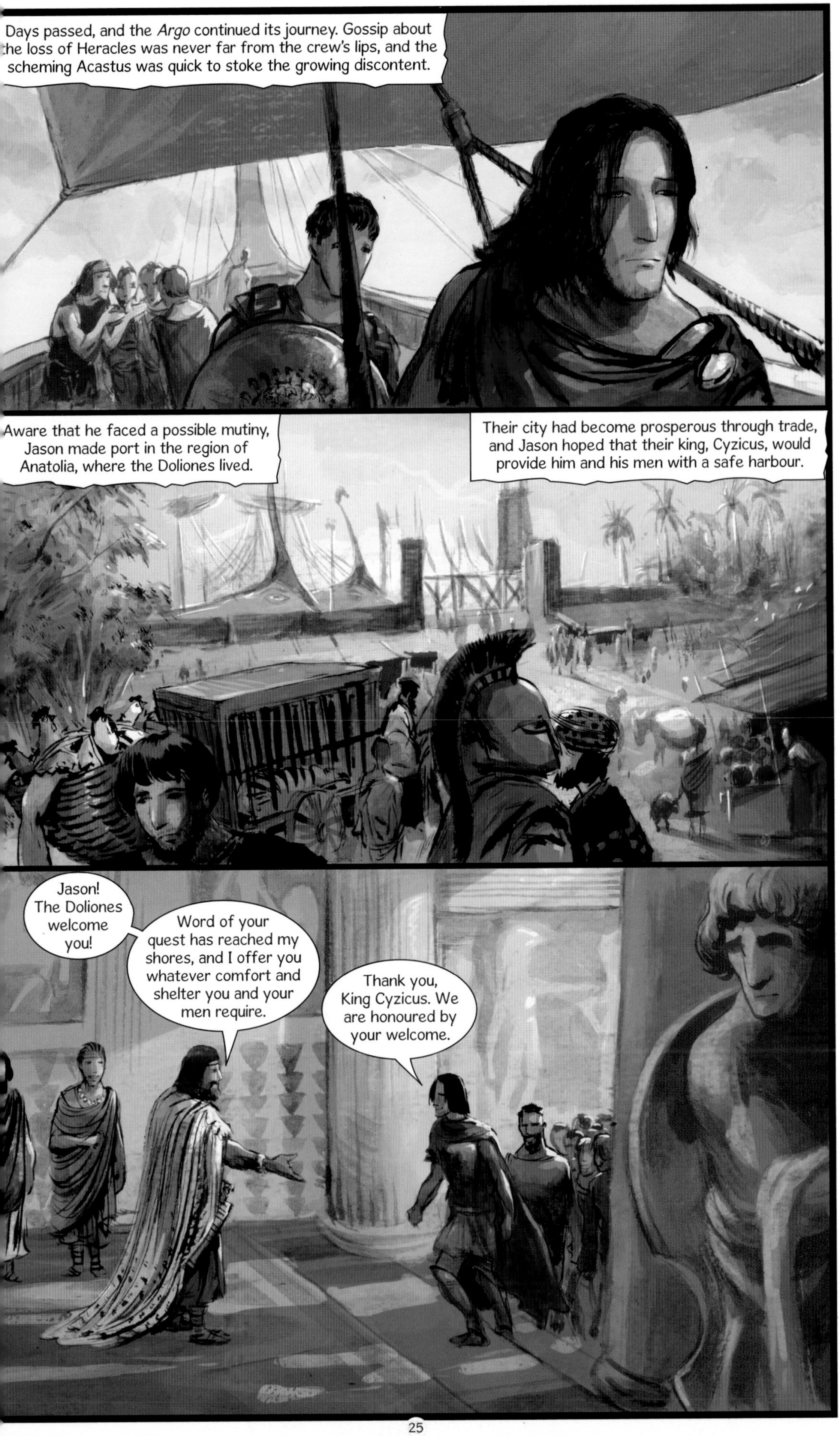
Days passed, and the *Argo* continued its journey. Gossip about the loss of Heracles was never far from the crew's lips, and the scheming Acastus was quick to stoke the growing discontent.
Aware that he faced a possible mutiny, Jason made port in the region of Anatolia, where the Doliones lived.
Their city had become prosperous through trade, and Jason hoped that their king, Cyzicus, would provide him and his men with a safe harbour.
Jason! The Doliones welcome you!
Word of your quest has reached my shores, and I offer you whatever comfort and shelter you and your men require.
Thank you, King Cyzicus. We are honoured by your welcome.

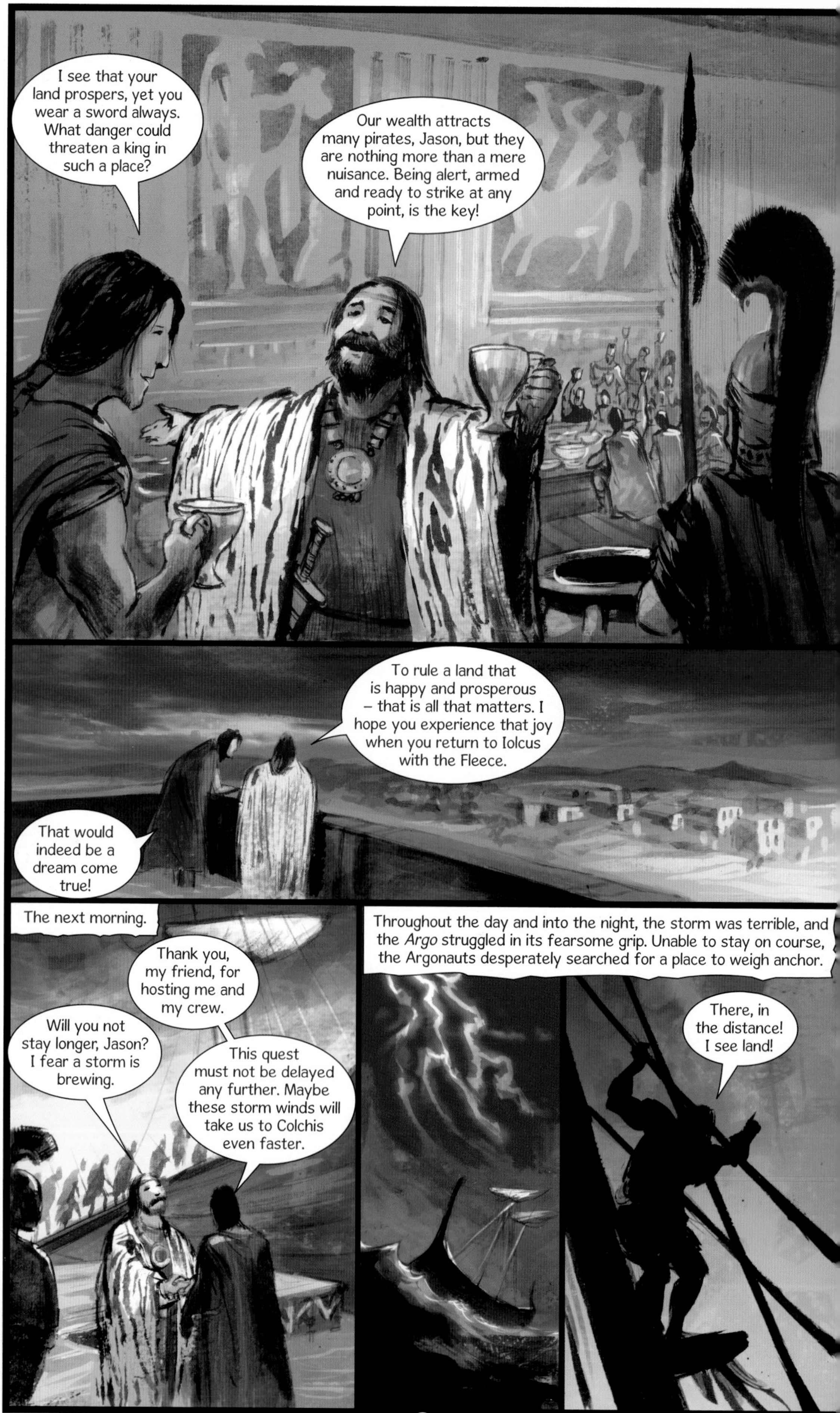
I see that your land prospers, yet you wear a sword always. What danger could threaten a king in such a place?
Our wealth attracts many pirates, Jason, but they are nothing more than a mere nuisance. Being alert, armed and ready to strike at any point, is the key!
To rule a land that is happy and prosperous – that is all that matters. I hope you experience that joy when you return to Iolcus with the Fleece.
That would indeed be a dream come true!
The next morning.
Thank you, my friend, for hosting me and my crew.
Will you not stay longer, Jason? I fear a storm is brewing.
This quest must not be delayed any further. Maybe these storm winds will take us to Colchis even faster.
Throughout the day and into the night, the storm was terrible, and the *Argo* struggled in its fearsome grip. Unable to stay on course, the Argonauts desperately searched for a place to weigh anchor.
There, in the distance! I see land!

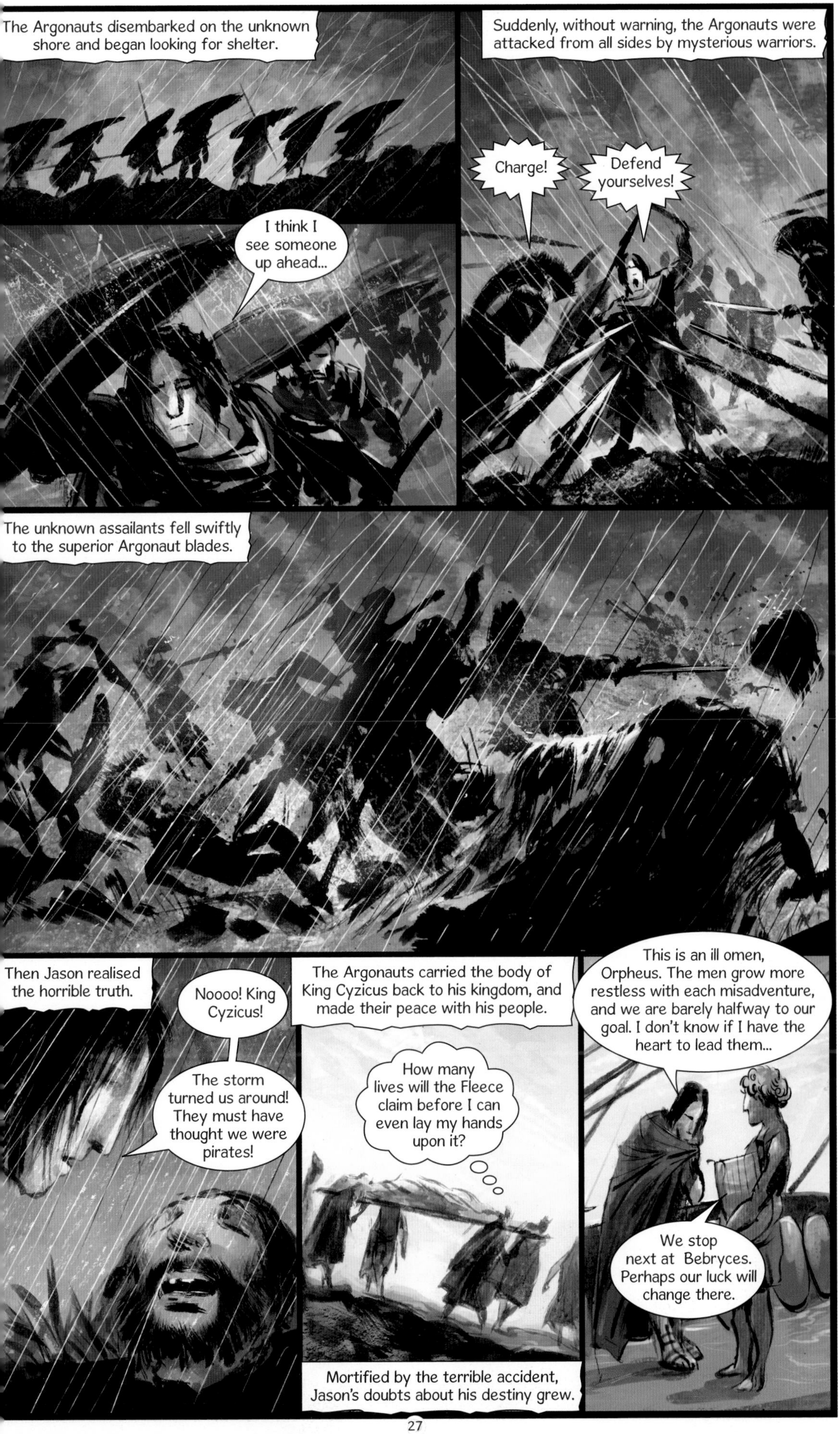

The Argonauts disembarked on the unknown shore and began looking for shelter.
I think I see someone up ahead...
Suddenly, without warning, the Argonauts were attacked from all sides by mysterious warriors.
Charge!
Defend yourselves!
The unknown assailants fell swiftly to the superior Argonaut blades.
Then Jason realised the horrible truth.
Noooo! King Cyzicus!
The storm turned us around! They must have thought we were pirates!
The Argonauts carried the body of King Cyzicus back to his kingdom, and made their peace with his people.
How many lives will the Fleece claim before I can even lay my hands upon it?
Mortified by the terrible accident, Jason's doubts about his destiny grew.
This is an ill omen, Orpheus. The men grow more restless with each misadventure, and we are barely halfway to our goal. I don't know if I have the heart to lead them...
We stop next at Bebryces. Perhaps our luck will change there.

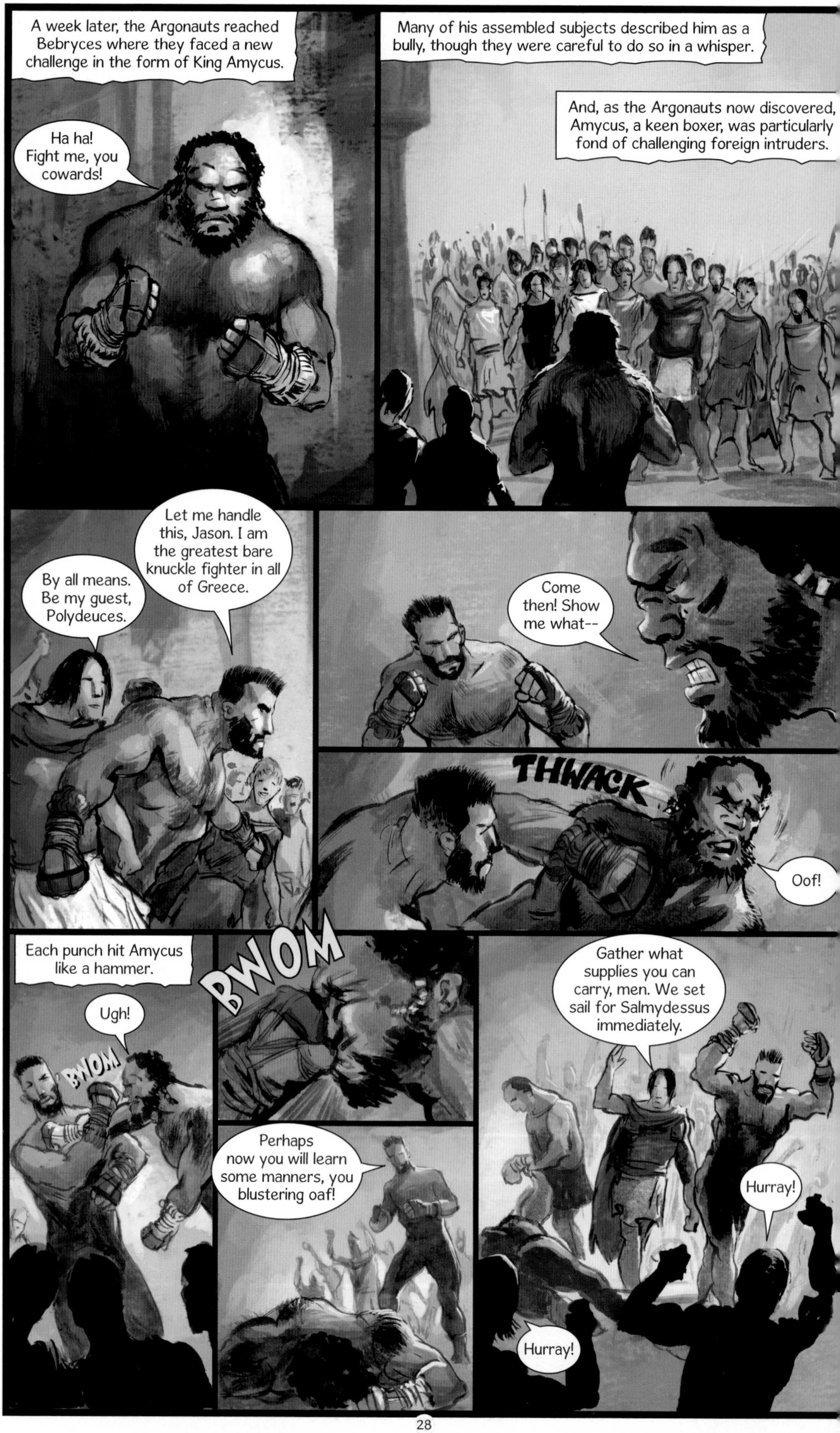
A week later, the Argonauts reached Bebryces where they faced a new challenge in the form of King Amycus.
Ha ha! Fight me, you cowards!
Many of his assembled subjects described him as a bully, though they were careful to do so in a whisper.
And, as the Argonauts now discovered, Amycus, a keen boxer, was particularly fond of challenging foreign intruders.
Let me handle this, Jason. I am the greatest bare knuckle fighter in all of Greece.
By all means. Be my guest, Polydeuces.
Come then! Show me what--
THWACK
Oof!
Each punch hit Amycus like a hammer.
Ugh!
BWOM
BWOM
Perhaps now you will learn some manners, you blustering oaf!
Gather what supplies you can carry, men. We set sail for Salmydessus immediately.
Hurray!
Hurray!

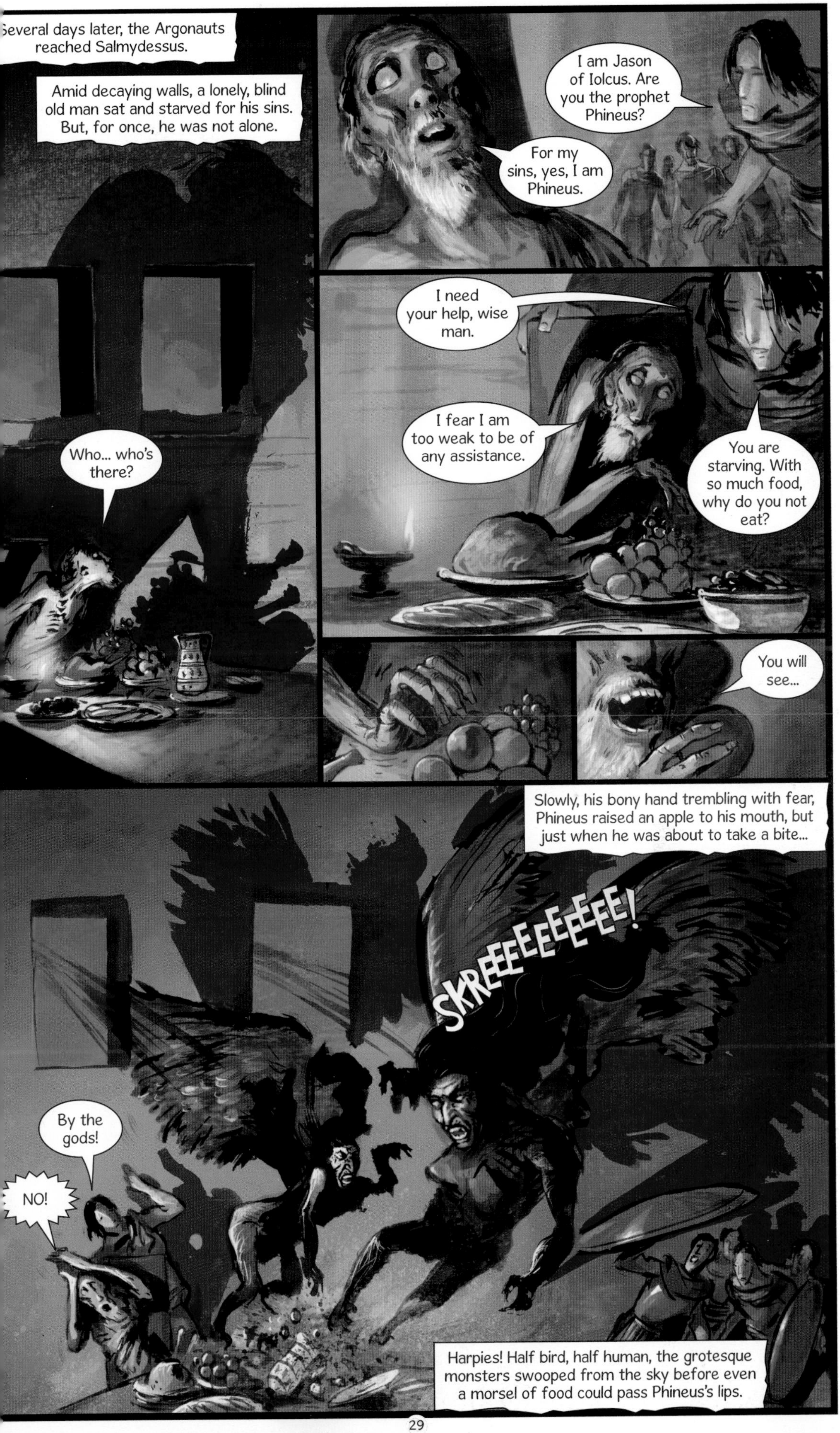
Several days later, the Argonauts reached Salmydessus.
Amid decaying walls, a lonely, blind old man sat and starved for his sins. But, for once, he was not alone.
Who... who's there?
I am Jason of Iolcus. Are you the prophet Phineus?
For my sins, yes, I am Phineus.
I need your help, wise man.
I fear I am too weak to be of any assistance.
You are starving. With so much food, why do you not eat?
You will see...
Slowly, his bony hand trembling with fear, Phineus raised an apple to his mouth, but just when he was about to take a bite...
SKREEEEEEEEE!
By the gods!
NO!
Harpies! Half bird, half human, the grotesque monsters swooped from the sky before even a morsel of food could pass Phineus's lips.

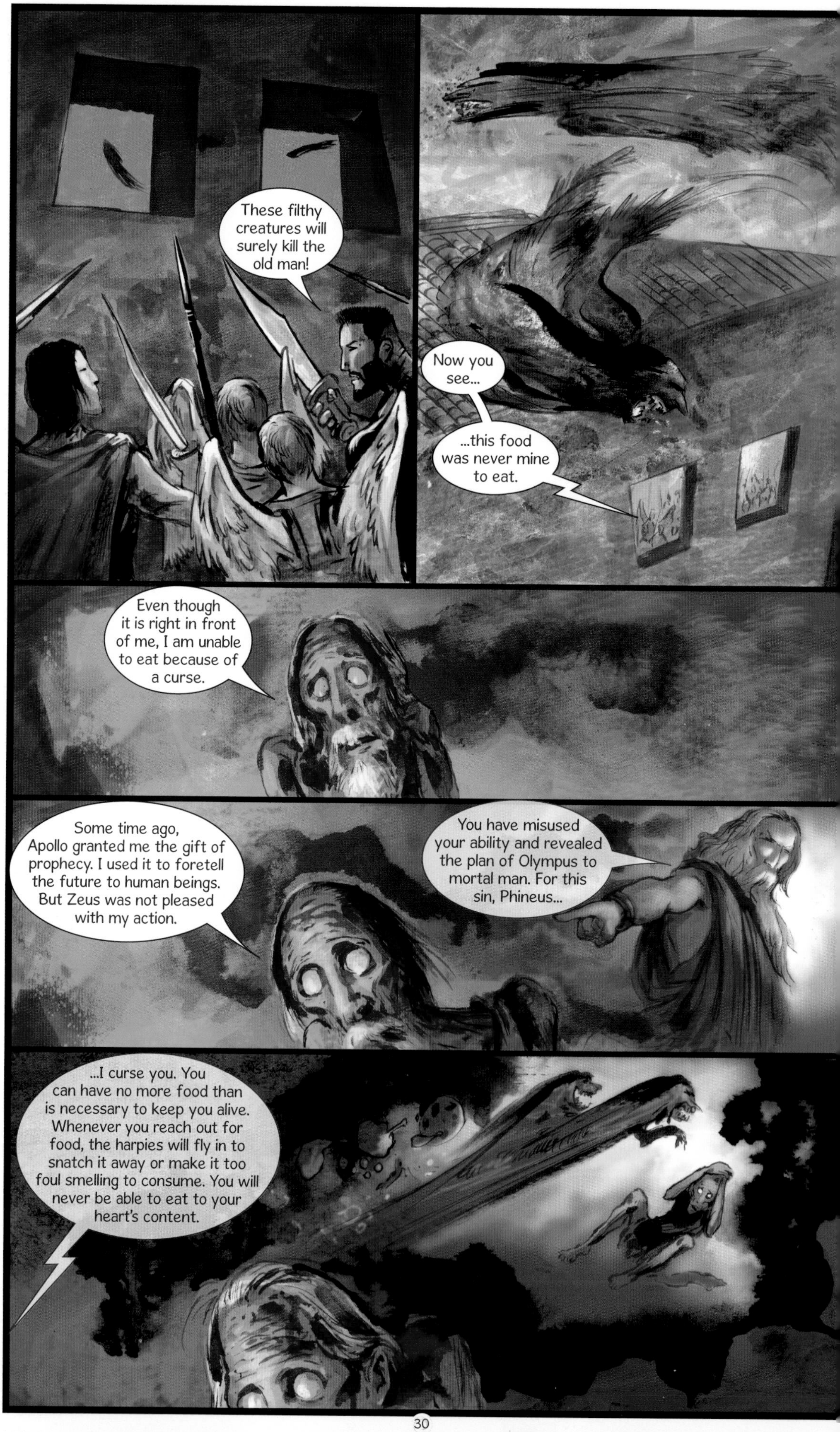
These filthy creatures will surely kill the old man!
Now you see...
...this food was never mine to eat.
Even though it is right in front of me, I am unable to eat because of a curse.
Some time ago, Apollo granted me the gift of prophecy. I used it to foretell the future to human beings. But Zeus was not pleased with my action.
You have misused your ability and revealed the plan of Olympus to mortal man. For this sin, Phineus...
...I curse you. You can have no more food than is necessary to keep you alive. Whenever you reach out for food, the harpies will fly in to snatch it away or make it too foul smelling to consume. You will never be able to eat to your heart's content.

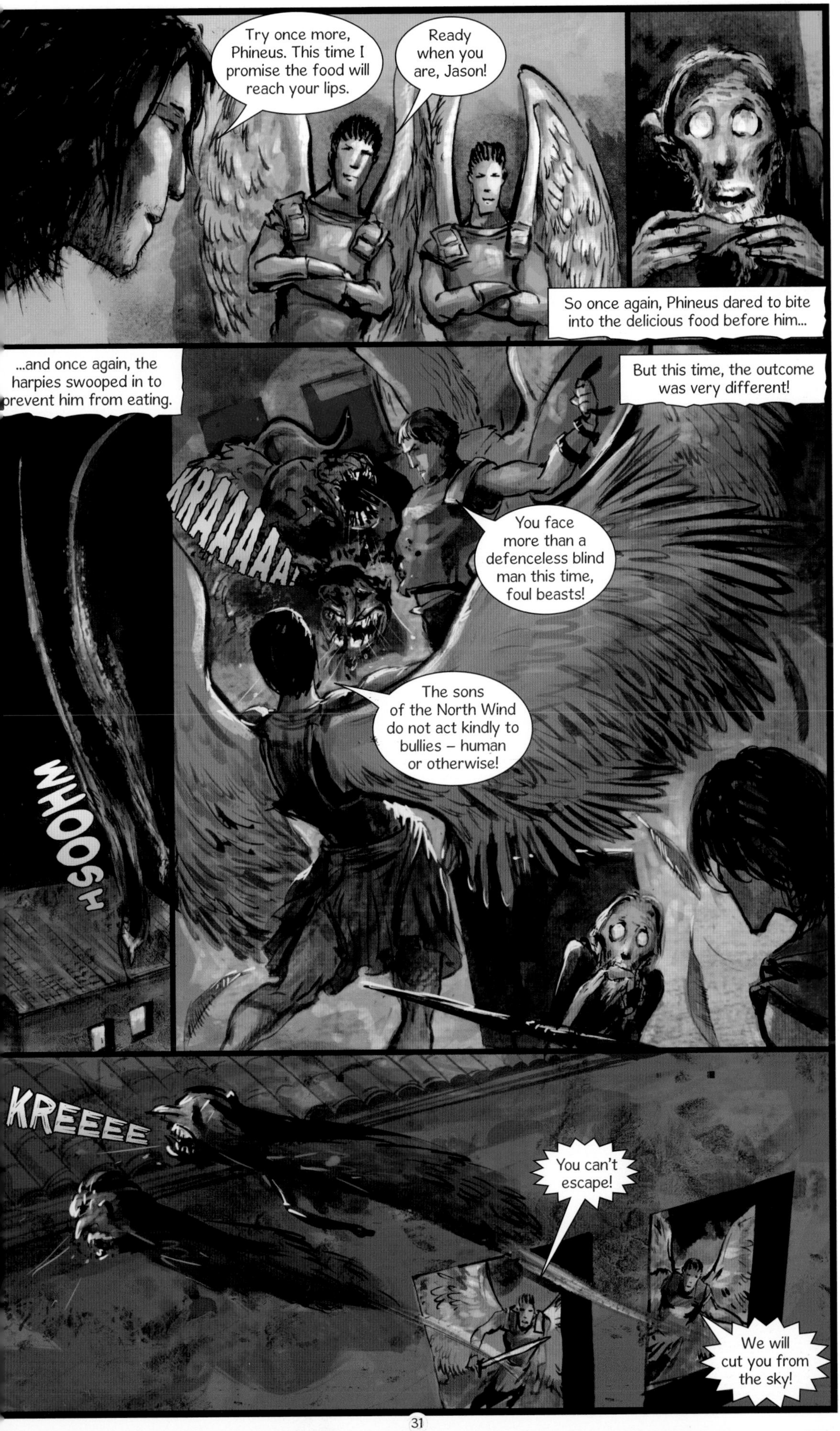
Try once more, Phineus. This time I promise the food will reach your lips.
Ready when you are, Jason!
So once again, Phineus dared to bite into the delicious food before him...
...and once again, the harpies swooped in to prevent him from eating.
But this time, the outcome was very different!
KRAAAAAA!
You face more than a defenceless blind man this time, foul beasts!
The sons of the North Wind do not act kindly to bullies – human or otherwise!
WHOOSH
KREEEEE
You can't escape!
We will cut you from the sky!

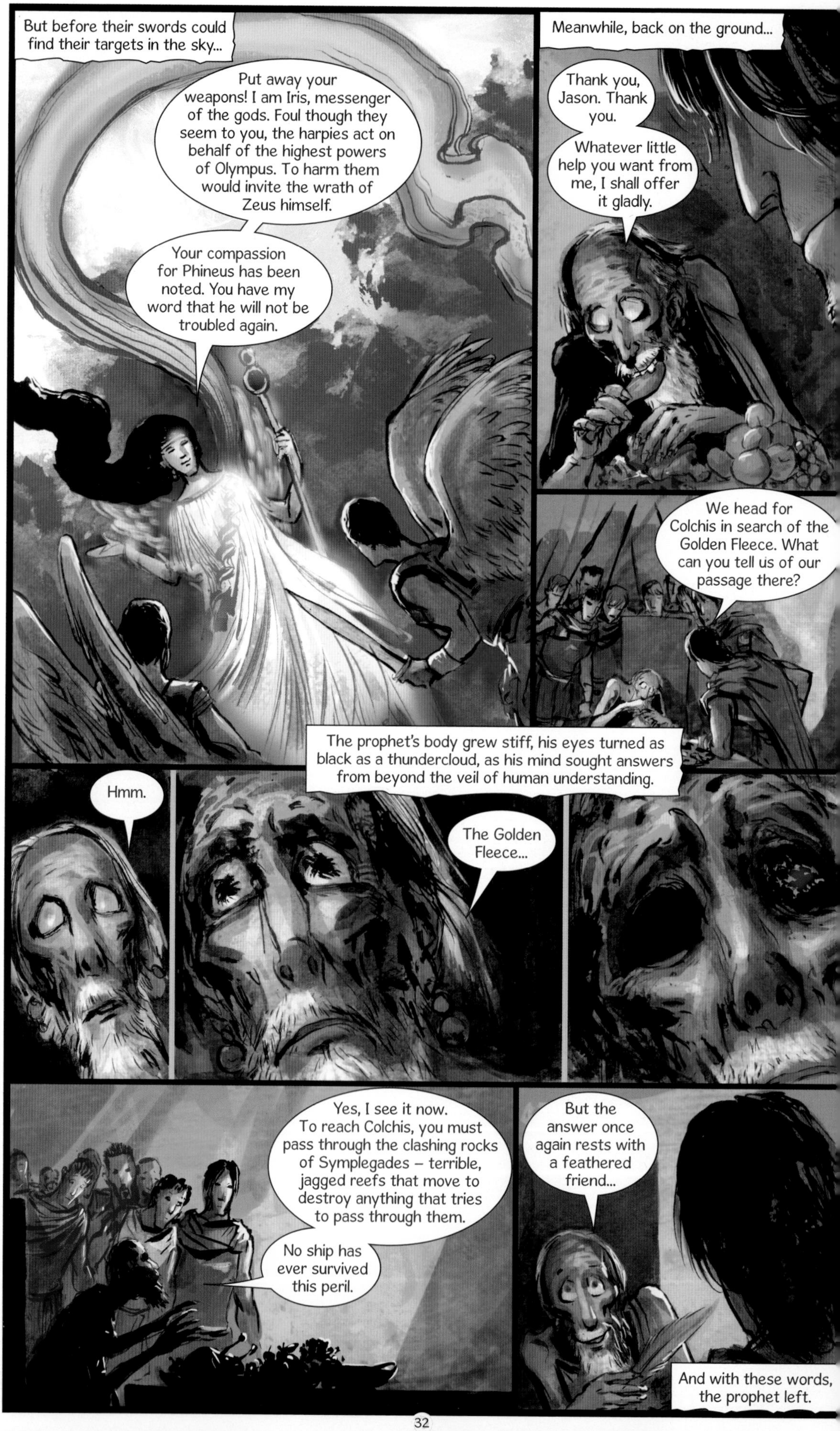

But before their swords could find their targets in the sky...
Put away your weapons! I am Iris, messenger of the gods. Foul though they seem to you, the harpies act on behalf of the highest powers of Olympus. To harm them would invite the wrath of Zeus himself.
Your compassion for Phineus has been noted. You have my word that he will not be troubled again.
Meanwhile, back on the ground...
Thank you, Jason. Thank you.
Whatever little help you want from me, I shall offer it gladly.
We head for Colchis in search of the Golden Fleece. What can you tell us of our passage there?
The prophet's body grew stiff, his eyes turned as black as a thundercloud, as his mind sought answers from beyond the veil of human understanding.
Hmm.
The Golden Fleece...
Yes, I see it now. To reach Colchis, you must pass through the clashing rocks of Symplegades – terrible, jagged reefs that move to destroy anything that tries to pass through them.
No ship has ever survived this peril.
But the answer once again rests with a feathered friend...
And with these words, the prophet left.

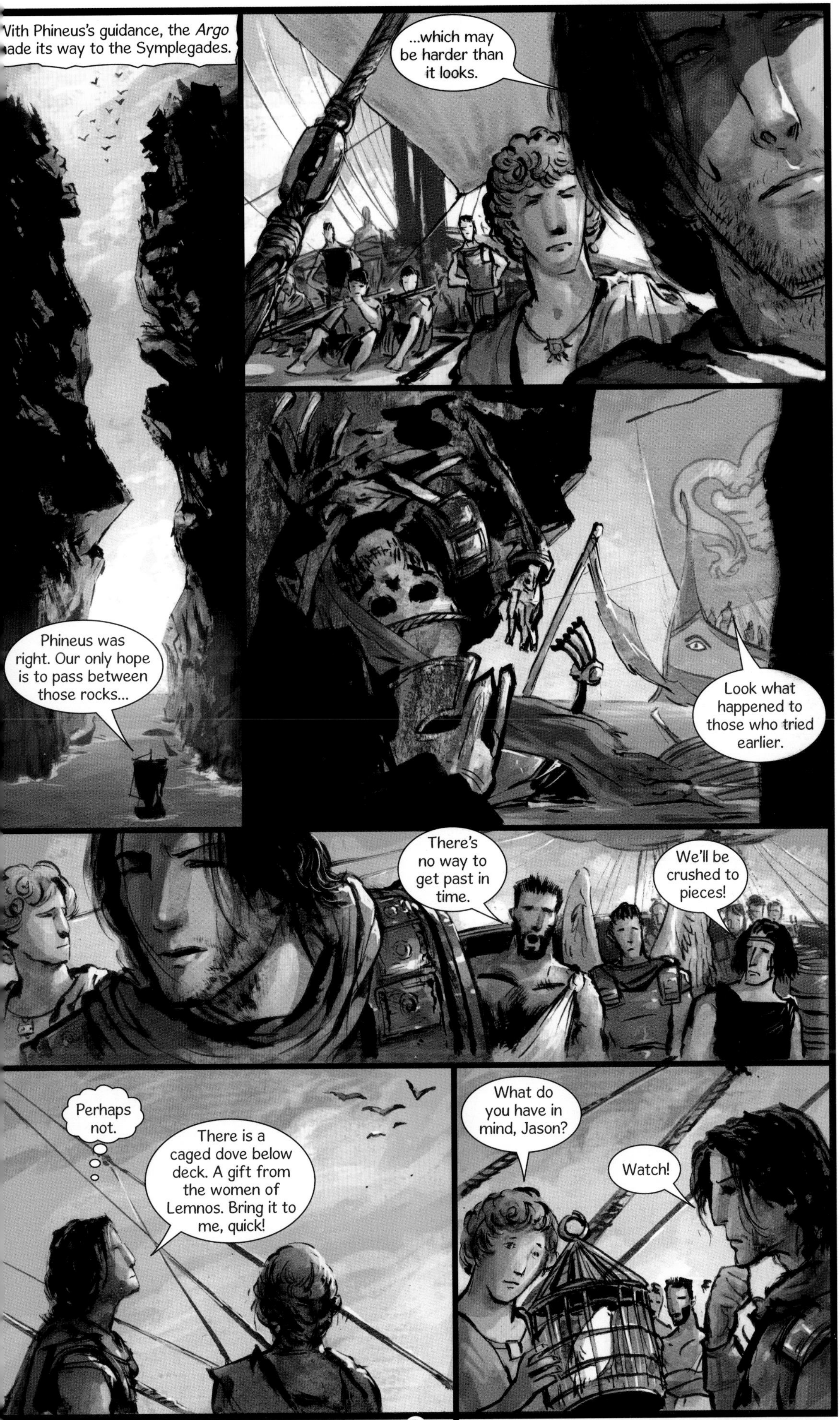

Vith Phineus's guidance, the *Argo* ıade its way to the Symplegades.
...which may be harder than it looks.
Phineus was right. Our only hope is to pass between those rocks...
Look what happened to those who tried earlier.
There's no way to get past in time.
We'll be crushed to pieces!
Perhaps not.
There is a caged dove below deck. A gift from the women of Lemnos. Bring it to me, quick!
What do you have in mind, Jason?
Watch!

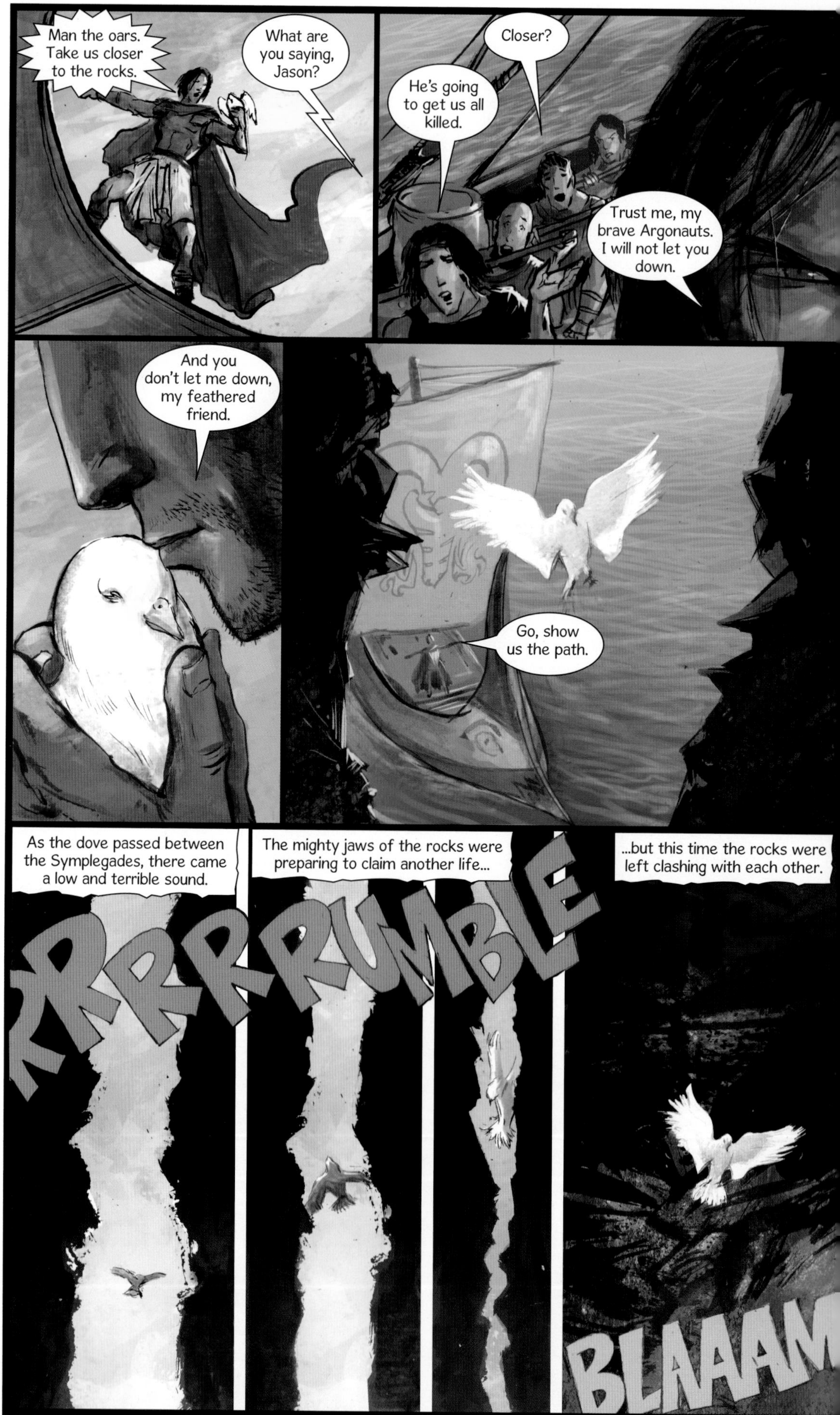
Man the oars. Take us closer to the rocks.
What are you saying, Jason?
Closer?
He's going to get us all killed.
Trust me, my brave Argonauts. I will not let you down.
And you don't let me down, my feathered friend.
Go, show us the path.
As the dove passed between the Symplegades, there came a low and terrible sound.
The mighty jaws of the rocks were preparing to claim another life...
...but this time the rocks were left clashing with each other.
RRRRUMBLE
BLAAAM

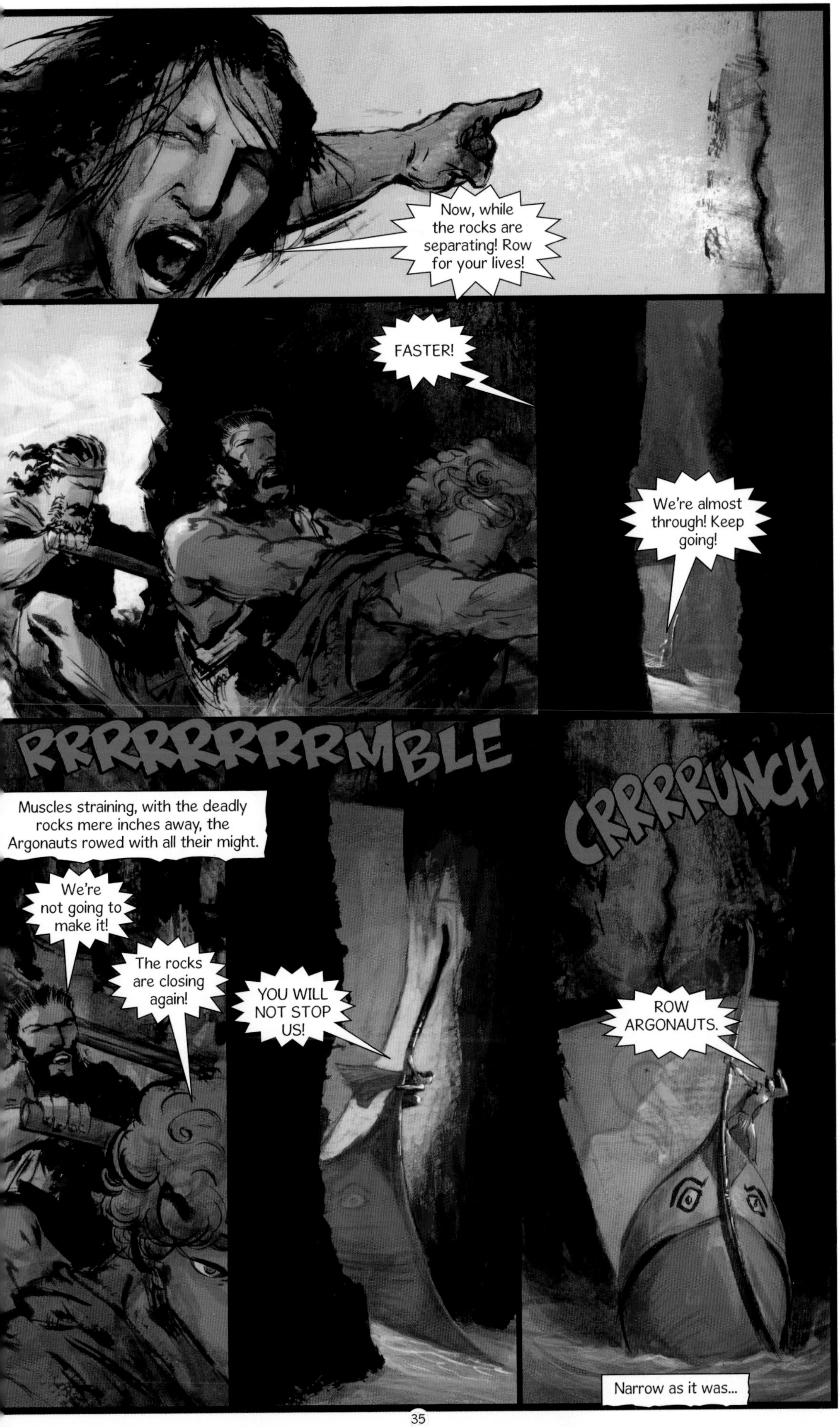
Now, while the rocks are separating! Row for your lives!
FASTER!
We're almost through! Keep going!
RRRRRRRRRMBLE
Muscles straining, with the deadly rocks mere inches away, the Argonauts rowed with all their might.
We're not going to make it!
The rocks are closing again!
YOU WILL NOT STOP US!
CRRRRUNCH
ROW ARGONAUTS.
Narrow as it was...

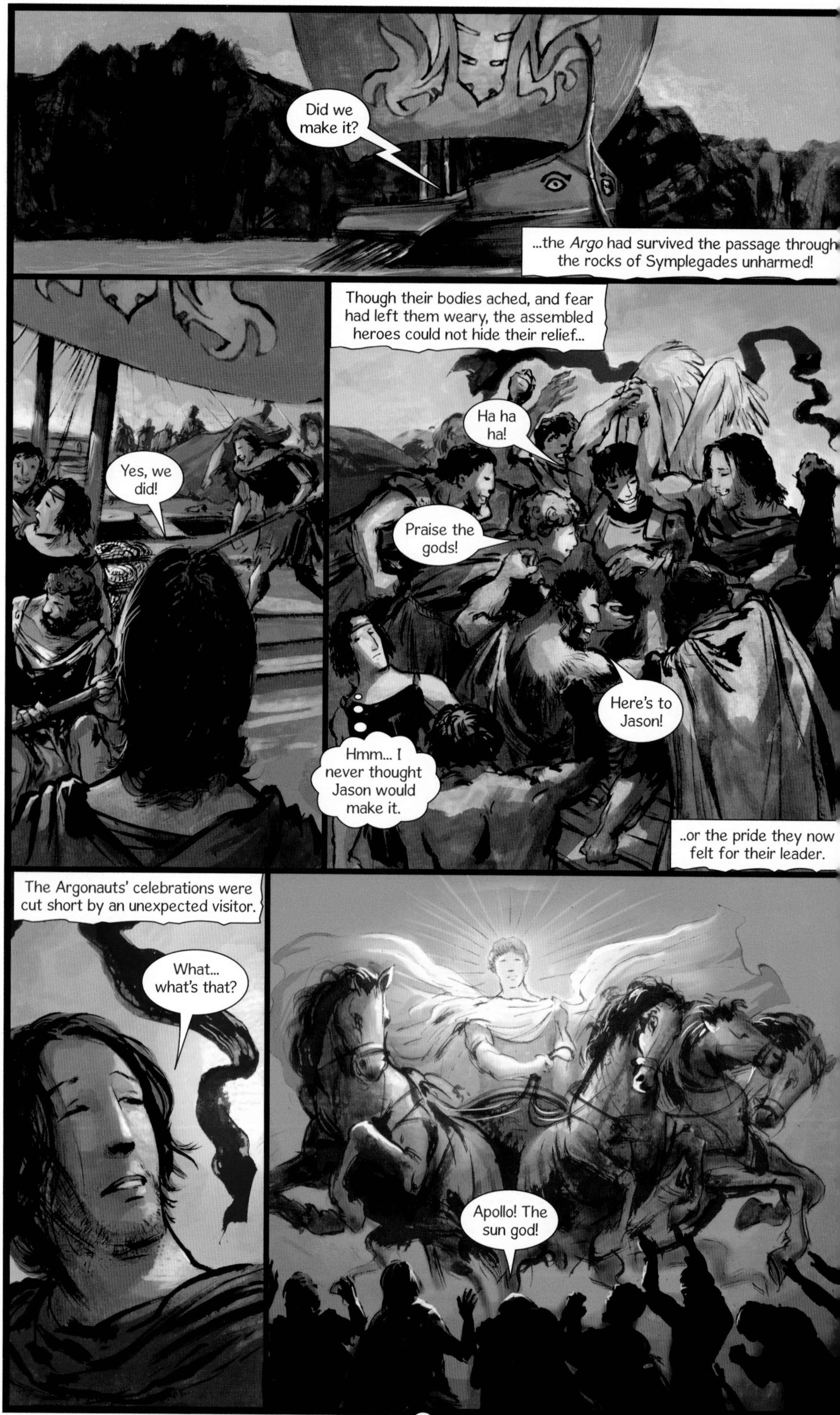
Did we make it?
...the *Argo* had survived the passage through the rocks of Symplegades unharmed!
Yes, we did!
Though their bodies ached, and fear had left them weary, the assembled heroes could not hide their relief...
Ha ha ha!
Praise the gods!
Here's to Jason!
Hmm... I never thought Jason would make it.
..or the pride they now felt for their leader.
The Argonauts' celebrations were cut short by an unexpected visitor.
What... what's that?
Apollo! The sun god!

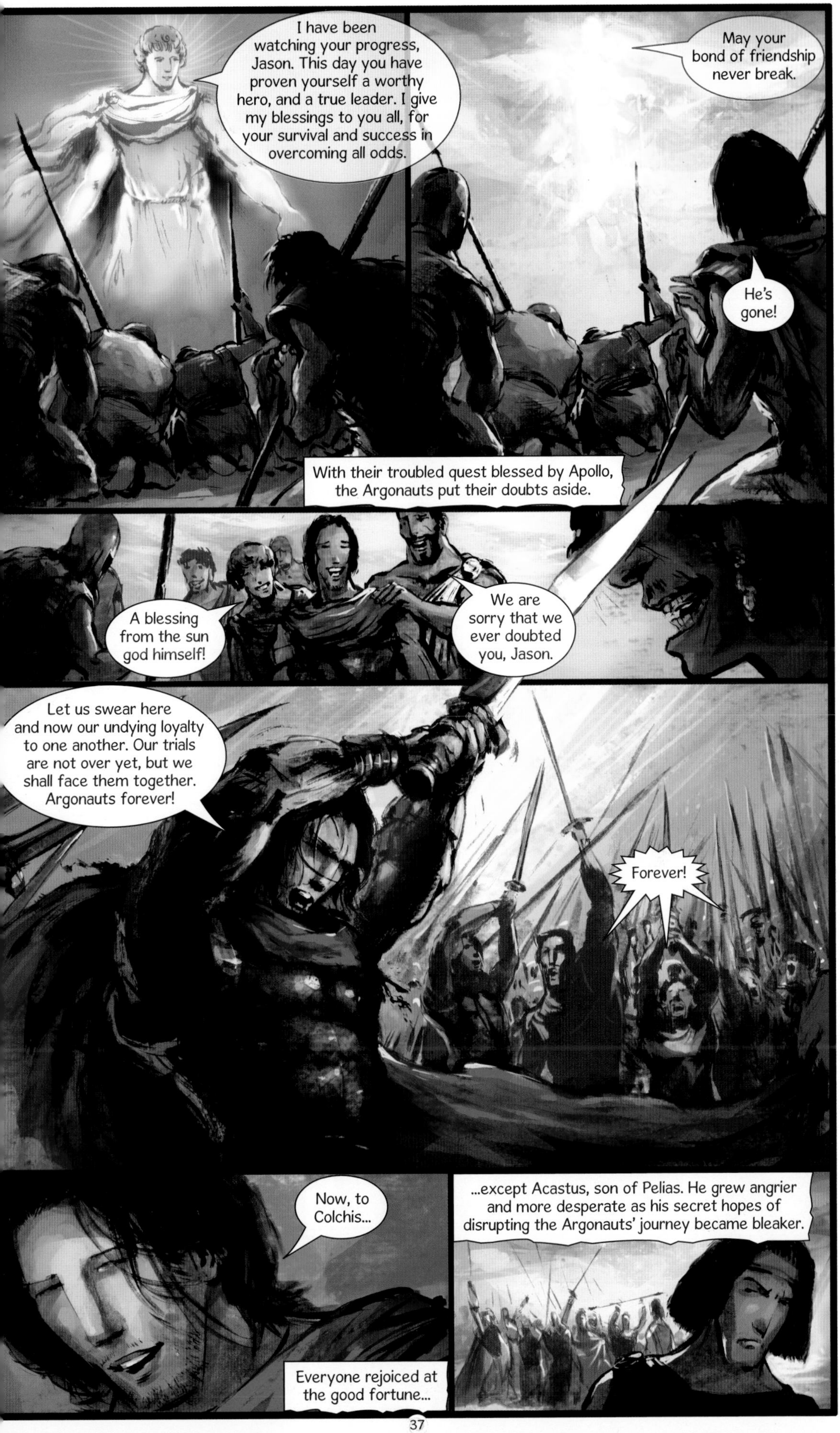

I have been watching your progress, Jason. This day you have proven yourself a worthy hero, and a true leader. I give my blessings to you all, for your survival and success in overcoming all odds.
May your bond of friendship never break.
He's gone!
With their troubled quest blessed by Apollo, the Argonauts put their doubts aside.
A blessing from the sun god himself!
We are sorry that we ever doubted you, Jason.
Let us swear here and now our undying loyalty to one another. Our trials are not over yet, but we shall face them together. Argonauts forever!
Forever!
Now, to Colchis...
Everyone rejoiced at the good fortune...
...except Acastus, son of Pelias. He grew angrier and more desperate as his secret hopes of disrupting the Argonauts' journey became bleaker.

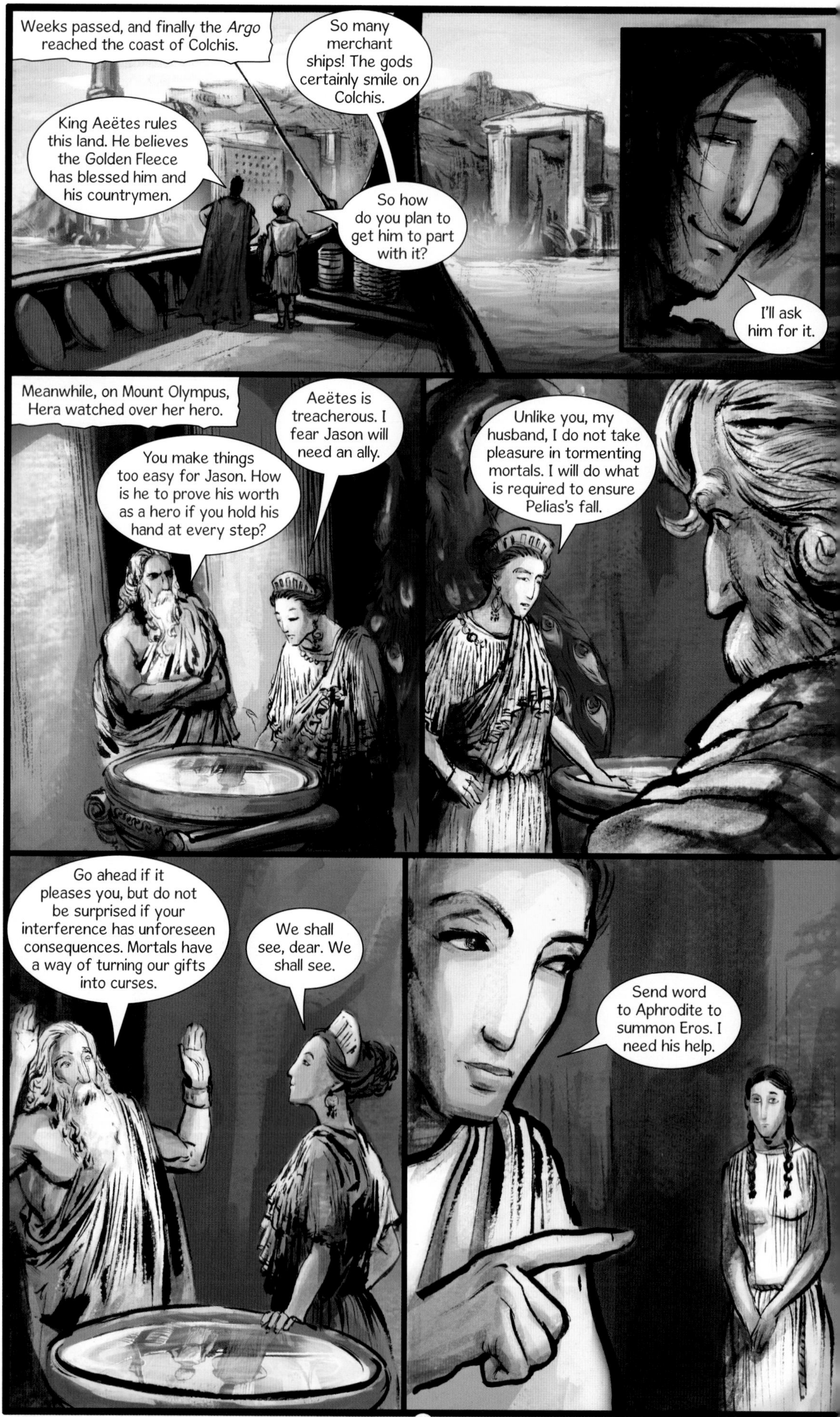

Weeks passed, and finally the *Argo* reached the coast of Colchis.
So many merchant ships! The gods certainly smile on Colchis.
King Aeëtes rules this land. He believes the Golden Fleece has blessed him and his countrymen.
So how do you plan to get him to part with it?
I'll ask him for it.
Meanwhile, on Mount Olympus, Hera watched over her hero.
Aeëtes is treacherous. I fear Jason will need an ally.
You make things too easy for Jason. How is he to prove his worth as a hero if you hold his hand at every step?
Unlike you, my husband, I do not take pleasure in tormenting mortals. I will do what is required to ensure Pelias's fall.
Go ahead if it pleases you, but do not be surprised if your interference has unforeseen consequences. Mortals have a way of turning our gifts into curses.
We shall see, dear. We shall see.
Send word to Aphrodite to summon Eros. I need his help.

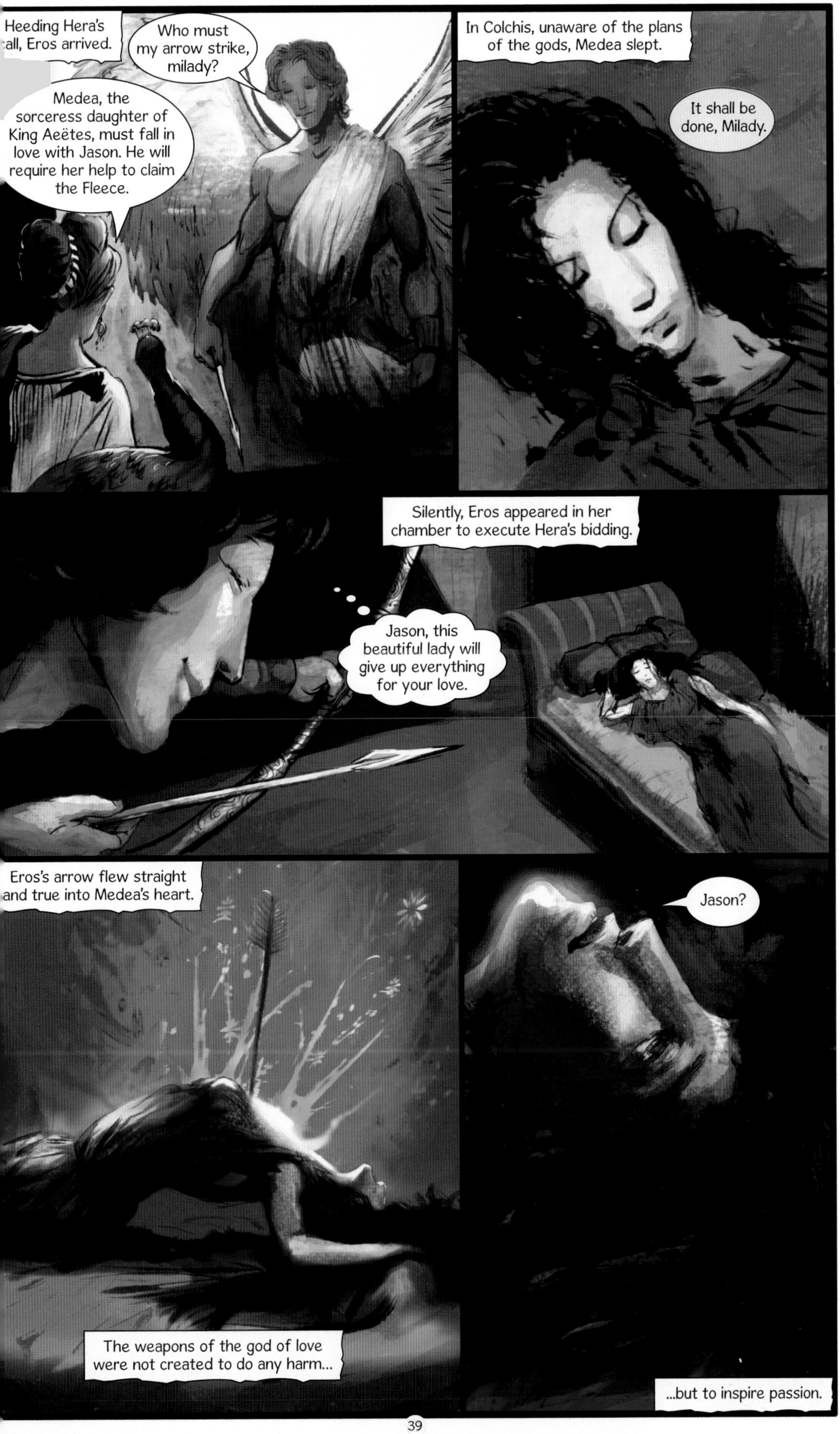
Heeding Hera's
call, Eros arrived.
Who must my arrow strike, milady?
Medea, the sorceress daughter of King Aeëtes, must fall in love with Jason. He will require her help to claim the Fleece.
In Colchis, unaware of the plans of the gods, Medea slept.
It shall be done, Milady.
Silently, Eros appeared in her chamber to execute Hera's bidding.
Jason, this beautiful lady will give up everything for your love.
Eros's arrow flew straight and true into Medea's heart.
The weapons of the god of love were not created to do any harm...
Jason?
...but to inspire passion.

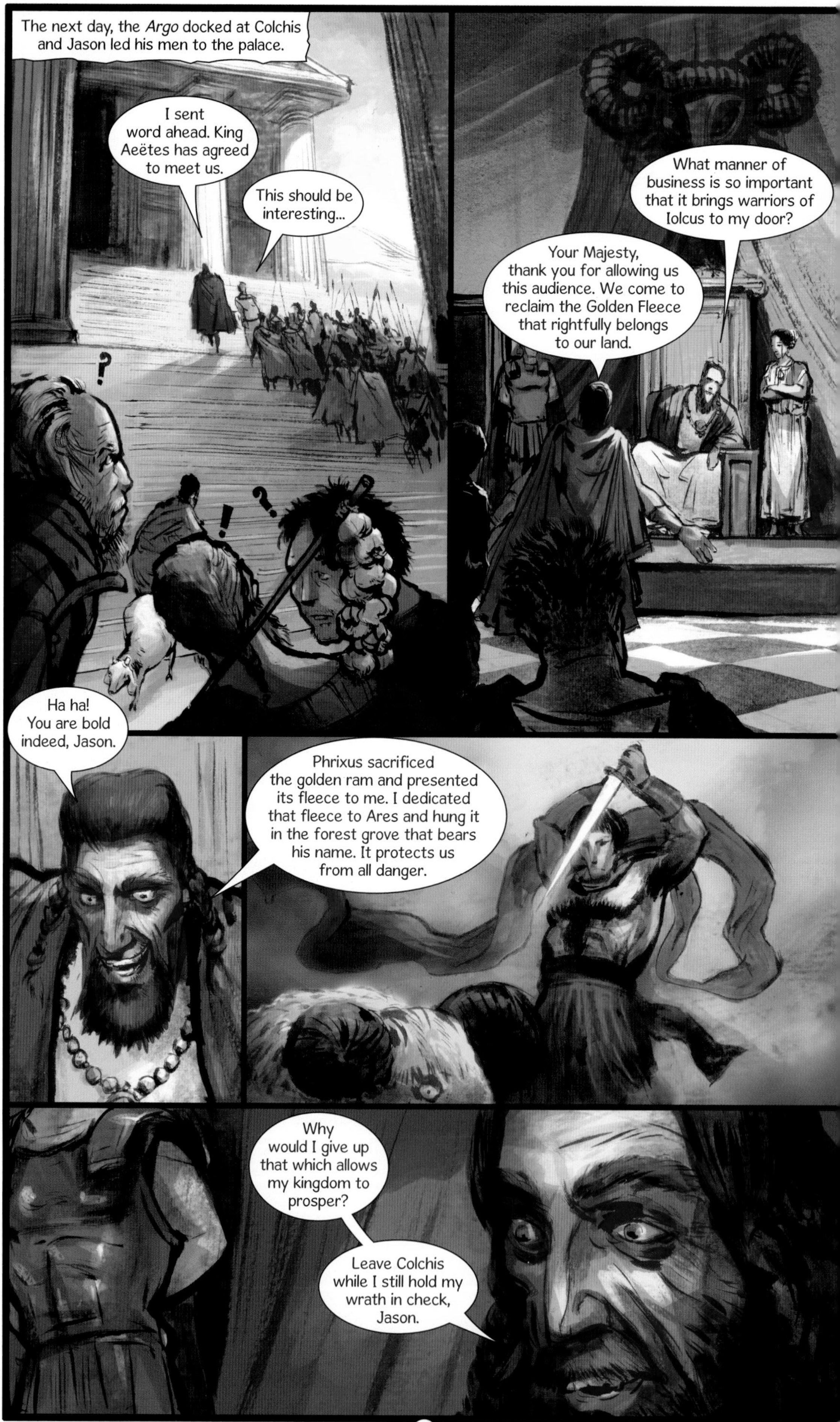
The next day, the Argo docked at Colchis and Jason led his men to the palace.
I sent word ahead. King Aeëtes has agreed to meet us.
This should be interesting...
?
!
?
What manner of business is so important that it brings warriors of Iolcus to my door?
Your Majesty, thank you for allowing us this audience. We come to reclaim the Golden Fleece that rightfully belongs to our land.
Ha ha! You are bold indeed, Jason.
Phrixus sacrificed the golden ram and presented its fleece to me. I dedicated that fleece to Ares and hung it in the forest grove that bears his name. It protects us from all danger.
Why would I give up that which allows my kingdom to prosper?
Leave Colchis while I still hold my wrath in check, Jason.

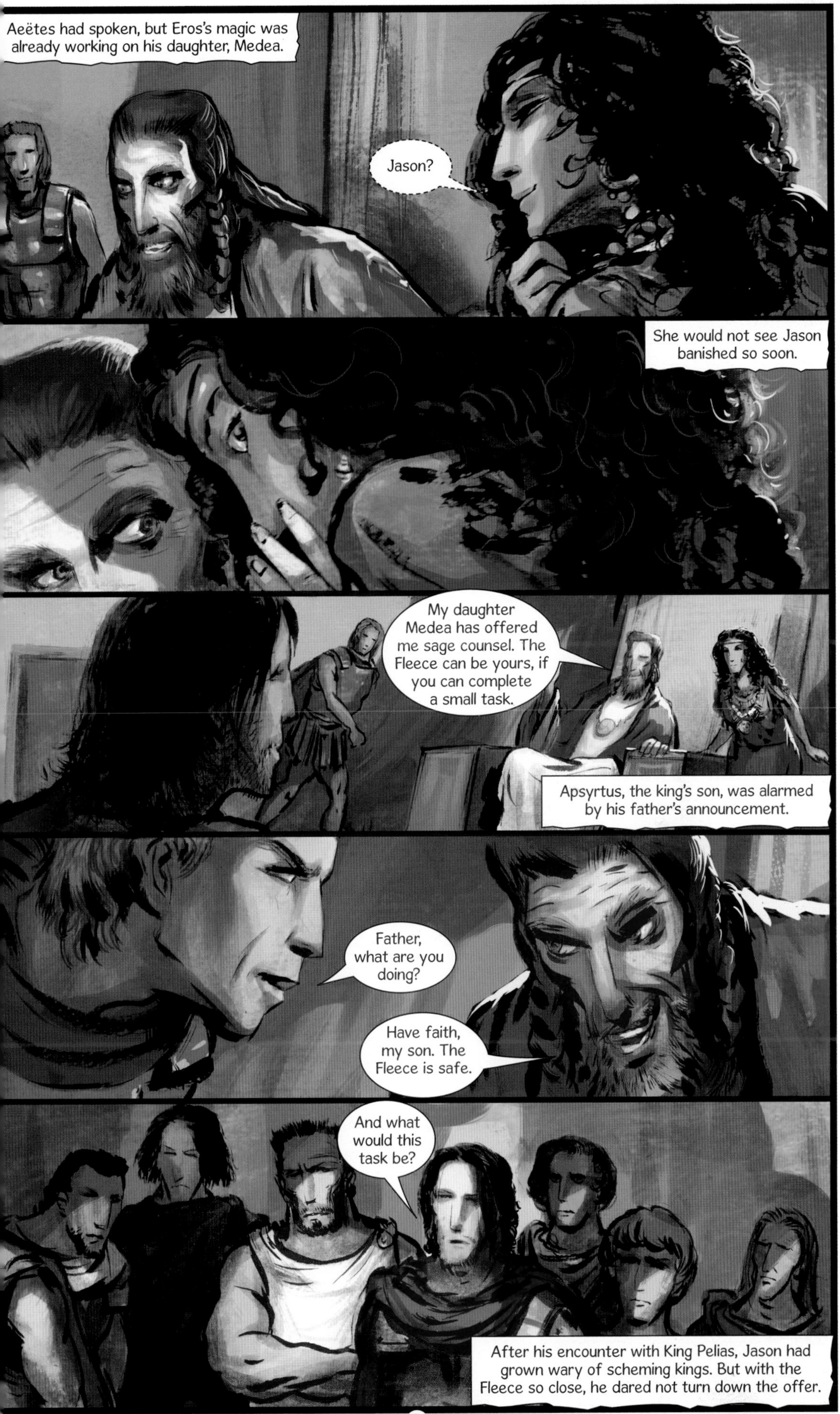

Aeëtes had spoken, but Eros's magic was already working on his daughter, Medea.
Jason?
She would not see Jason banished so soon.
My daughter Medea has offered me sage counsel. The Fleece can be yours, if you can complete a small task.
Apsyrtus, the king's son, was alarmed by his father's announcement.
Father, what are you doing?
Have faith, my son. The Fleece is safe.
And what would this task be?
After his encounter with King Pelias, Jason had grown wary of scheming kings. But with the Fleece so close, he dared not turn down the offer.

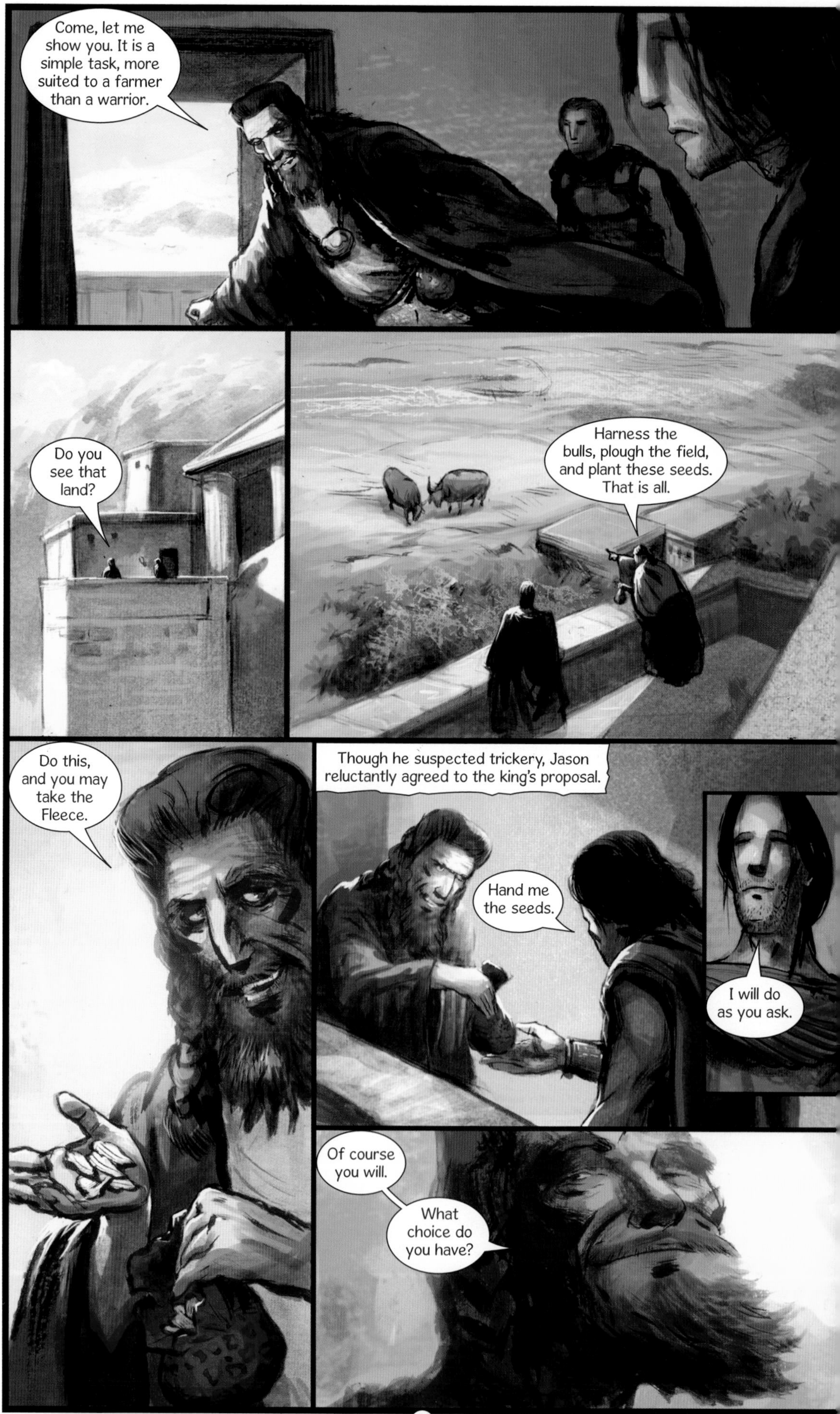

Come, let me show you. It is a simple task, more suited to a farmer than a warrior.
Do you see that land?
Harness the bulls, plough the field, and plant these seeds. That is all.
Do this, and you may take the Fleece.
Though he suspected trickery, Jason reluctantly agreed to the king's proposal.
Hand me the seeds.
I will do as you ask.
Of course you will.
What choice do you have?

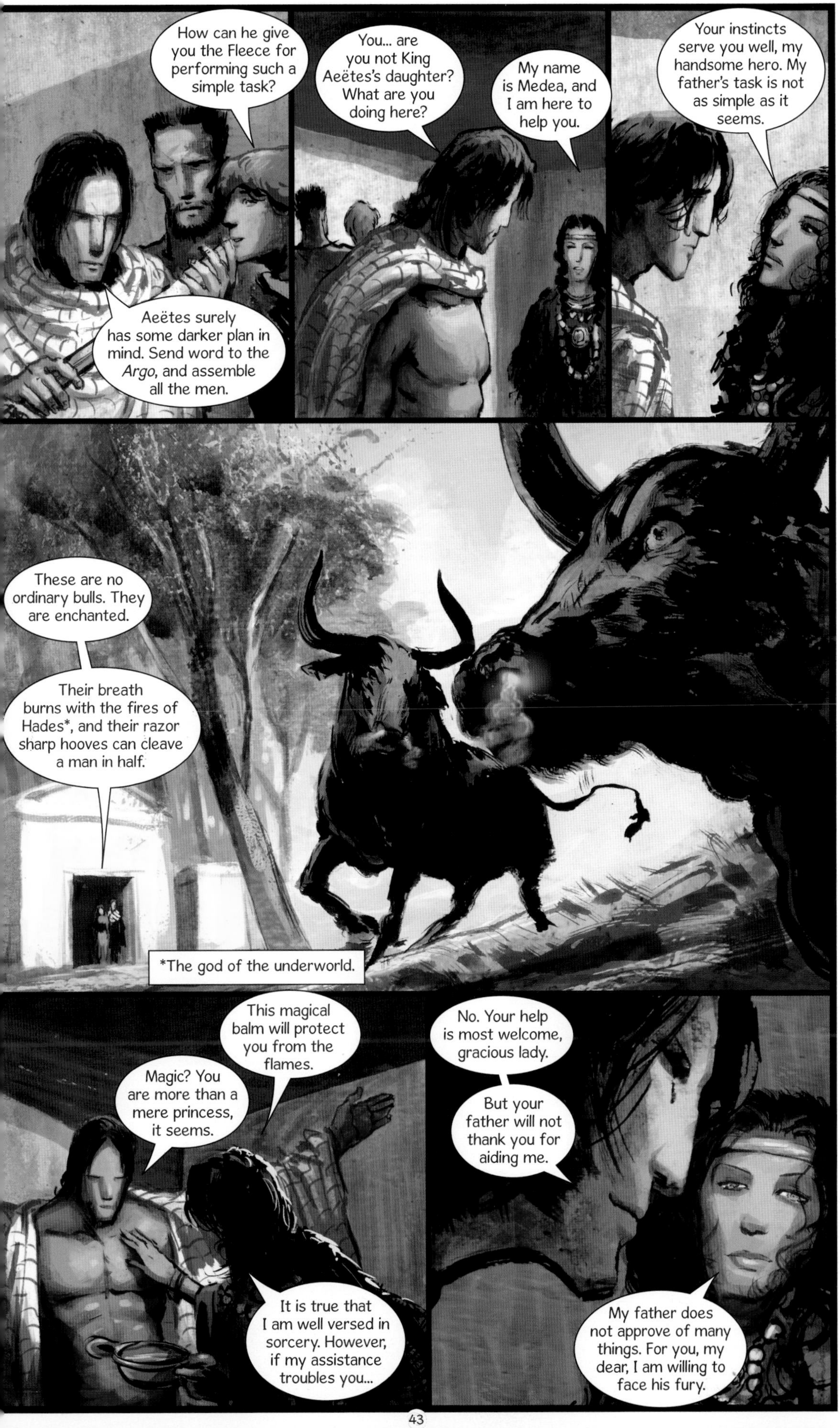
How can he give you the Fleece for performing such a simple task?
Aeëtes surely has some darker plan in mind. Send word to the *Argo*, and assemble all the men.
You... are you not King Aeëtes's daughter? What are you doing here?
My name is Medea, and I am here to help you.
Your instincts serve you well, my handsome hero. My father's task is not as simple as it seems.
These are no ordinary bulls. They are enchanted.
Their breath burns with the fires of Hades*, and their razor sharp hooves can cleave a man in half.
*The god of the underworld.
Magic? You are more than a mere princess, it seems.
This magical balm will protect you from the flames.
It is true that I am well versed in sorcery. However, if my assistance troubles you...
No. Your help is most welcome, gracious lady.
But your father will not thank you for aiding me.
My father does not approve of many things. For you, my dear, I am willing to face his fury.

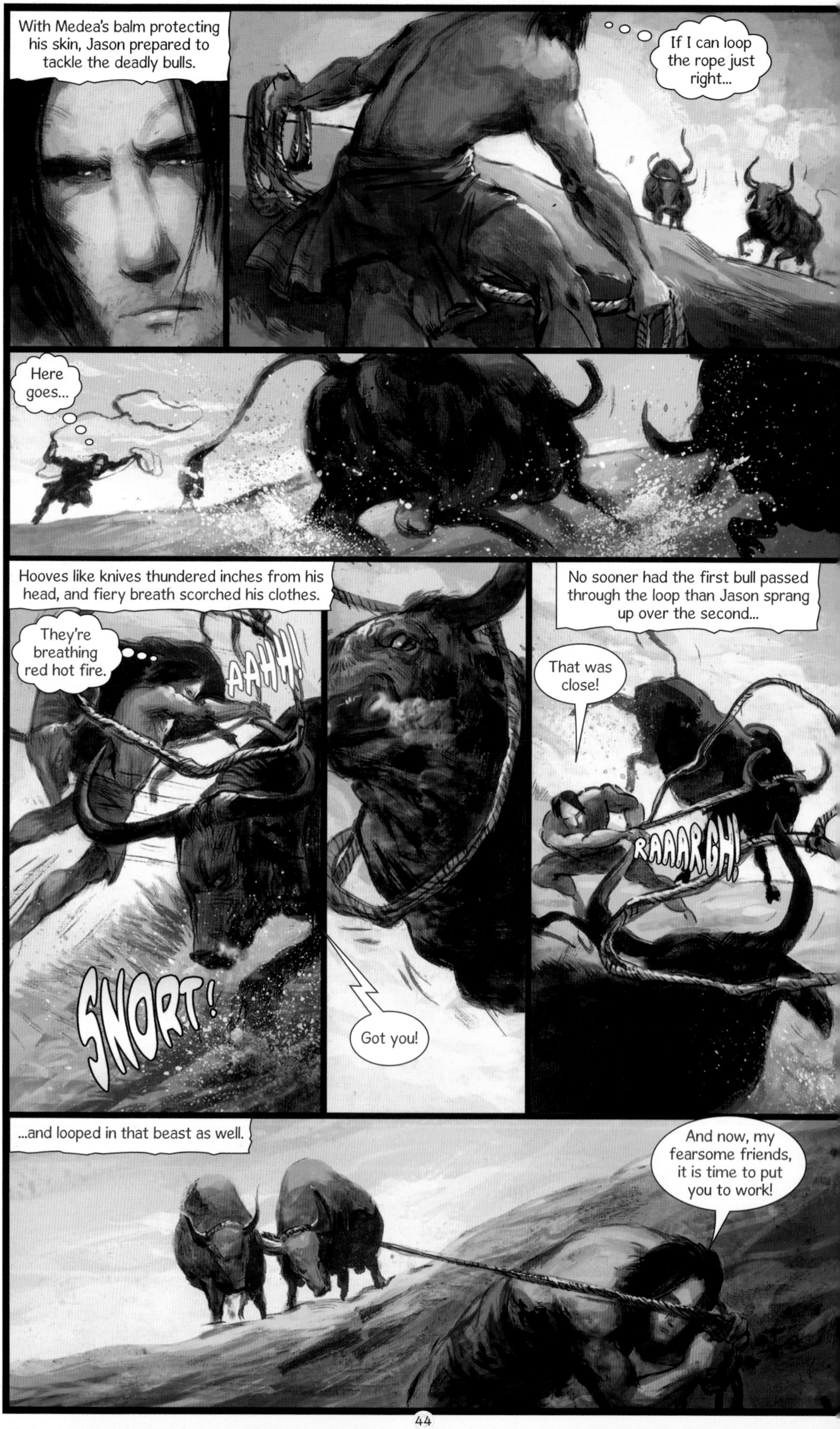
With Medea's balm protecting his skin, Jason prepared to tackle the deadly bulls.
If I can loop the rope just right...
Here goes...
Hooves like knives thundered inches from his head, and fiery breath scorched his clothes.
They're breathing red hot fire.
AAHH!
SNORT!
Got you!
No sooner had the first bull passed through the loop than Jason sprang up over the second...
That was close!
RAAARGH!
...and looped in that beast as well.
And now, my fearsome friends, it is time to put you to work!

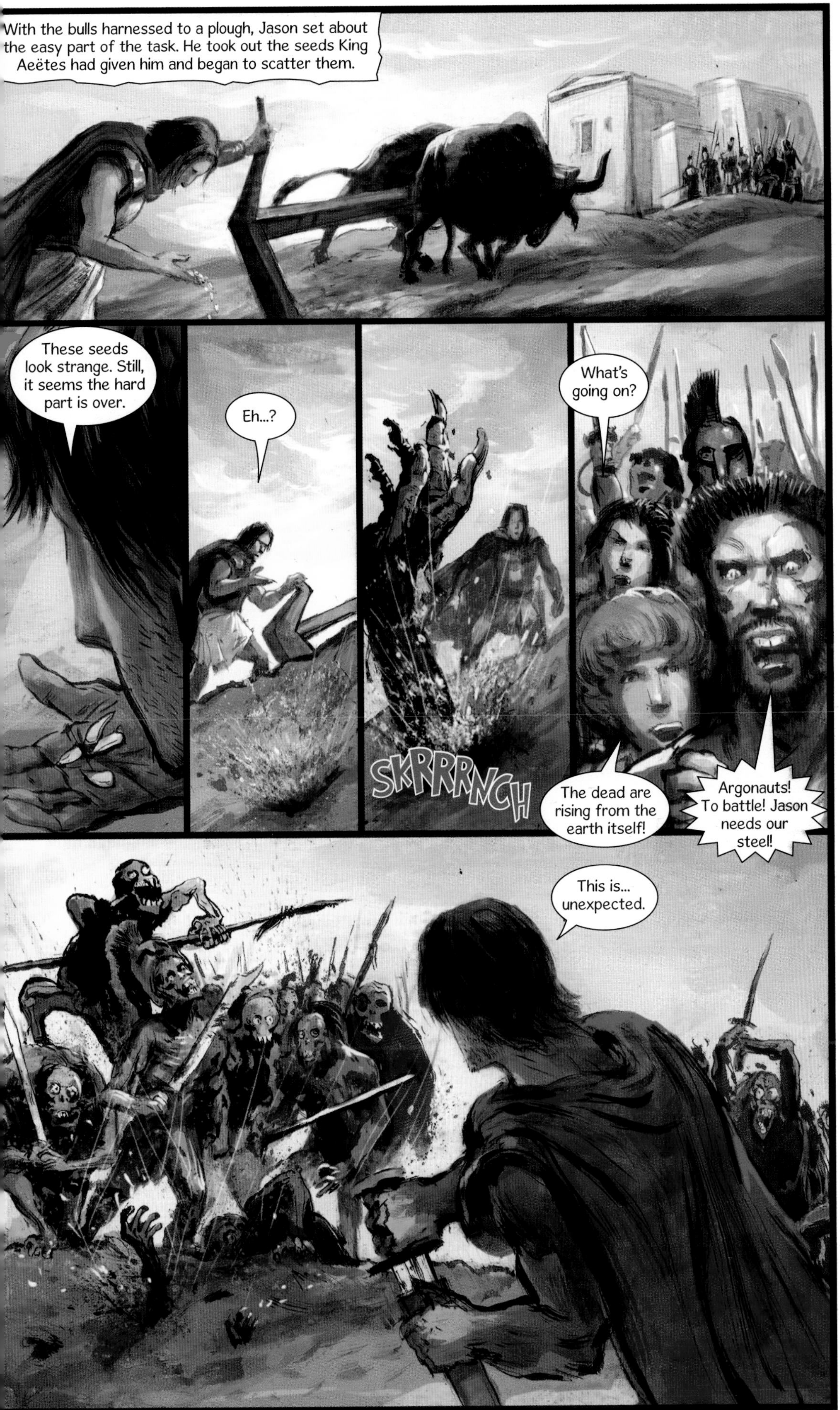
With the bulls harnessed to a plough, Jason set about the easy part of the task. He took out the seeds King Aeëtes had given him and began to scatter them.
These seeds look strange. Still, it seems the hard part is over.
Eh...?
SKRRRNCH
What's going on?
The dead are rising from the earth itself!
Argonauts! To battle! Jason needs our steel!
This is... unexpected.

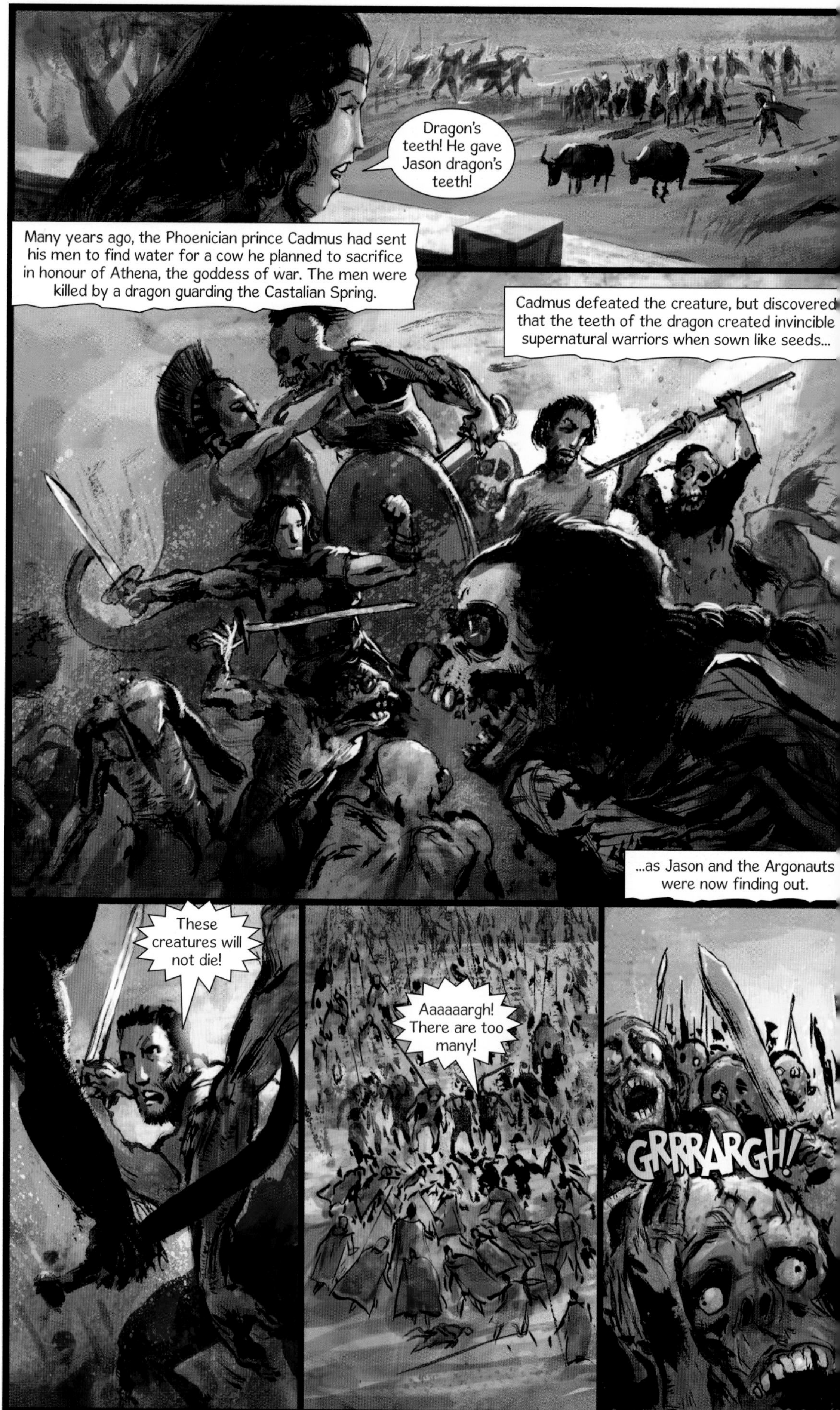

Dragon's teeth! He gave Jason dragon's teeth!
Many years ago, the Phoenician prince Cadmus had sent his men to find water for a cow he planned to sacrifice in honour of Athena, the goddess of war. The men were killed by a dragon guarding the Castalian Spring.
Cadmus defeated the creature, but discovered that the teeth of the dragon created invincible supernatural warriors when sown like seeds...
...as Jason and the Argonauts were now finding out.
These creatures will not die!
Aaaaaargh! There are too many!
GRRRARGH!

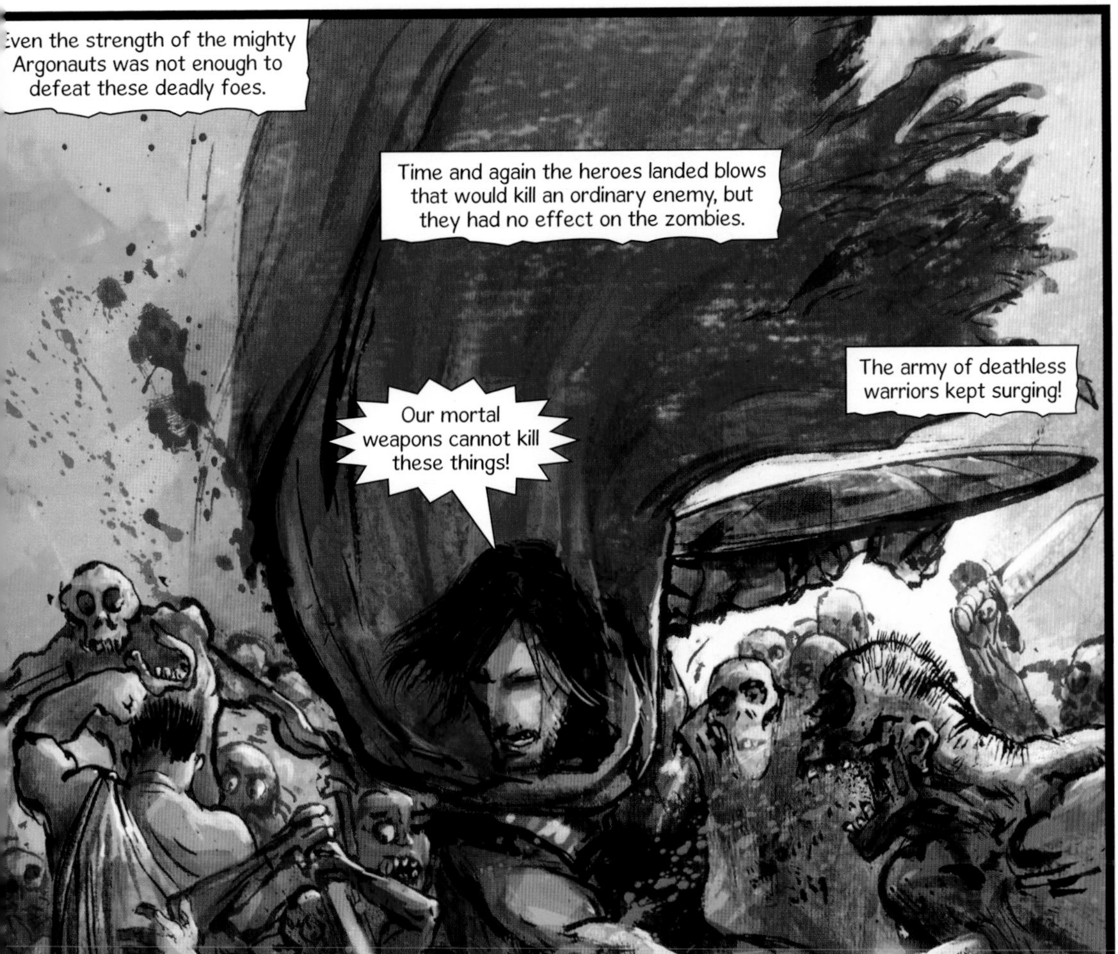
:ven the strength of the mighty Argonauts was not enough to defeat these deadly foes.
Time and again the heroes landed blows that would kill an ordinary enemy, but they had no effect on the zombies.
The army of deathless warriors kept surging!
Our mortal weapons cannot kill these things!

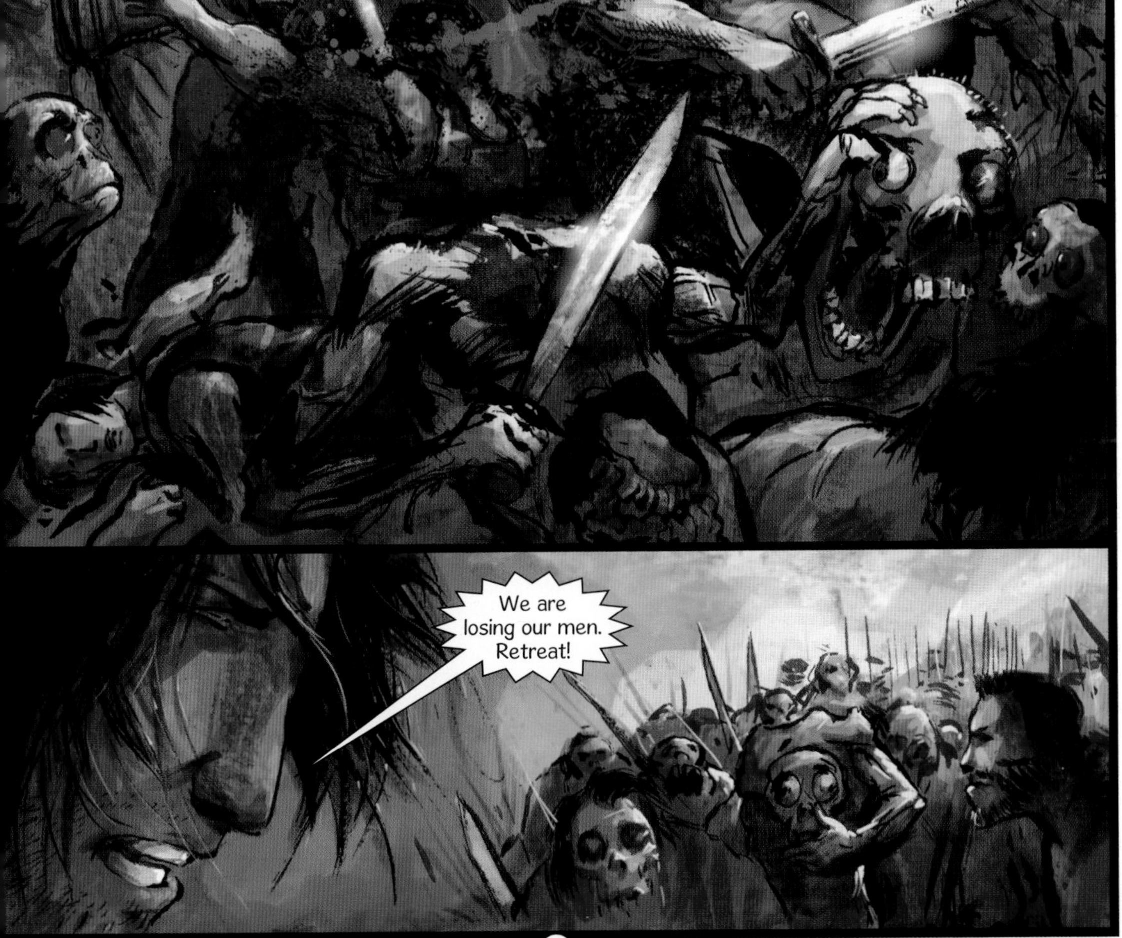
We are losing our men. Retreat!

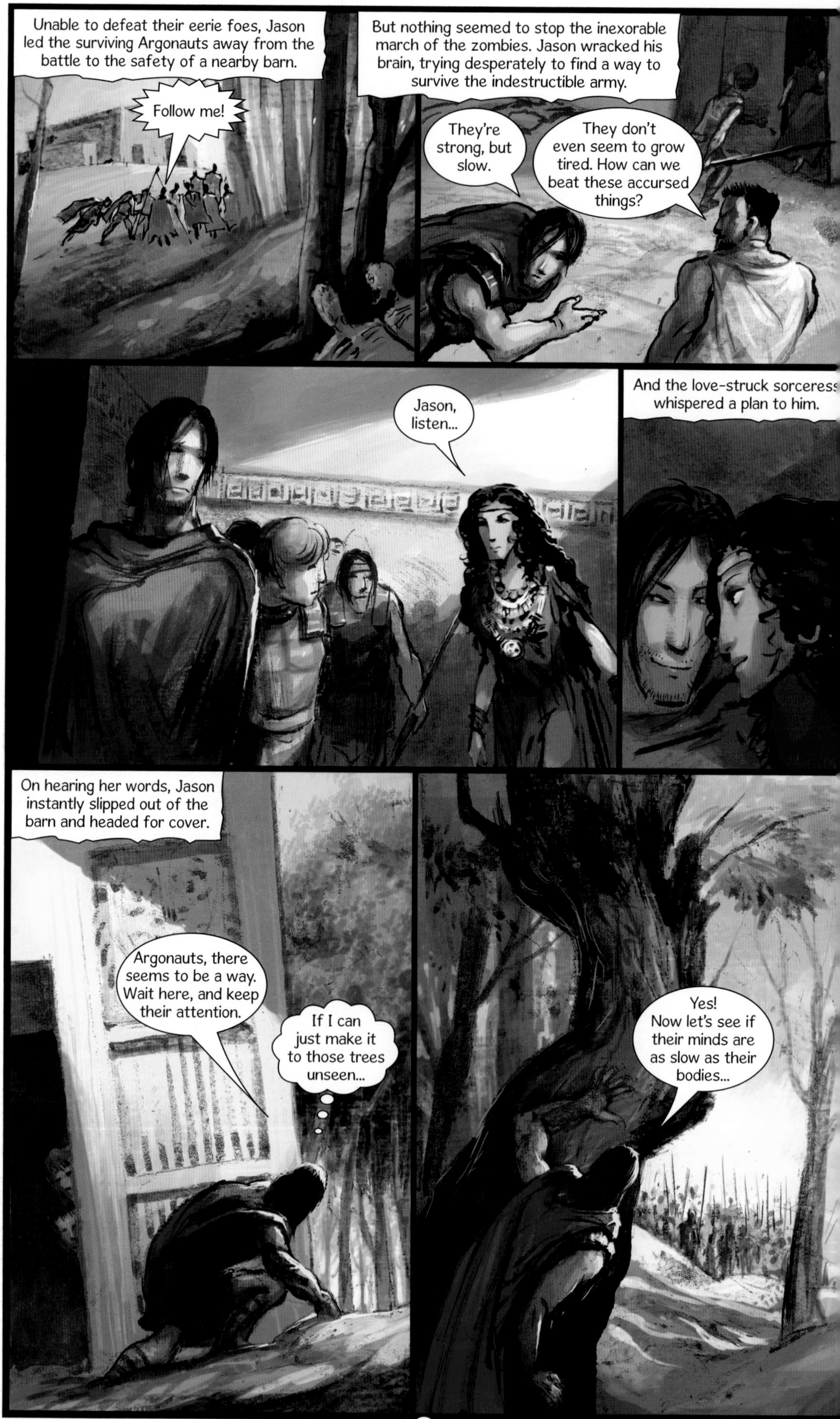
Unable to defeat their eerie foes, Jason led the surviving Argonauts away from the battle to the safety of a nearby barn.
Follow me!
But nothing seemed to stop the inexorable march of the zombies. Jason wracked his brain, trying desperately to find a way to survive the indestructible army.
They're strong, but slow.
They don't even seem to grow tired. How can we beat these accursed things?
Jason, listen...
And the love-struck sorceress whispered a plan to him.
On hearing her words, Jason instantly slipped out of the barn and headed for cover.
Argonauts, there seems to be a way. Wait here, and keep their attention.
If I can just make it to those trees unseen...
Yes! Now let's see if their minds are as slow as their bodies...

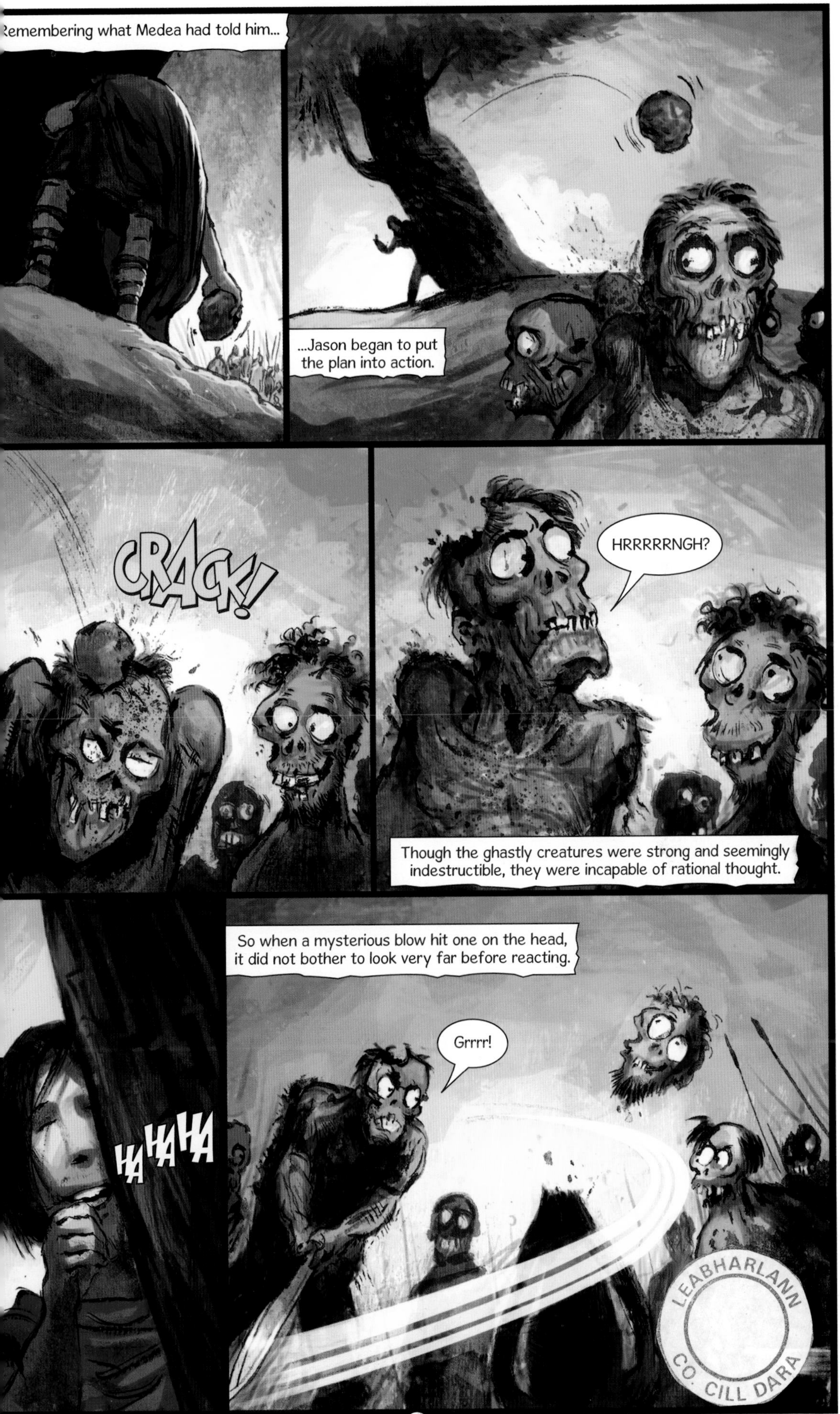
Remembering what Medea had told him...
...Jason began to put the plan into action.
CRACK!
HRRRRRNGH?
Though the ghastly creatures were strong and seemingly indestructible, they were incapable of rational thought.
So when a mysterious blow hit one on the head, it did not bother to look very far before reacting.
HAHAHA
Grrrr!

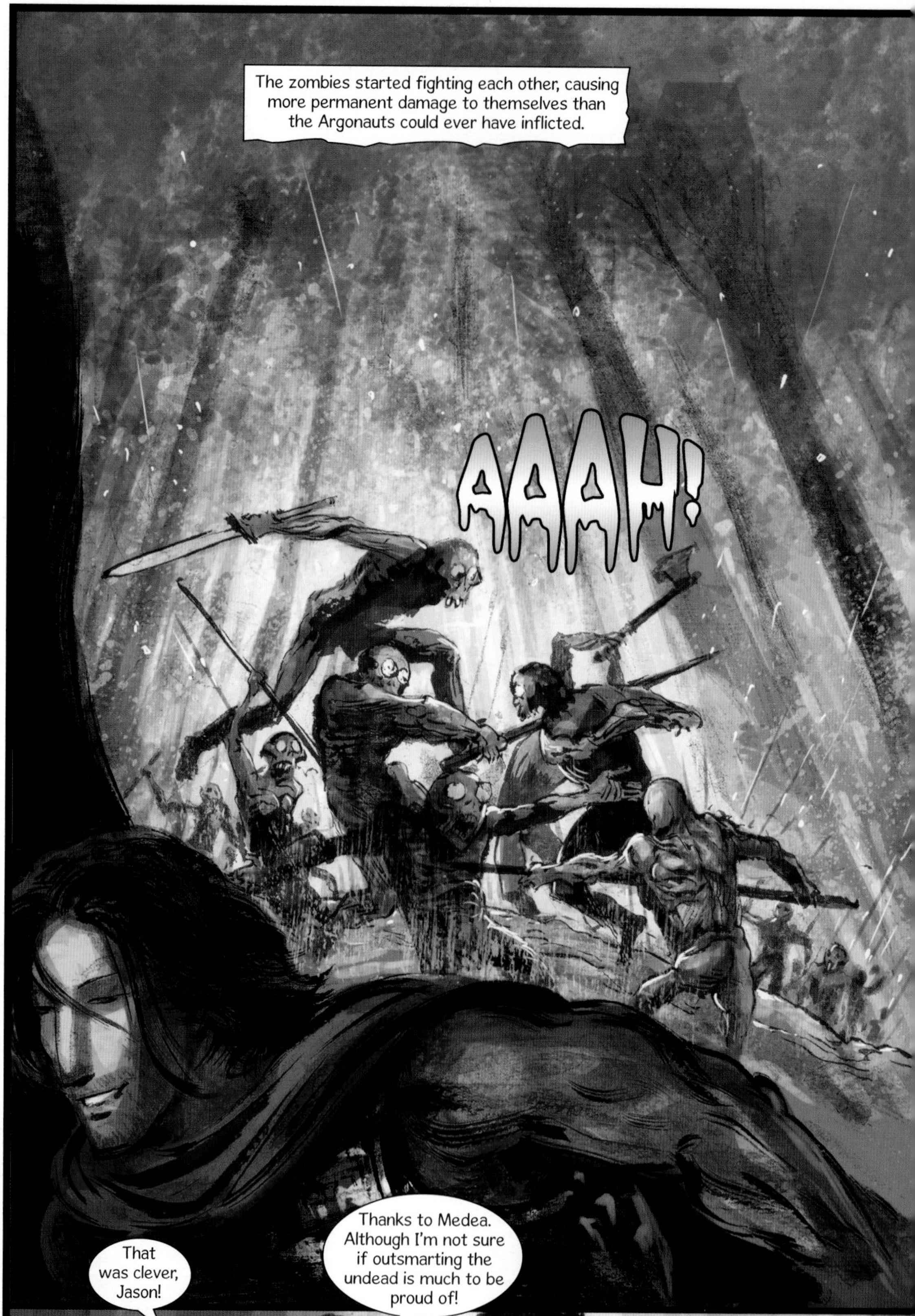
The zombies started fighting each other, causing more permanent damage to themselves than the Argonauts could ever have inflicted.
AAAH!

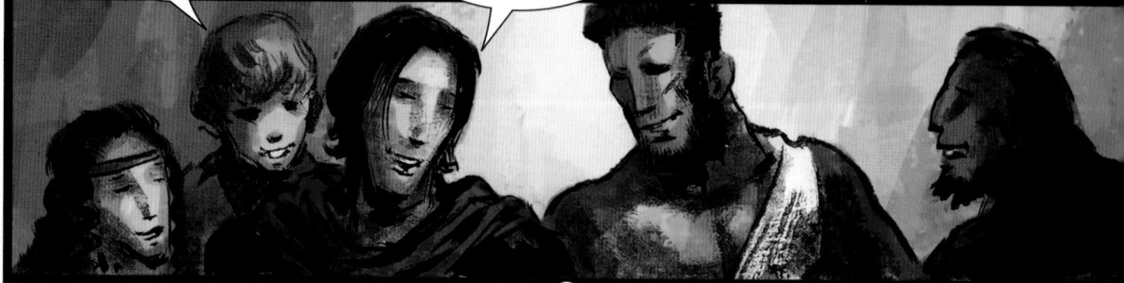
That was clever, Jason!
Thanks to Medea. Although I'm not sure if outsmarting the undead is much to be proud of!

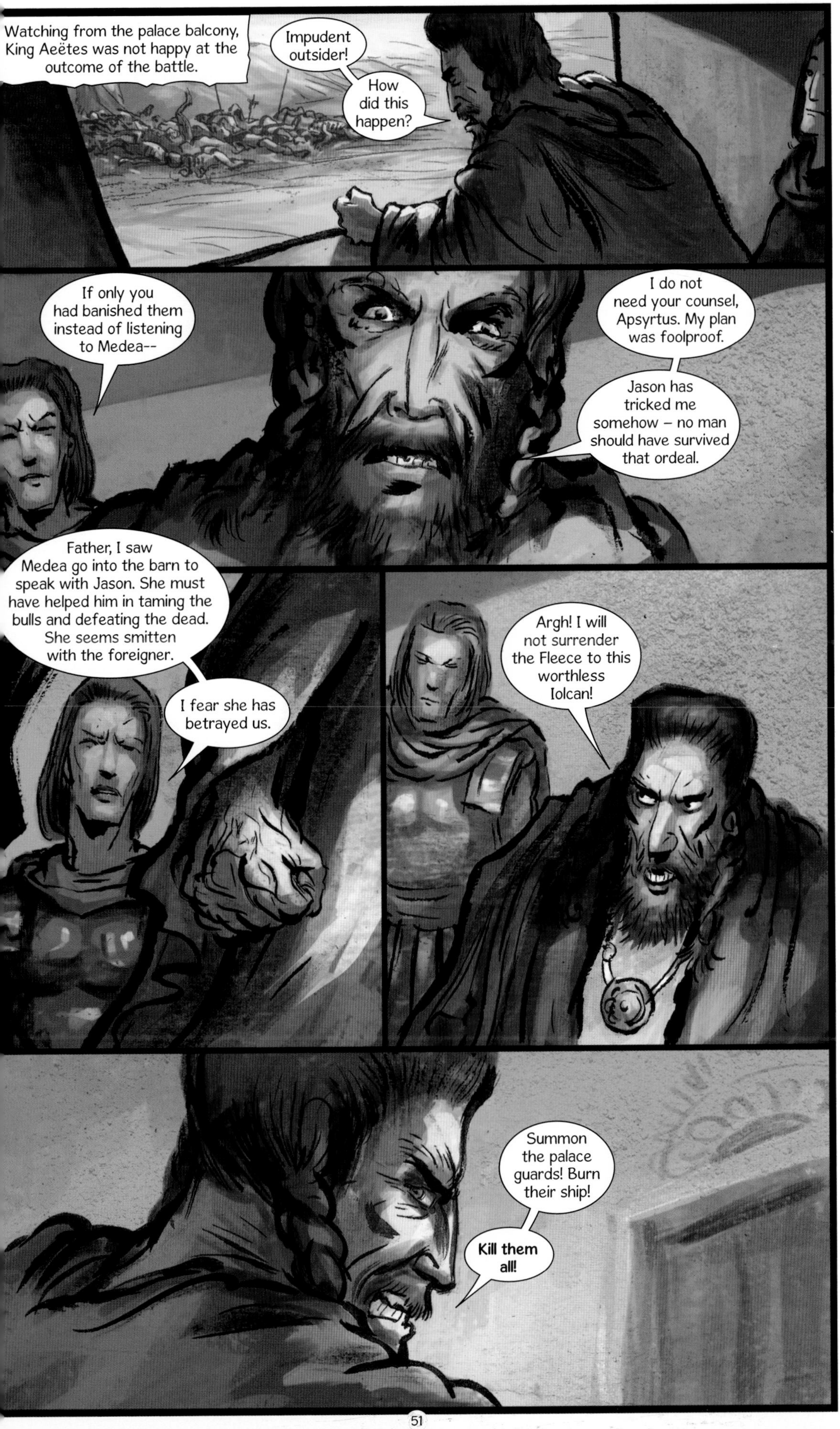

Watching from the palace balcony, King Aeëtes was not happy at the outcome of the battle.
Impudent outsider!
How did this happen?
If only you had banished them instead of listening to Medea--
I do not need your counsel, Apsyrtus. My plan was foolproof.
Jason has tricked me somehow – no man should have survived that ordeal.
Father, I saw Medea go into the barn to speak with Jason. She must have helped him in taming the bulls and defeating the dead. She seems smitten with the foreigner.
I fear she has betrayed us.
Argh! I will not surrender the Fleece to this worthless Iolcan!
Summon the palace guards! Burn their ship!
Kill them all!

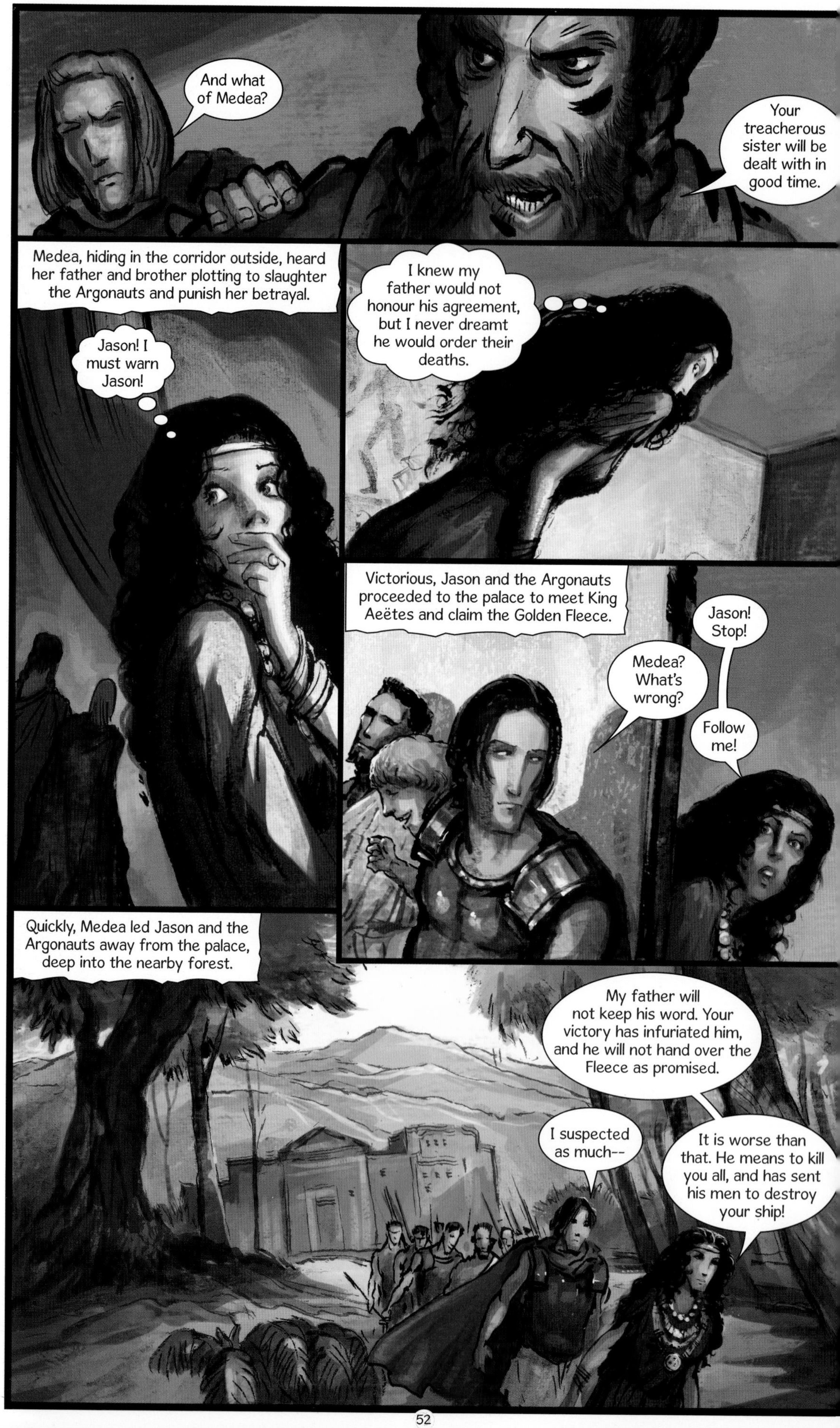
And what of Medea?
Your treacherous sister will be dealt with in good time.
Medea, hiding in the corridor outside, heard her father and brother plotting to slaughter the Argonauts and punish her betrayal.
Jason! I must warn Jason!
I knew my father would not honour his agreement, but I never dreamt he would order their deaths.
Victorious, Jason and the Argonauts proceeded to the palace to meet King Aeëtes and claim the Golden Fleece.
Jason! Stop!
Medea? What's wrong?
Follow me!
Quickly, Medea led Jason and the Argonauts away from the palace, deep into the nearby forest.
My father will not keep his word. Your victory has infuriated him, and he will not hand over the Fleece as promised.
I suspected as much--
It is worse than that. He means to kill you all, and has sent his men to destroy your ship!

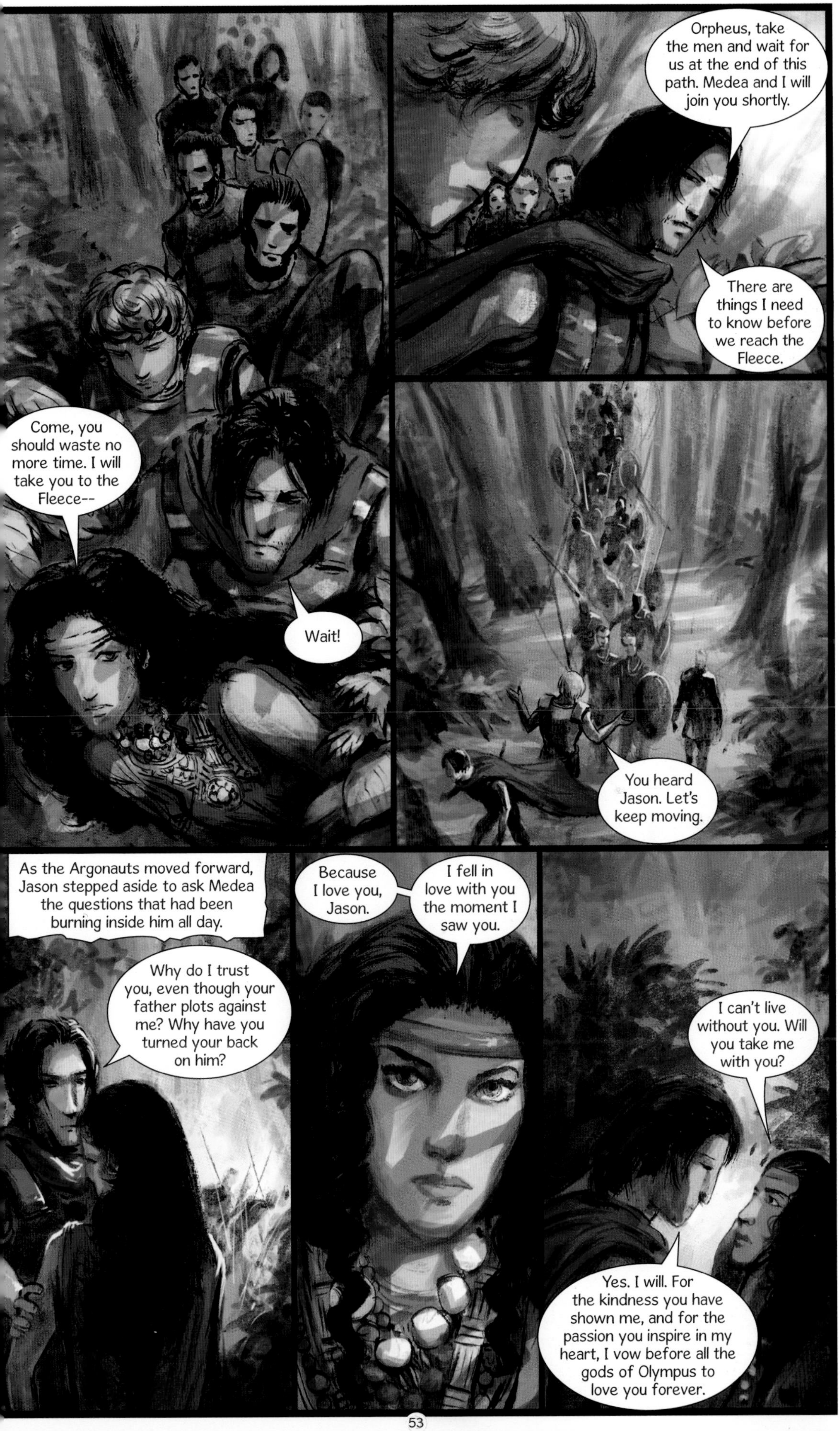
Come, you should waste no more time. I will take you to the Fleece--
Wait!
Orpheus, take the men and wait for us at the end of this path. Medea and I will join you shortly.
There are things I need to know before we reach the Fleece.
You heard Jason. Let's keep moving.
As the Argonauts moved forward, Jason stepped aside to ask Medea the questions that had been burning inside him all day.
Why do I trust you, even though your father plots against me? Why have you turned your back on him?
Because I love you, Jason.
I fell in love with you the moment I saw you.
I can't live without you. Will you take me with you?
Yes. I will. For the kindness you have shown me, and for the passion you inspire in my heart, I vow before all the gods of Olympus to love you forever.

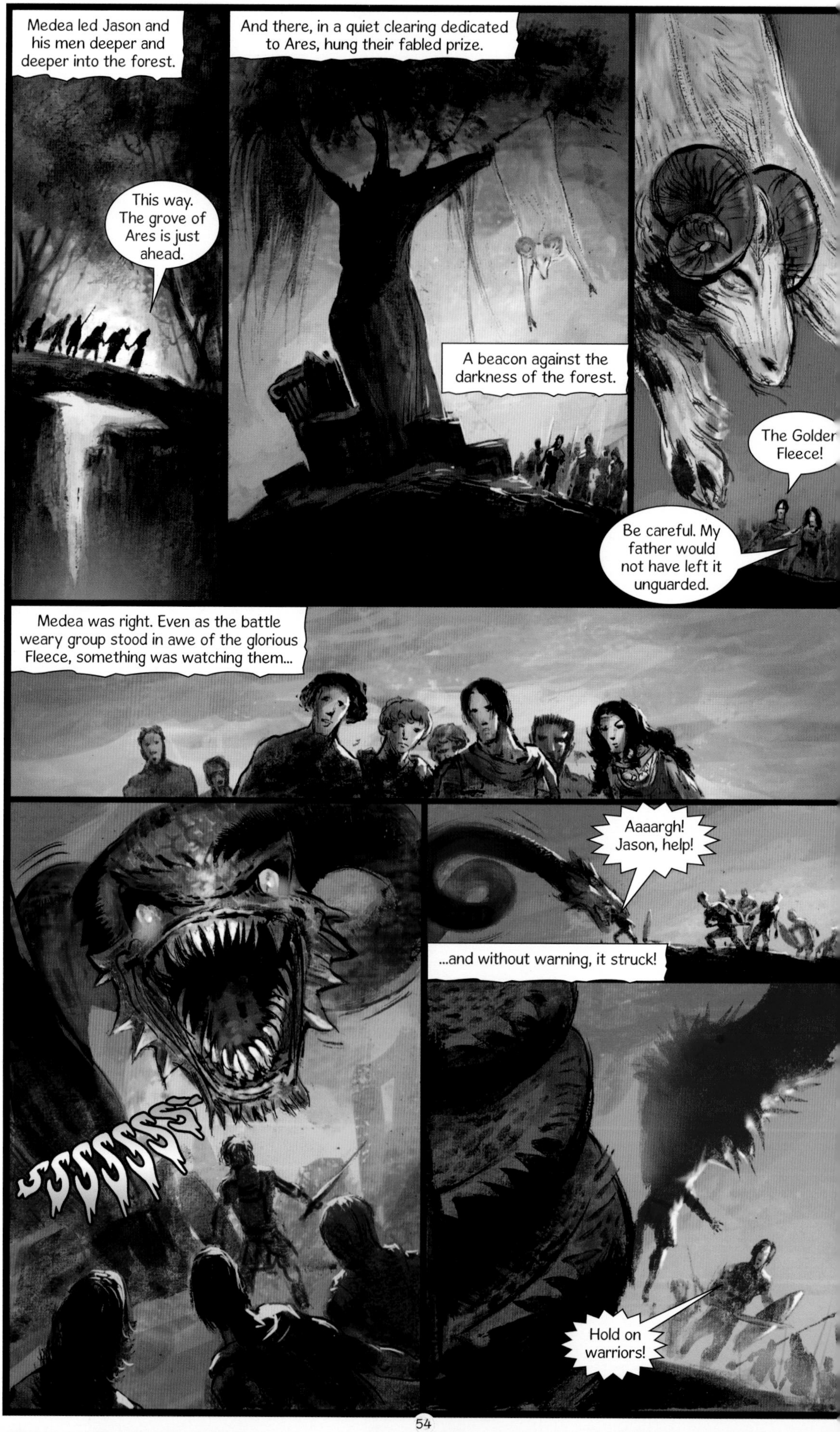

Medea led Jason and his men deeper and deeper into the forest.
This way. The grove of Ares is just ahead.
And there, in a quiet clearing dedicated to Ares, hung their fabled prize.
A beacon against the darkness of the forest.
The Golden Fleece!
Be careful. My father would not have left it unguarded.
Medea was right. Even as the battle weary group stood in awe of the glorious Fleece, something was watching them...
SSSSSSS
Aaaargh! Jason, help!
...and without warning, it struck!
Hold on warriors!

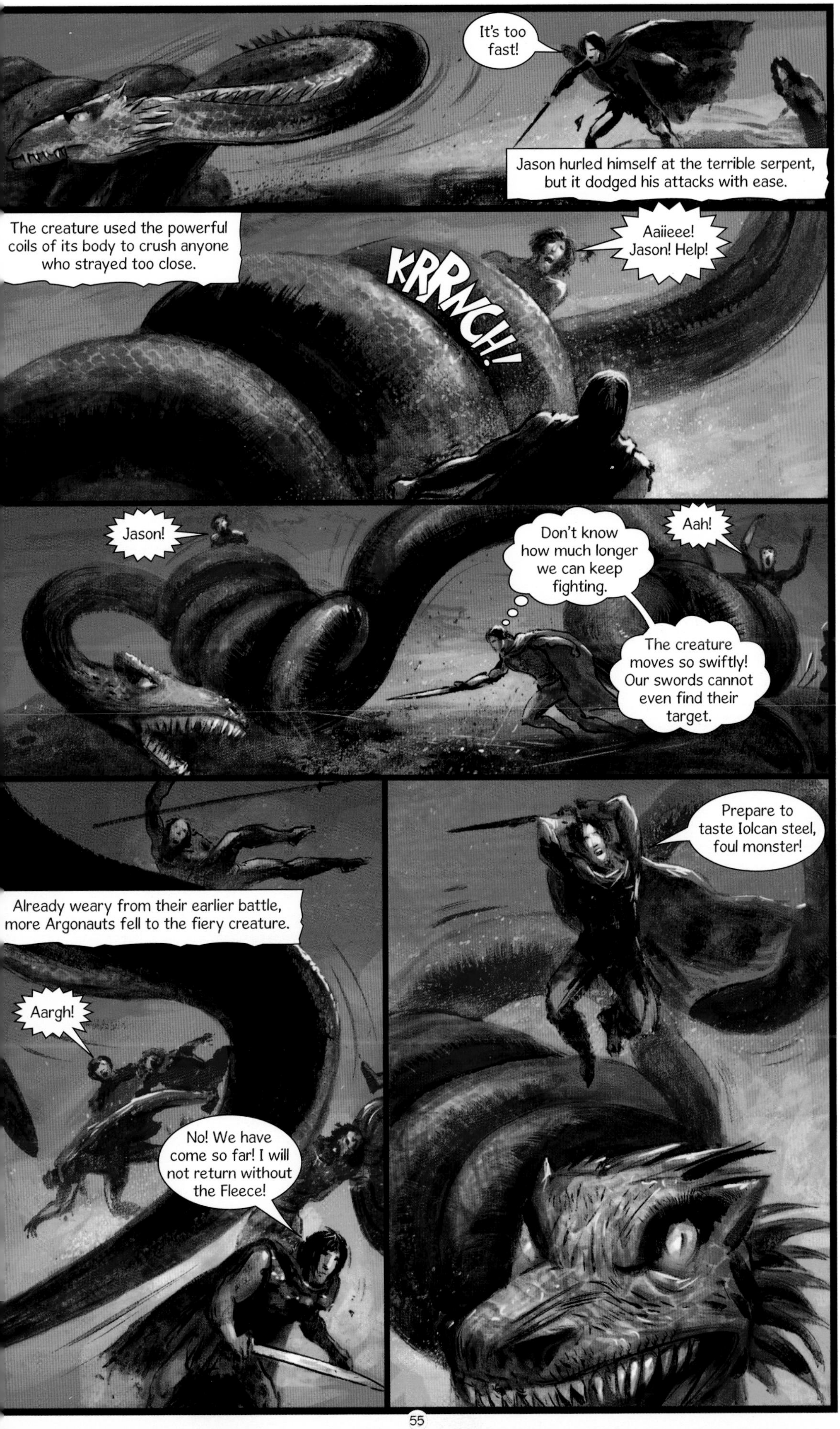
It's too fast!
Jason hurled himself at the terrible serpent, but it dodged his attacks with ease.
The creature used the powerful coils of its body to crush anyone who strayed too close.
KRRNCH!
Aaiieee! Jason! Help!
Jason!
Don't know how much longer we can keep fighting.
Aah!
The creature moves so swiftly! Our swords cannot even find their target.
Already weary from their earlier battle, more Argonauts fell to the fiery creature.
Aargh!
No! We have come so far! I will not return without the Fleece!
Prepare to taste Iolcan steel, foul monster!

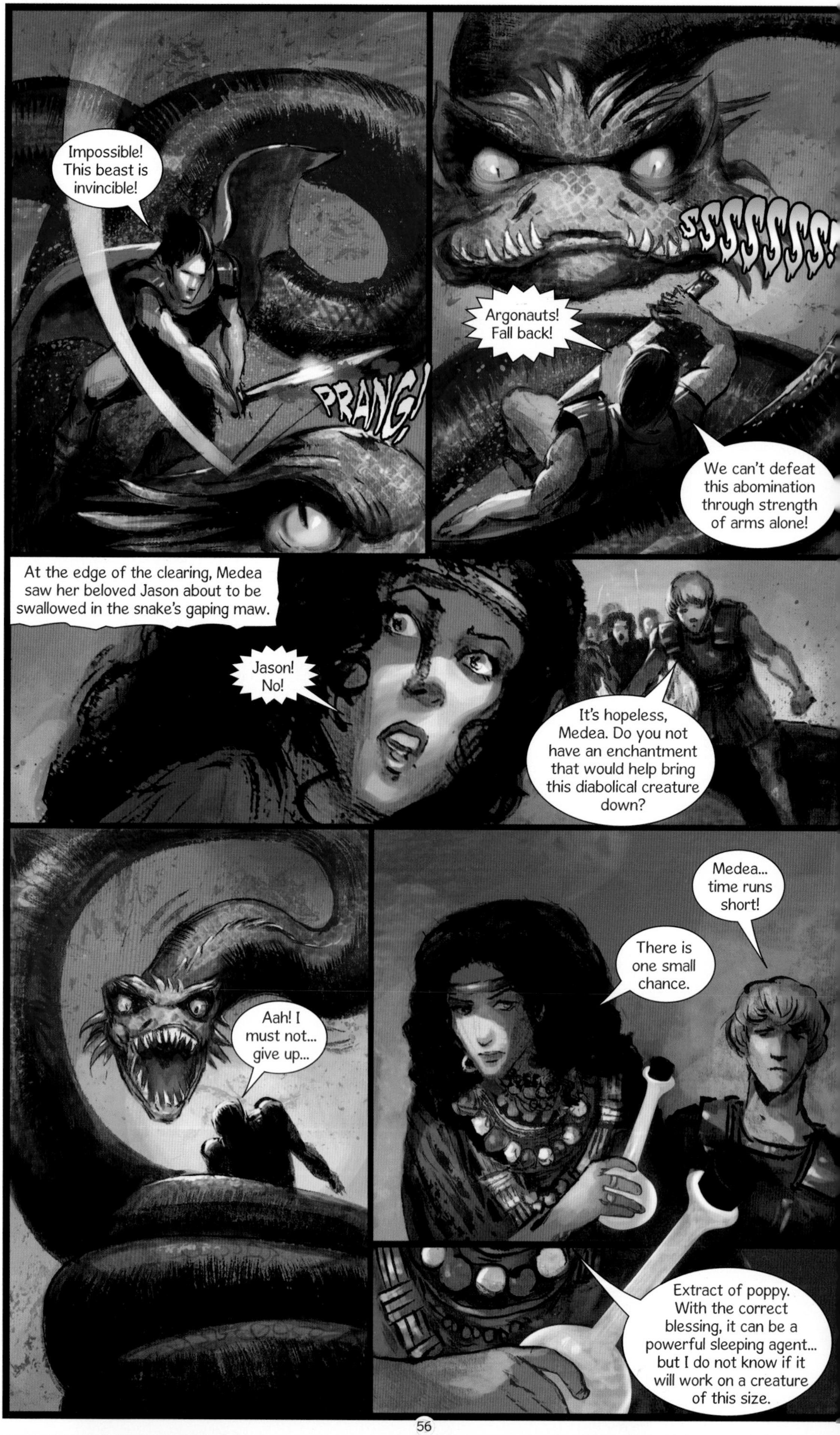
Impossible! This beast is invincible!
PRANG!
SSSSSSS!
Argonauts! Fall back!
We can't defeat this abomination through strength of arms alone!
At the edge of the clearing, Medea saw her beloved Jason about to be swallowed in the snake's gaping maw.
Jason! No!
It's hopeless, Medea. Do you not have an enchantment that would help bring this diabolical creature down?
Aah! I must not... give up...
Medea... time runs short!
There is one small chance.
Extract of poppy. With the correct blessing, it can be a powerful sleeping agent... but I do not know if it will work on a creature of this size.

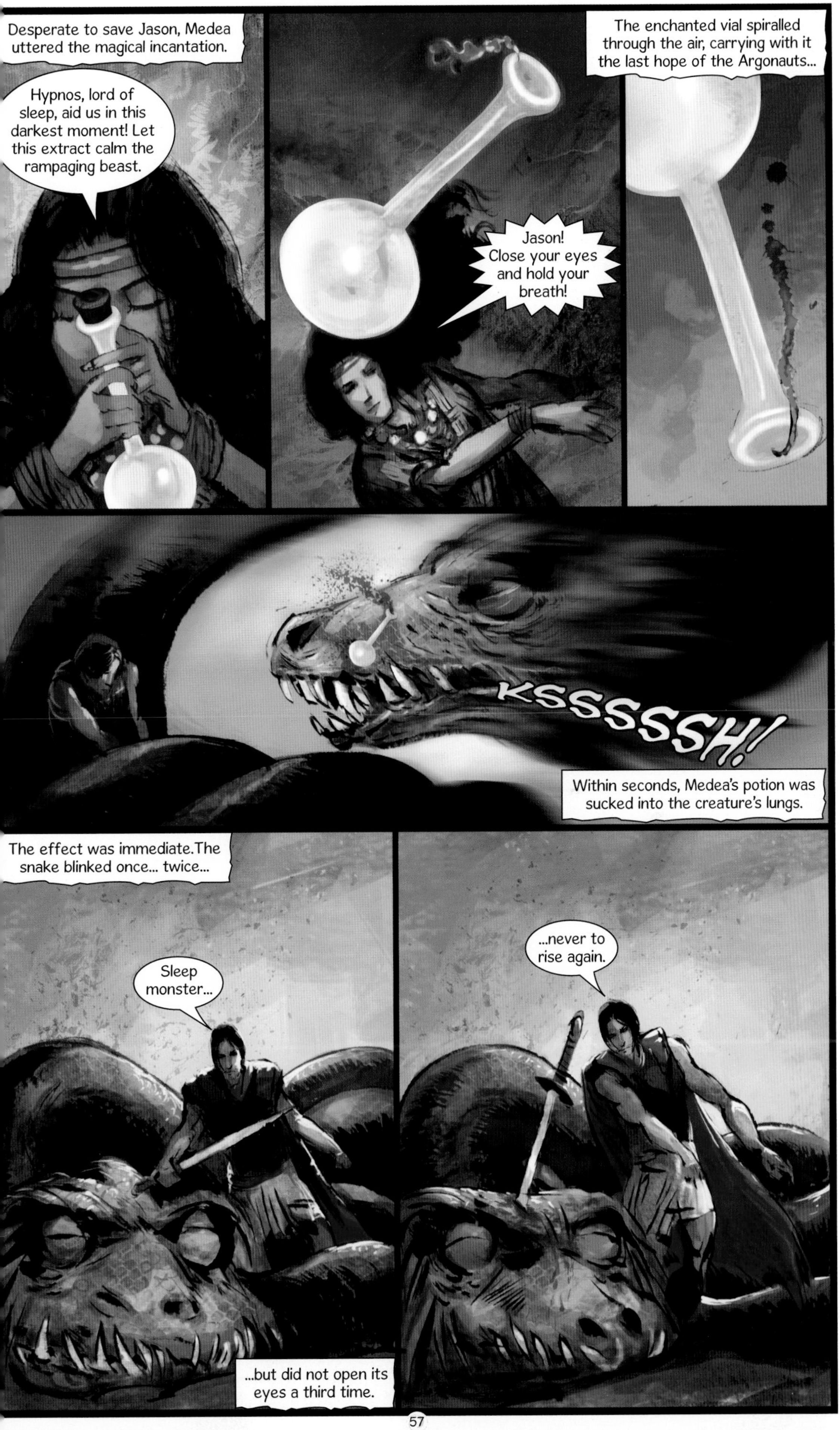
Desperate to save Jason, Medea uttered the magical incantation.
Hypnos, lord of sleep, aid us in this darkest moment! Let this extract calm the rampaging beast.
Jason! Close your eyes and hold your breath!
The enchanted vial spiralled through the air, carrying with it the last hope of the Argonauts...
KSSSSSH!
Within seconds, Medea's potion was sucked into the creature's lungs.
The effect was immediate.The snake blinked once... twice...
Sleep monster...
...but did not open its eyes a third time.
...never to rise again.

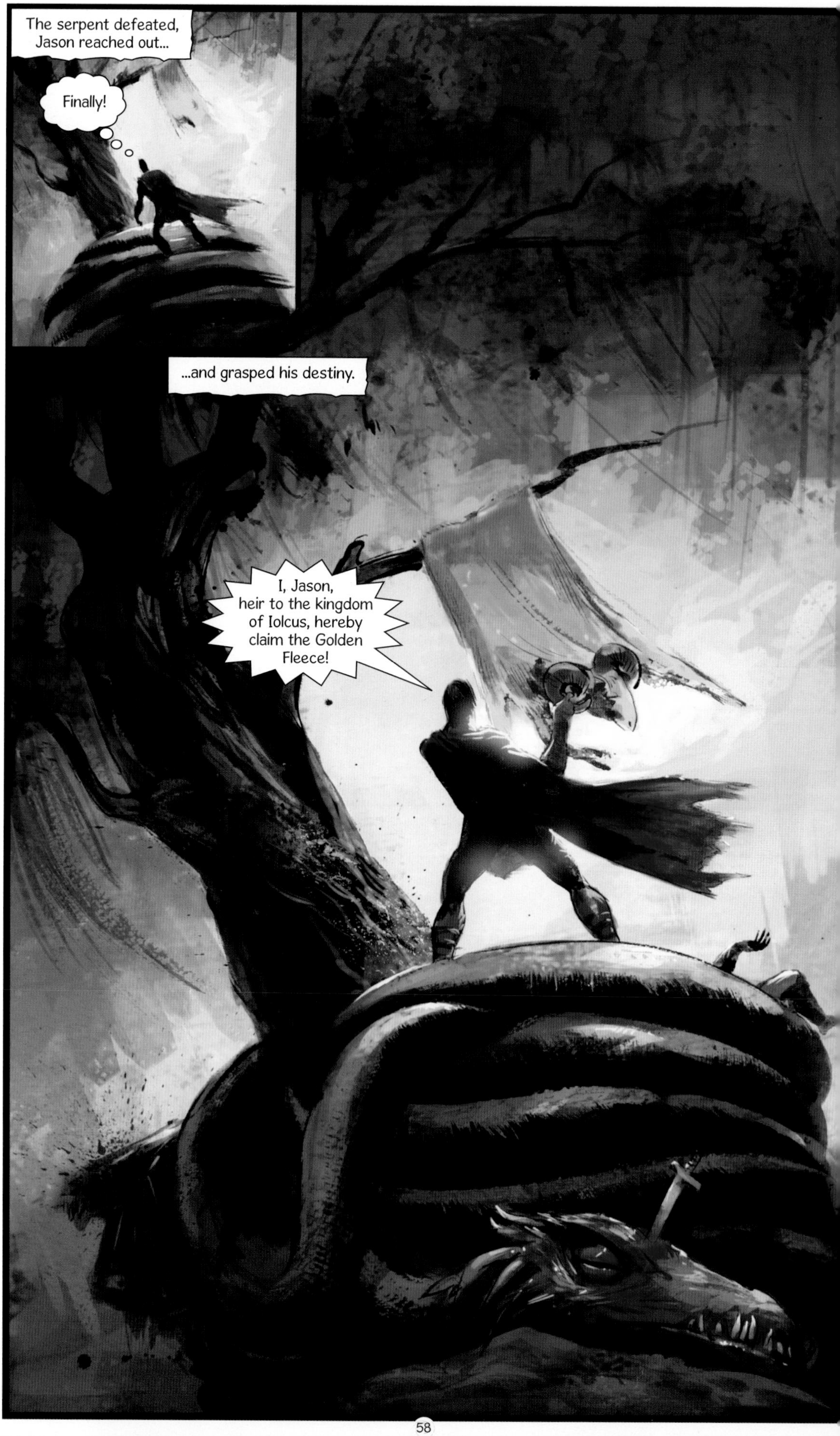
The serpent defeated, Jason reached out...
Finally!
...and grasped his destiny.
I, Jason, heir to the kingdom of Iolcus, hereby claim the Golden Fleece!

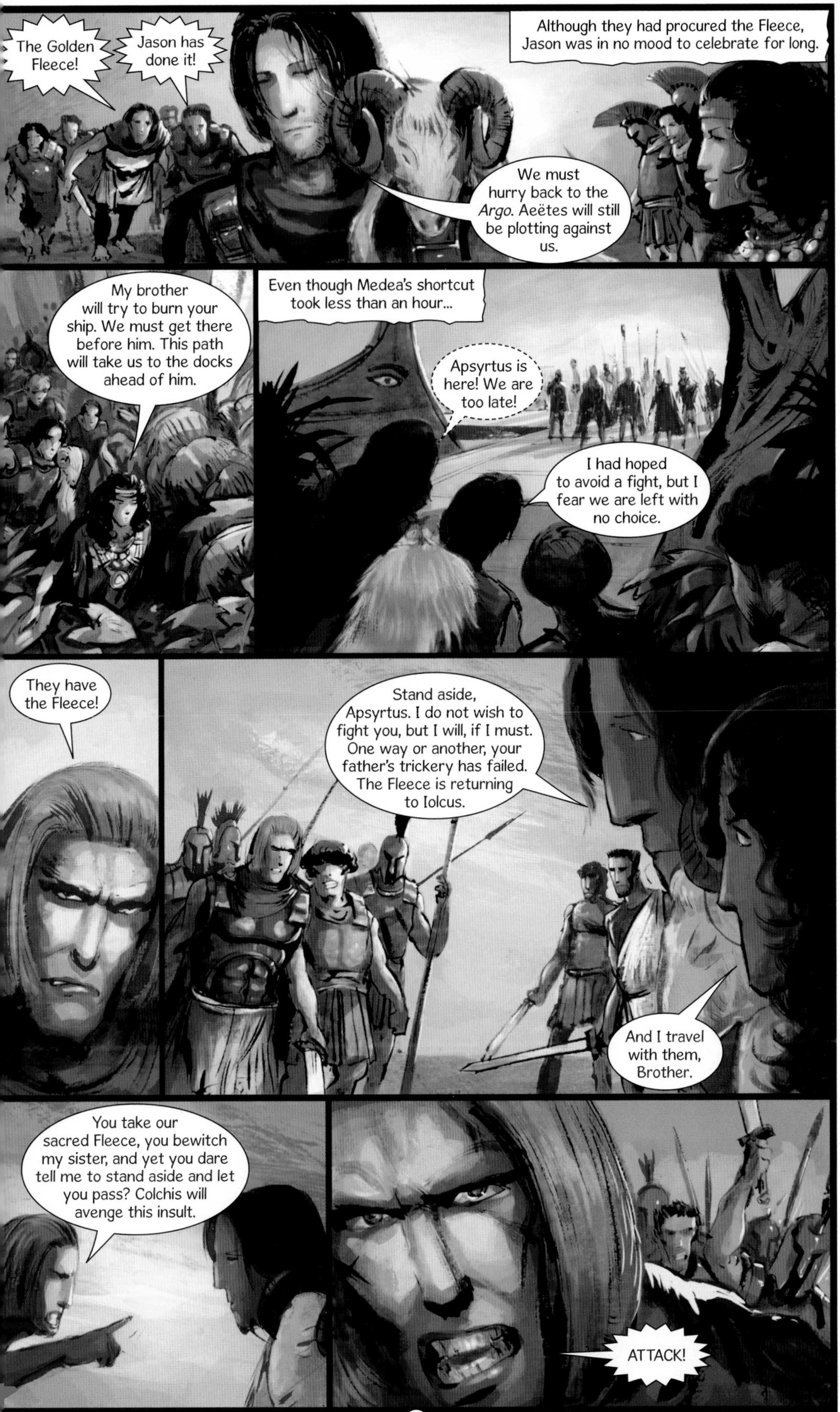
Although they had procured the Fleece, Jason was in no mood to celebrate for long.
The Golden Fleece!
Jason has done it!
We must hurry back to the Argo. Aeëtes will still be plotting against us.
My brother will try to burn your ship. We must get there before him. This path will take us to the docks ahead of him.
Even though Medea's shortcut took less than an hour...
Apsyrtus is here! We are too late!
I had hoped to avoid a fight, but I fear we are left with no choice.
They have the Fleece!
Stand aside, Apsyrtus. I do not wish to fight you, but I will, if I must. One way or another, your father's trickery has failed. The Fleece is returning to Iolcus.
And I travel with them, Brother.
You take our sacred Fleece, you bewitch my sister, and yet you dare tell me to stand aside and let you pass? Colchis will avenge this insult.
ATTACK!

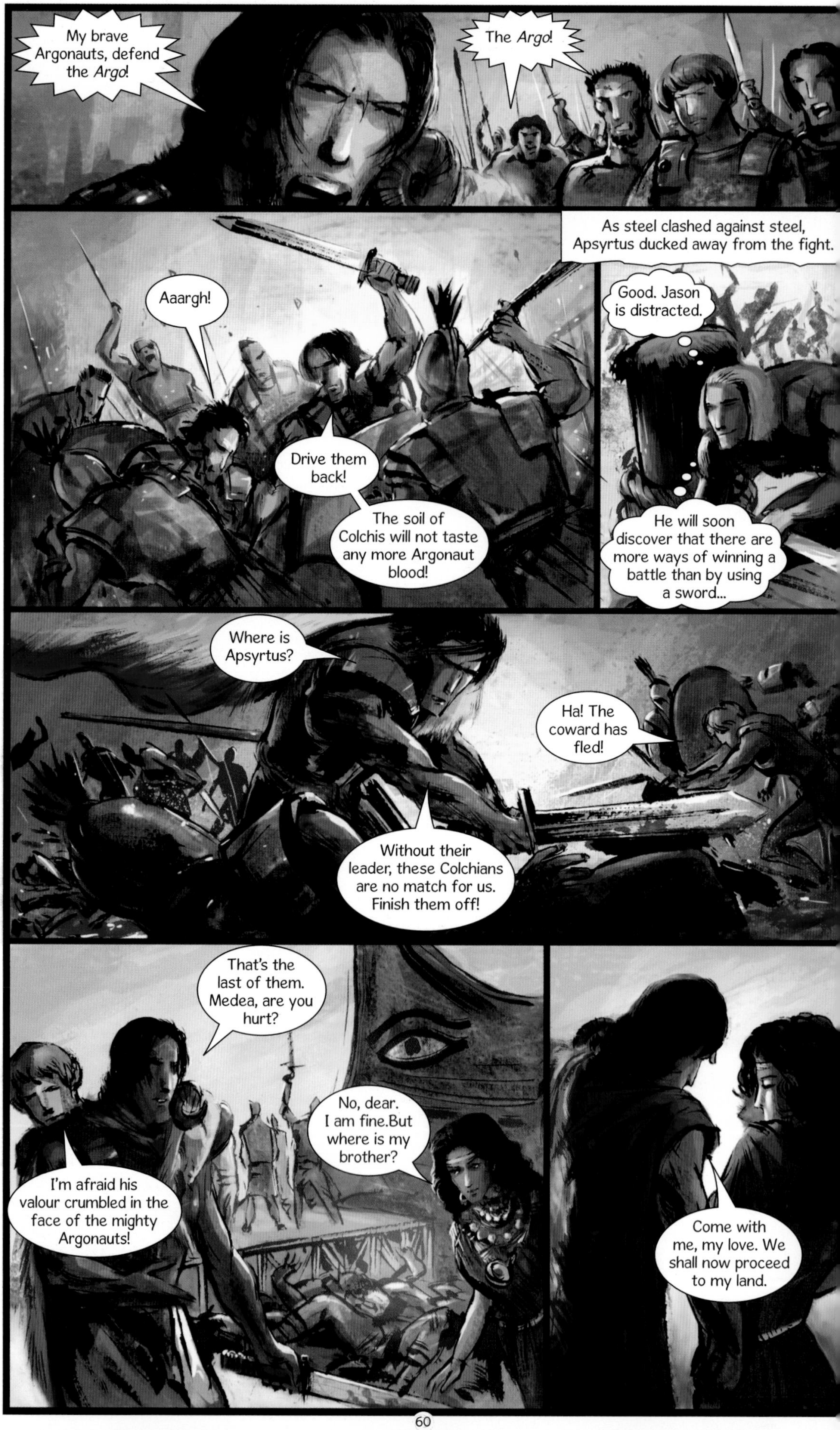

My brave Argonauts, defend the *Argo*!
The *Argo*!
As steel clashed against steel, Apsyrtus ducked away from the fight.
Aaargh!
Drive them back!
The soil of Colchis will not taste any more Argonaut blood!
Good. Jason is distracted.
He will soon discover that there are more ways of winning a battle than by using a sword...
Where is Apsyrtus?
Ha! The coward has fled!
Without their leader, these Colchians are no match for us. Finish them off!
That's the last of them. Medea, are you hurt?
No, dear. I am fine.But where is my brother?
I'm afraid his valour crumbled in the face of the mighty Argonauts!
Come with me, my love. We shall now proceed to my land.

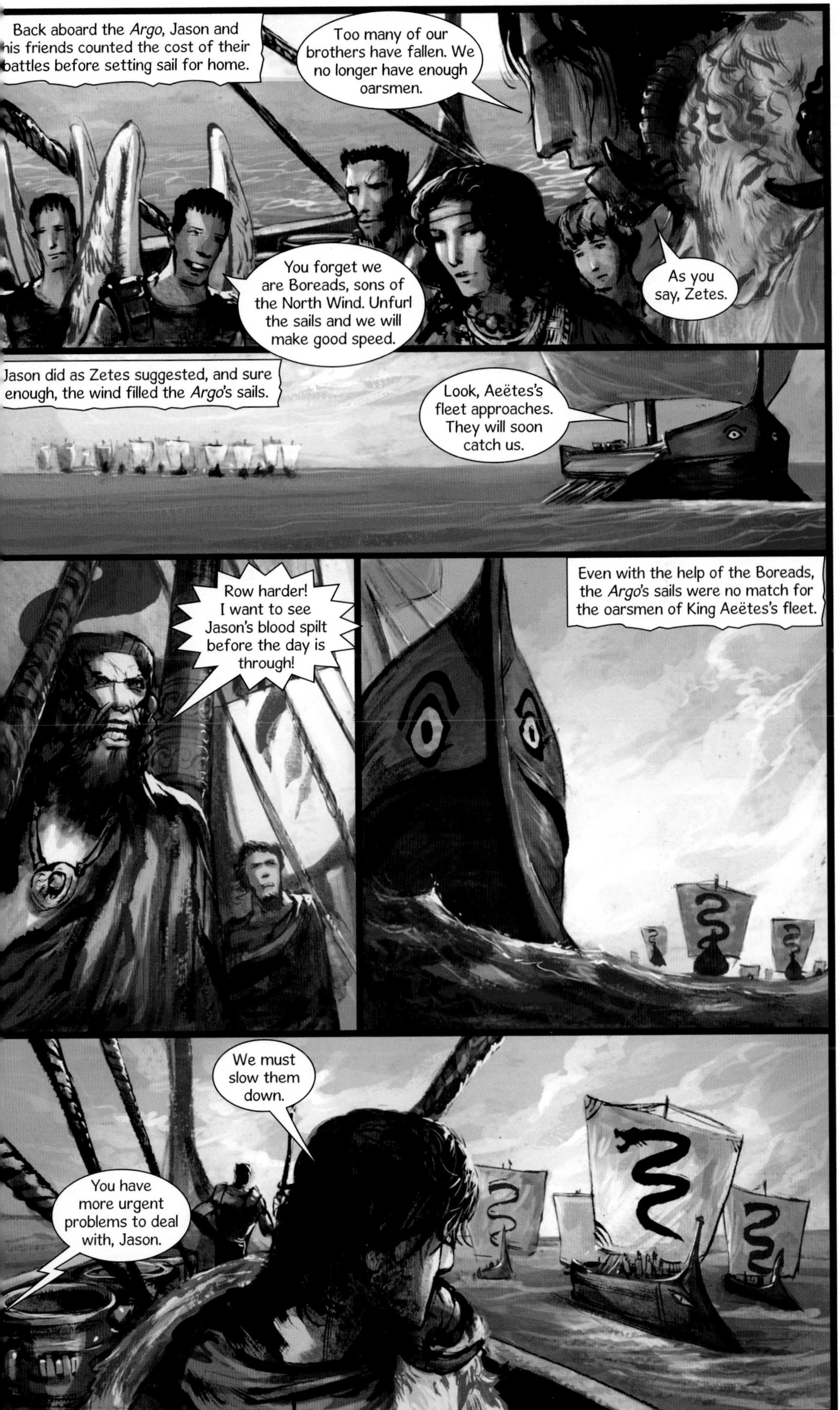
Back aboard the *Argo*, Jason and his friends counted the cost of their battles before setting sail for home.
Too many of our brothers have fallen. We no longer have enough oarsmen.
You forget we are Boreads, sons of the North Wind. Unfurl the sails and we will make good speed.
As you say, Zetes.
Jason did as Zetes suggested, and sure enough, the wind filled the *Argo*'s sails.
Look, Aeëtes's fleet approaches. They will soon catch us.
Row harder! I want to see Jason's blood spilt before the day is through!
Even with the help of the Boreads, the *Argo*'s sails were no match for the oarsmen of King Aeëtes's fleet.
We must slow them down.
You have more urgent problems to deal with, Jason.

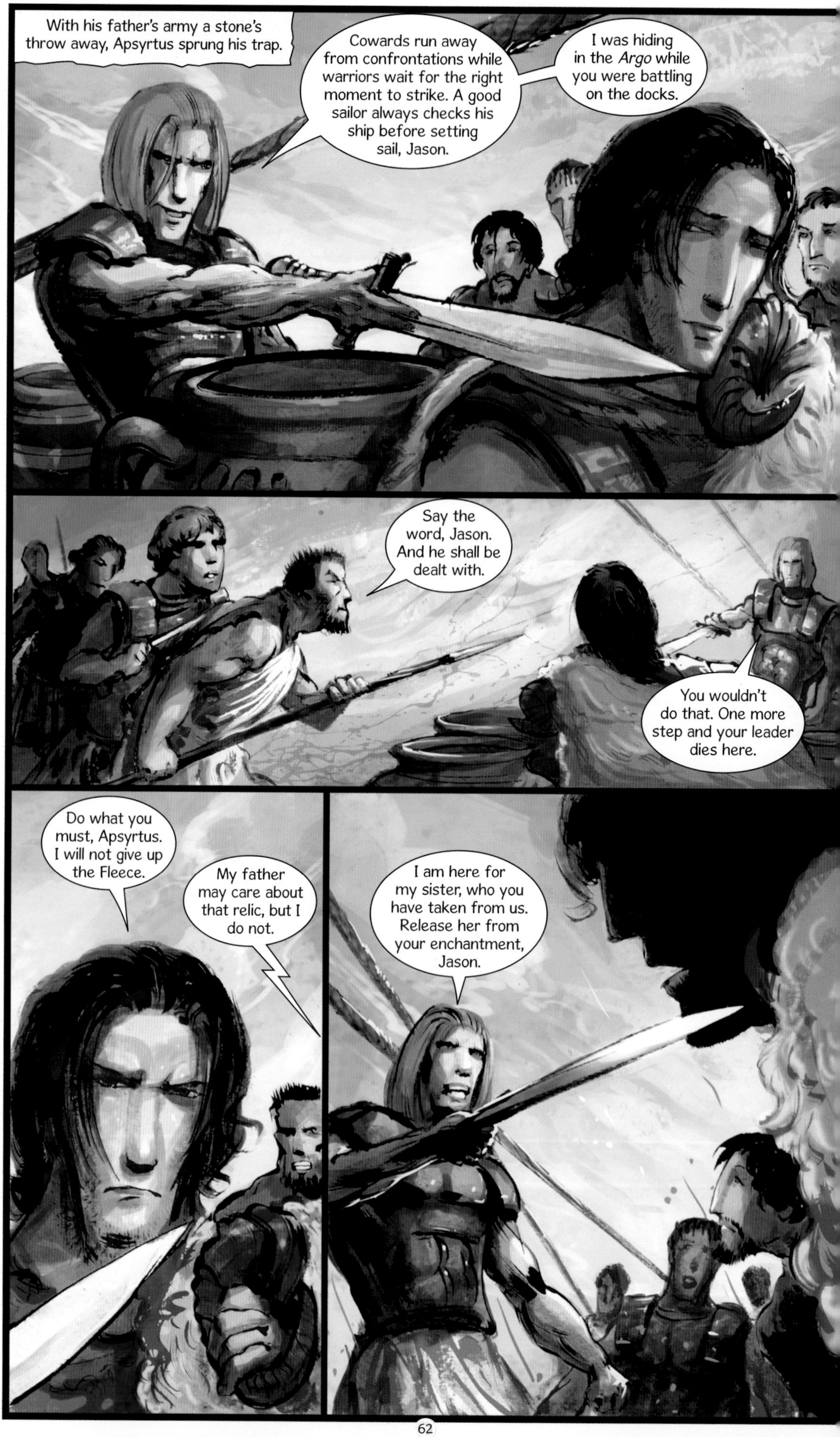

With his father's army a stone's throw away, Apsyrtus sprung his trap.
Cowards run away from confrontations while warriors wait for the right moment to strike. A good sailor always checks his ship before setting sail, Jason.
I was hiding in the *Argo* while you were battling on the docks.
Say the word, Jason. And he shall be dealt with.
You wouldn't do that. One more step and your leader dies here.
Do what you must, Apsyrtus. I will not give up the Fleece.
My father may care about that relic, but I do not.
I am here for my sister, who you have taken from us. Release her from your enchantment, Jason.

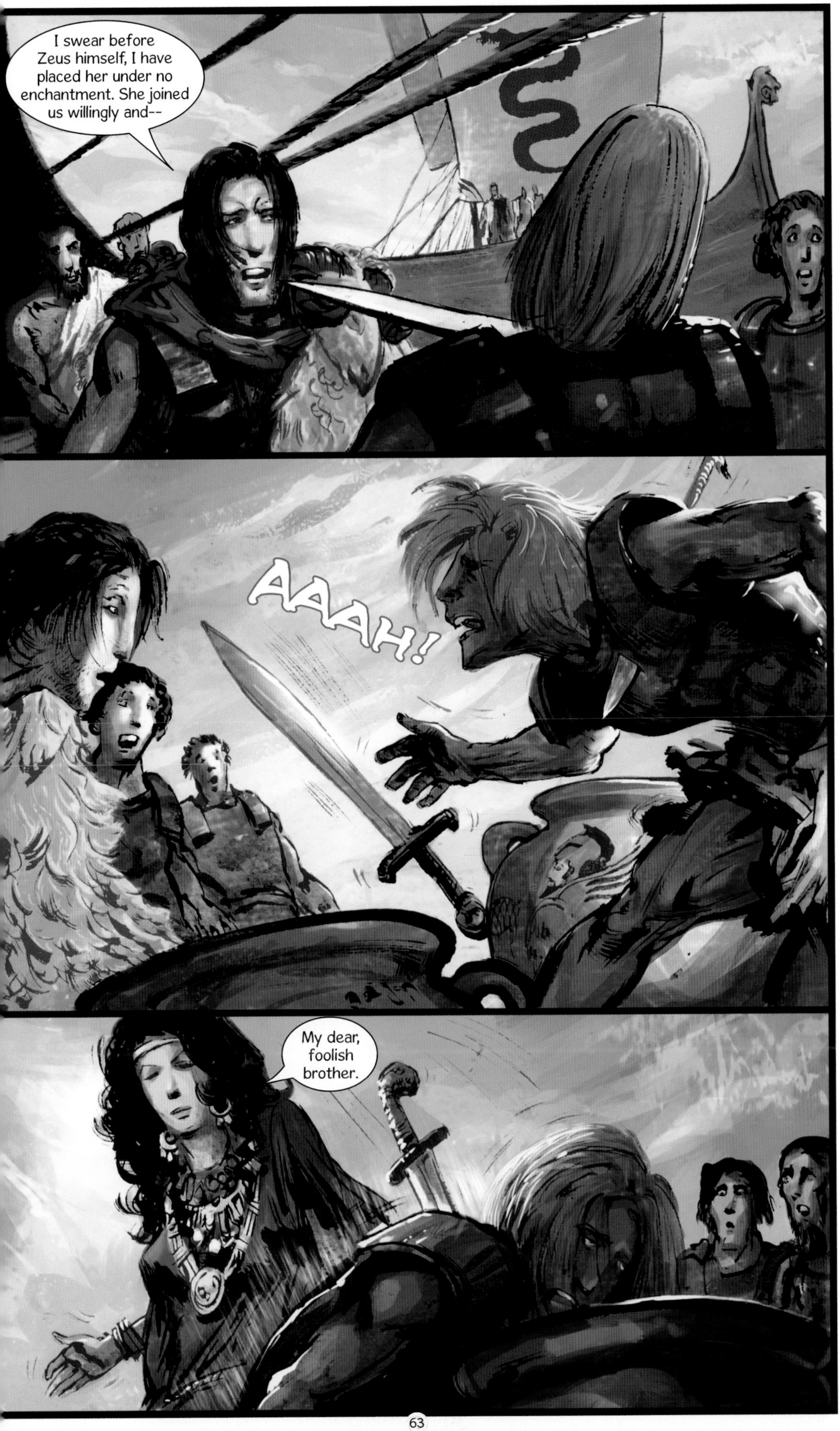
I swear before Zeus himself, I have placed her under no enchantment. She joined us willingly and--
AAAAH!
My dear, foolish brother.

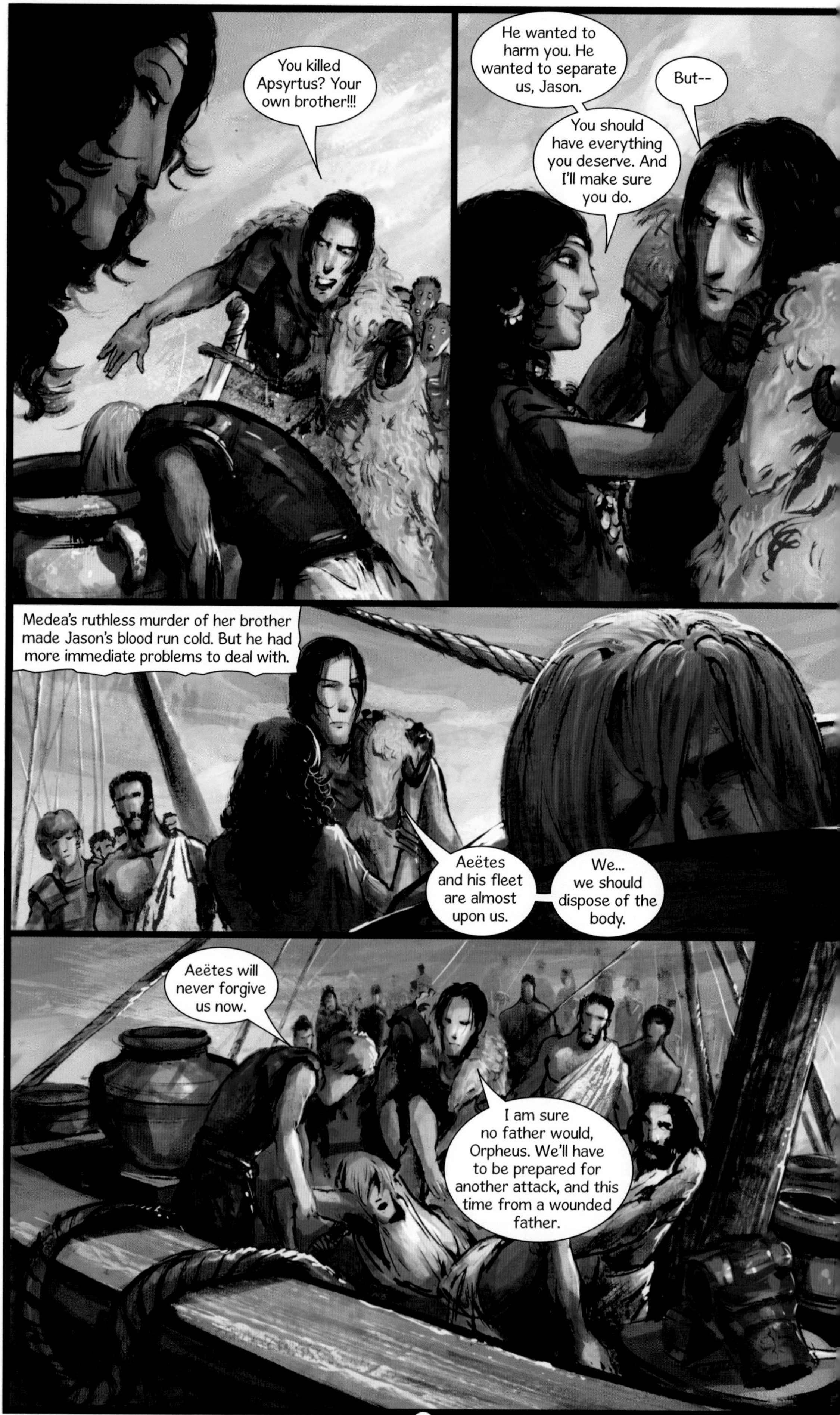
You killed Apsyrtus? Your own brother!!!
He wanted to harm you. He wanted to separate us, Jason.
But--
You should have everything you deserve. And I'll make sure you do.
Medea's ruthless murder of her brother made Jason's blood run cold. But he had more immediate problems to deal with.
Aeëtes and his fleet are almost upon us.
We... we should dispose of the body.
Aeëtes will never forgive us now.
I am sure no father would, Orpheus. We'll have to be prepared for another attack, and this time from a wounded father.

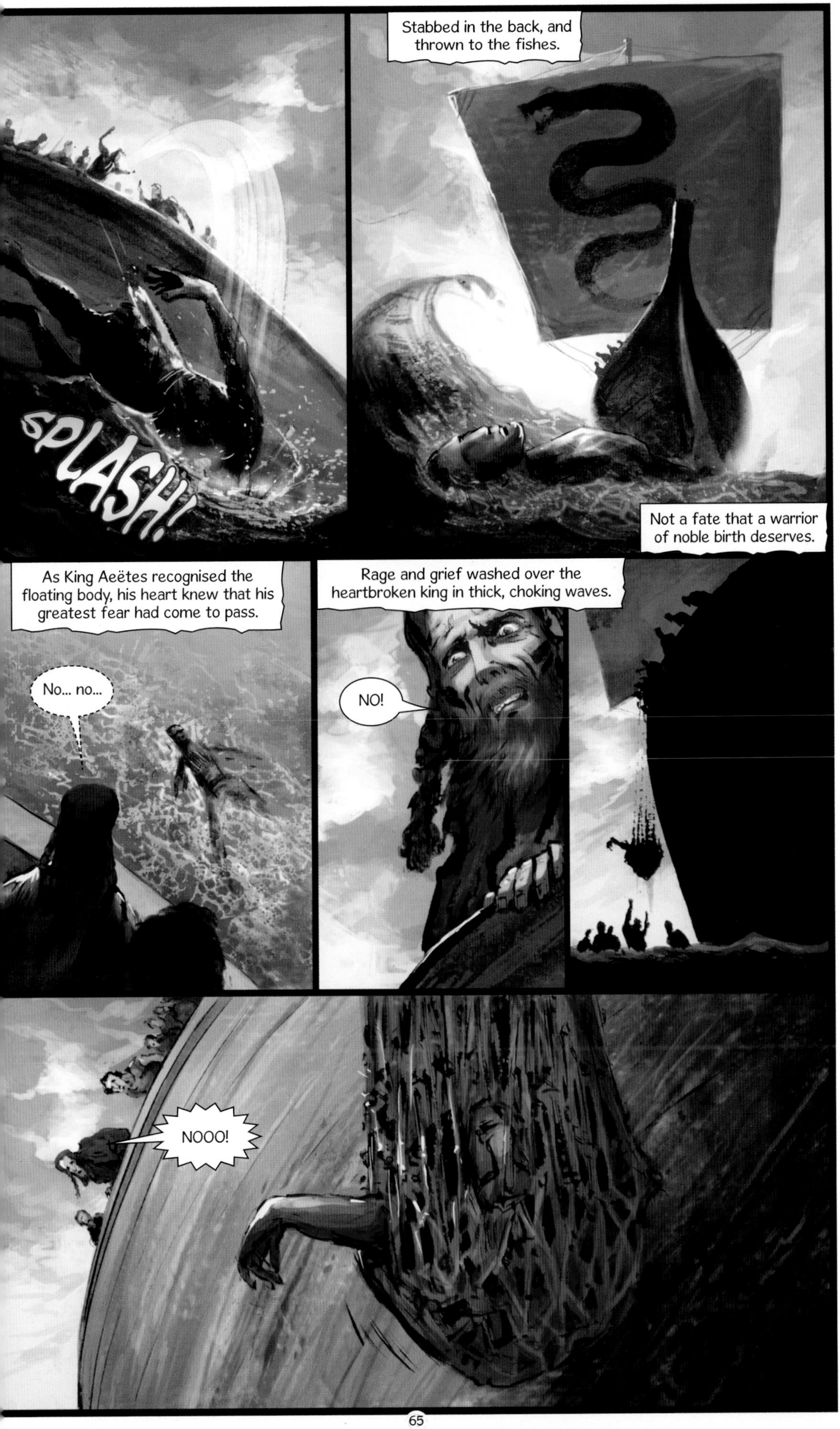
SPLASH!
Stabbed in the back, and thrown to the fishes.
Not a fate that a warrior of noble birth deserves.
As King Aeëtes recognised the floating body, his heart knew that his greatest fear had come to pass.
No... no...
Rage and grief washed over the heartbroken king in thick, choking waves.
NO!
NOOO!

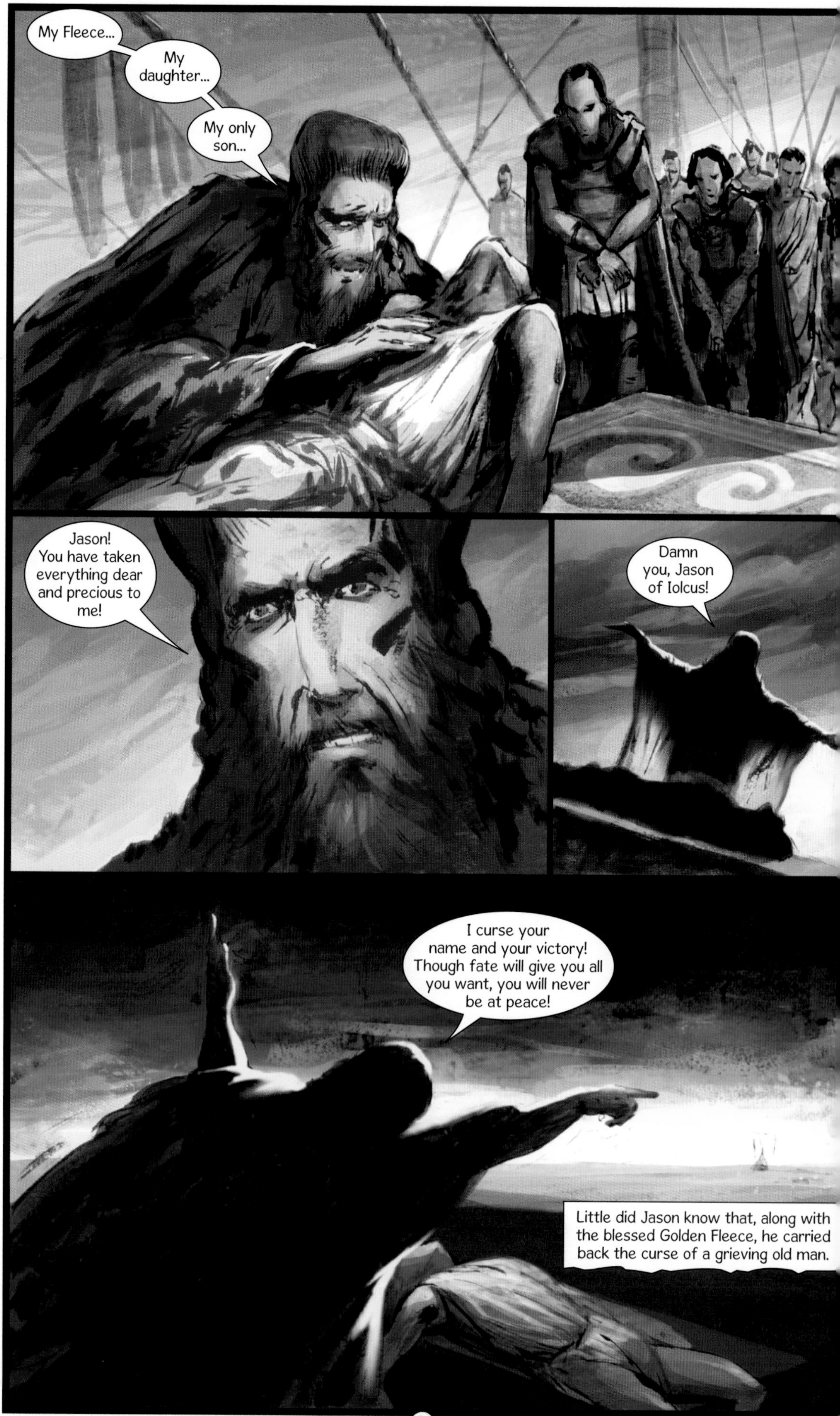
My Fleece...
My daughter...
My only son...
Jason! You have taken everything dear and precious to me!
Damn you, Jason of Iolcus!
I curse your name and your victory! Though fate will give you all you want, you will never be at peace!
Little did Jason know that, along with the blessed Golden Fleece, he carried back the curse of a grieving old man.

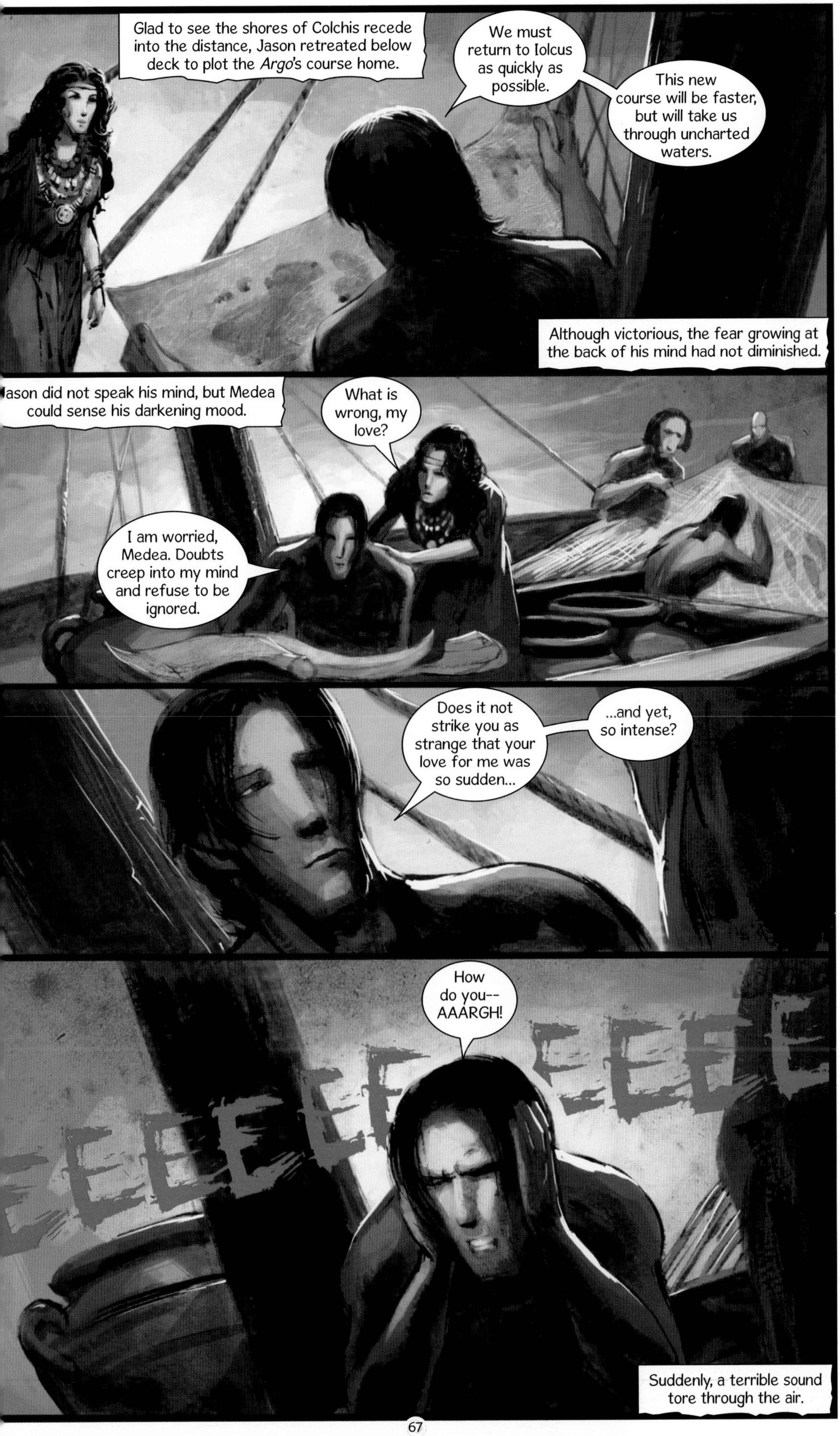

Glad to see the shores of Colchis recede into the distance, Jason retreated below deck to plot the *Argo*'s course home.
We must return to Iolcus as quickly as possible.
This new course will be faster, but will take us through uncharted waters.
Although victorious, the fear growing at the back of his mind had not diminished.
Jason did not speak his mind, but Medea could sense his darkening mood.
What is wrong, my love?
I am worried, Medea. Doubts creep into my mind and refuse to be ignored.
Does it not strike you as strange that your love for me was so sudden...
...and yet, so intense?
How do you-- AAARGH!
EEEEEEEEEEE
Suddenly, a terrible sound tore through the air.

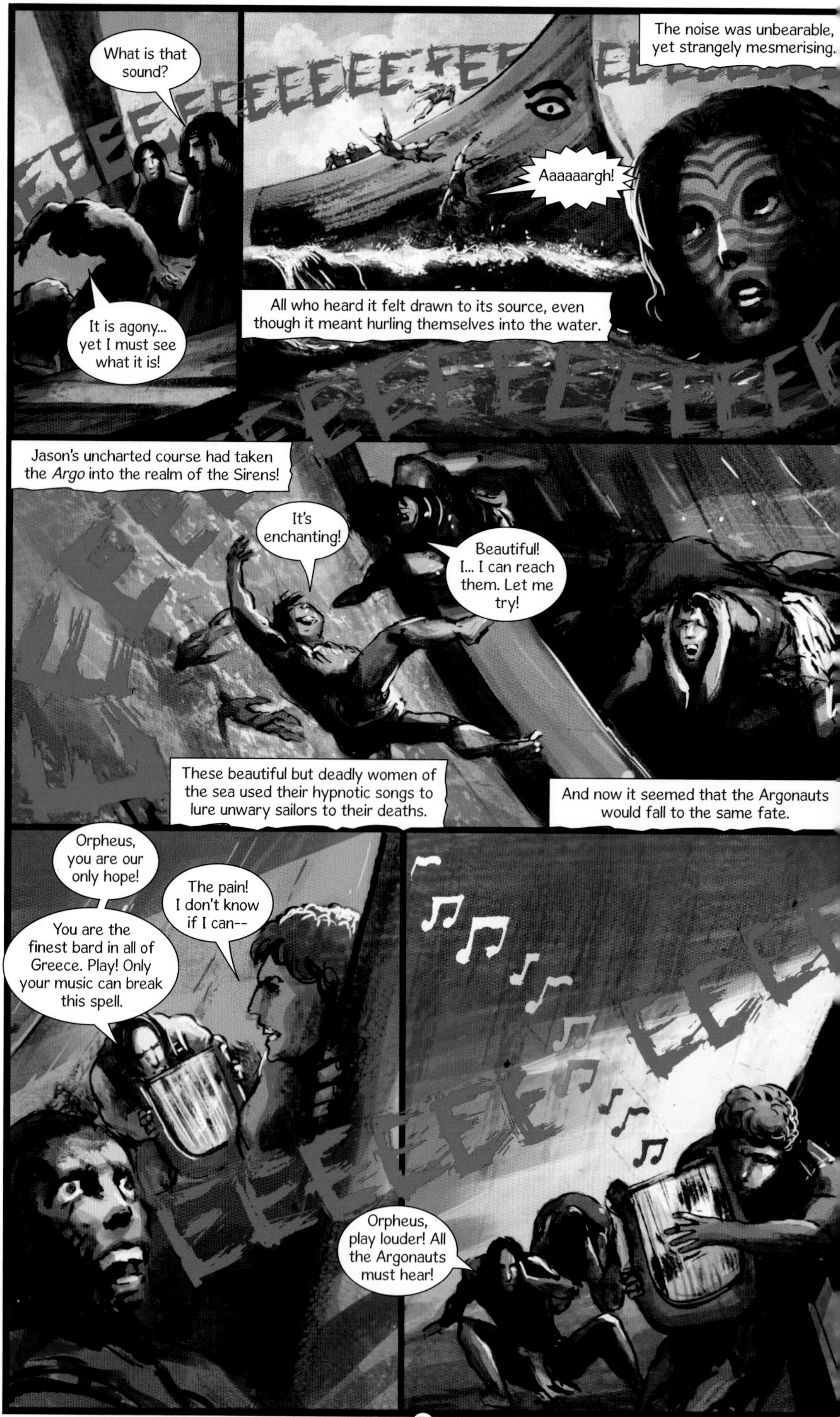

What is that sound?
It is agony... yet I must see what it is!
The noise was unbearable, yet strangely mesmerising.
Aaaaaargh!
All who heard it felt drawn to its source, even though it meant hurling themselves into the water.
Jason's uncharted course had taken the *Argo* into the realm of the Sirens!
It's enchanting!
Beautiful! I... I can reach them. Let me try!
These beautiful but deadly women of the sea used their hypnotic songs to lure unwary sailors to their deaths.
And now it seemed that the Argonauts would fall to the same fate.
Orpheus, you are our only hope!
You are the finest bard in all of Greece. Play! Only your music can break this spell.
The pain! I don't know if I can--
Orpheus, play louder! All the Argonauts must hear!

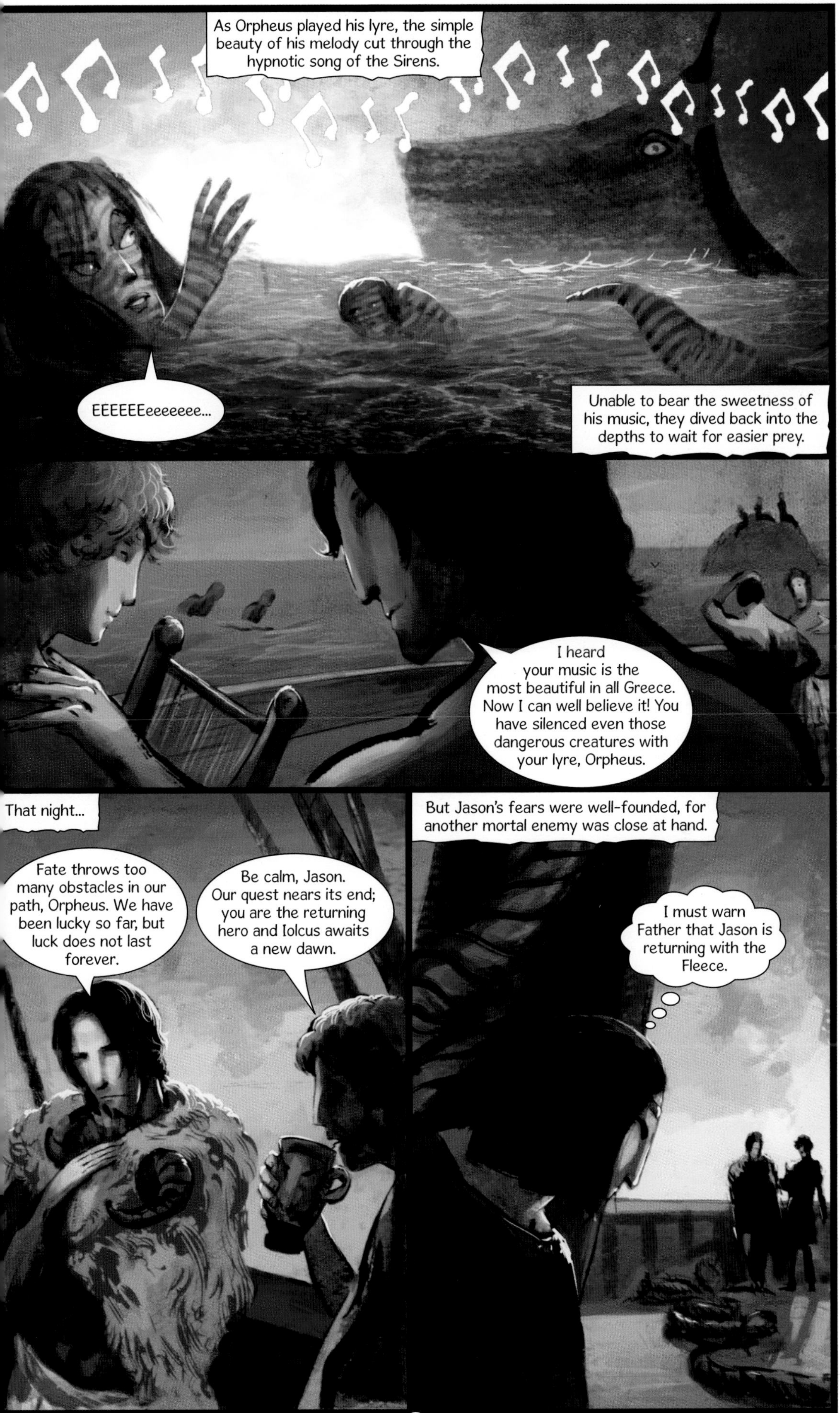
As Orpheus played his lyre, the simple beauty of his melody cut through the hypnotic song of the Sirens.
EEEEEEeeeeeee...
Unable to bear the sweetness of his music, they dived back into the depths to wait for easier prey.
I heard your music is the most beautiful in all Greece. Now I can well believe it! You have silenced even those dangerous creatures with your lyre, Orpheus.
That night...
Fate throws too many obstacles in our path, Orpheus. We have been lucky so far, but luck does not last forever.
Be calm, Jason. Our quest nears its end; you are the returning hero and Iolcus awaits a new dawn.
But Jason's fears were well-founded, for another mortal enemy was close at hand.
I must warn Father that Jason is returning with the Fleece.

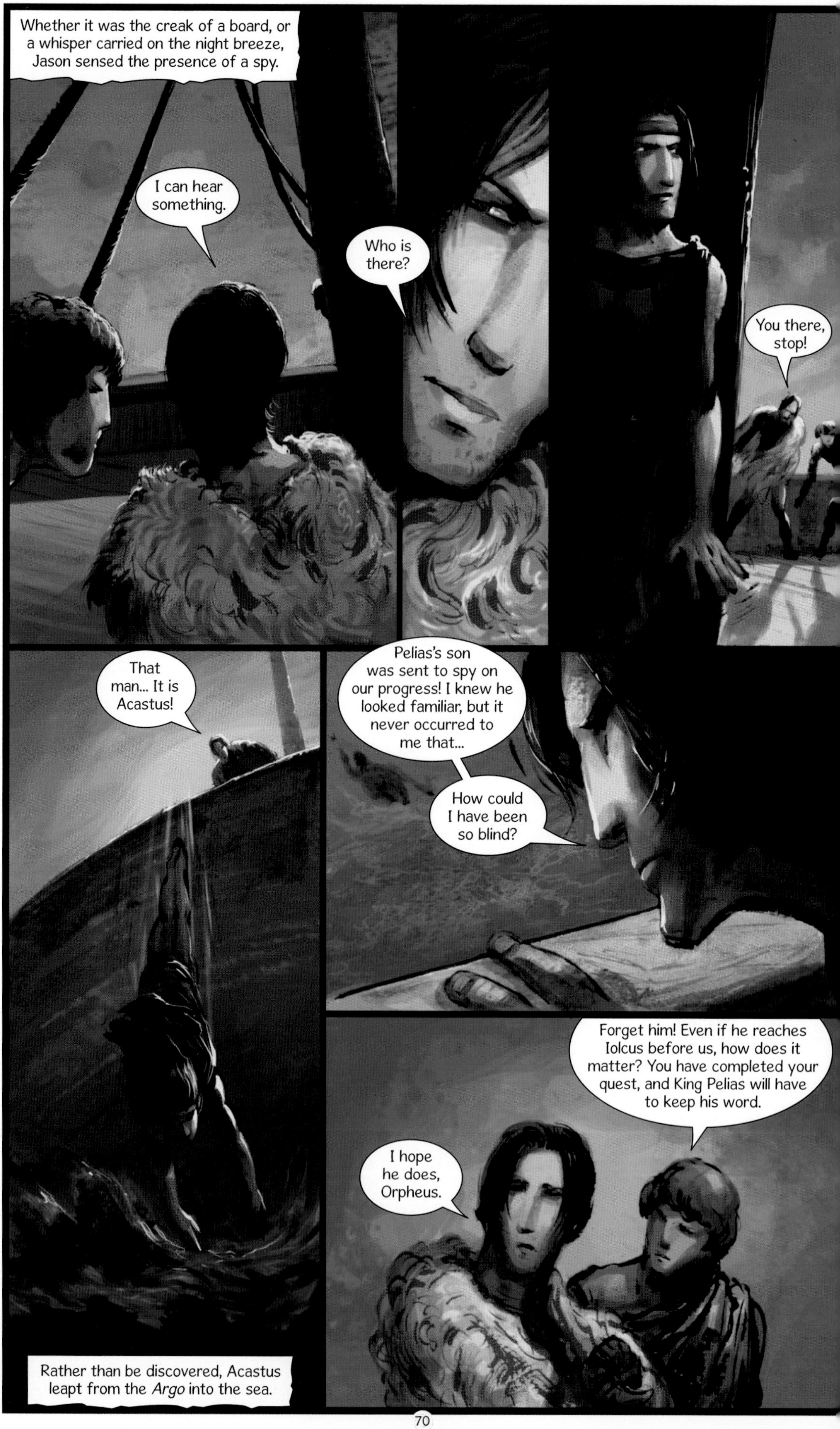
Whether it was the creak of a board, or a whisper carried on the night breeze, Jason sensed the presence of a spy.
I can hear something.
Who is there?
You there, stop!
That man... It is Acastus!
Pelias's son was sent to spy on our progress! I knew he looked familiar, but it never occurred to me that...
How could I have been so blind?
Forget him! Even if he reaches Iolcus before us, how does it matter? You have completed your quest, and King Pelias will have to keep his word.
I hope he does, Orpheus.
Rather than be discovered, Acastus leapt from the *Argo* into the sea.

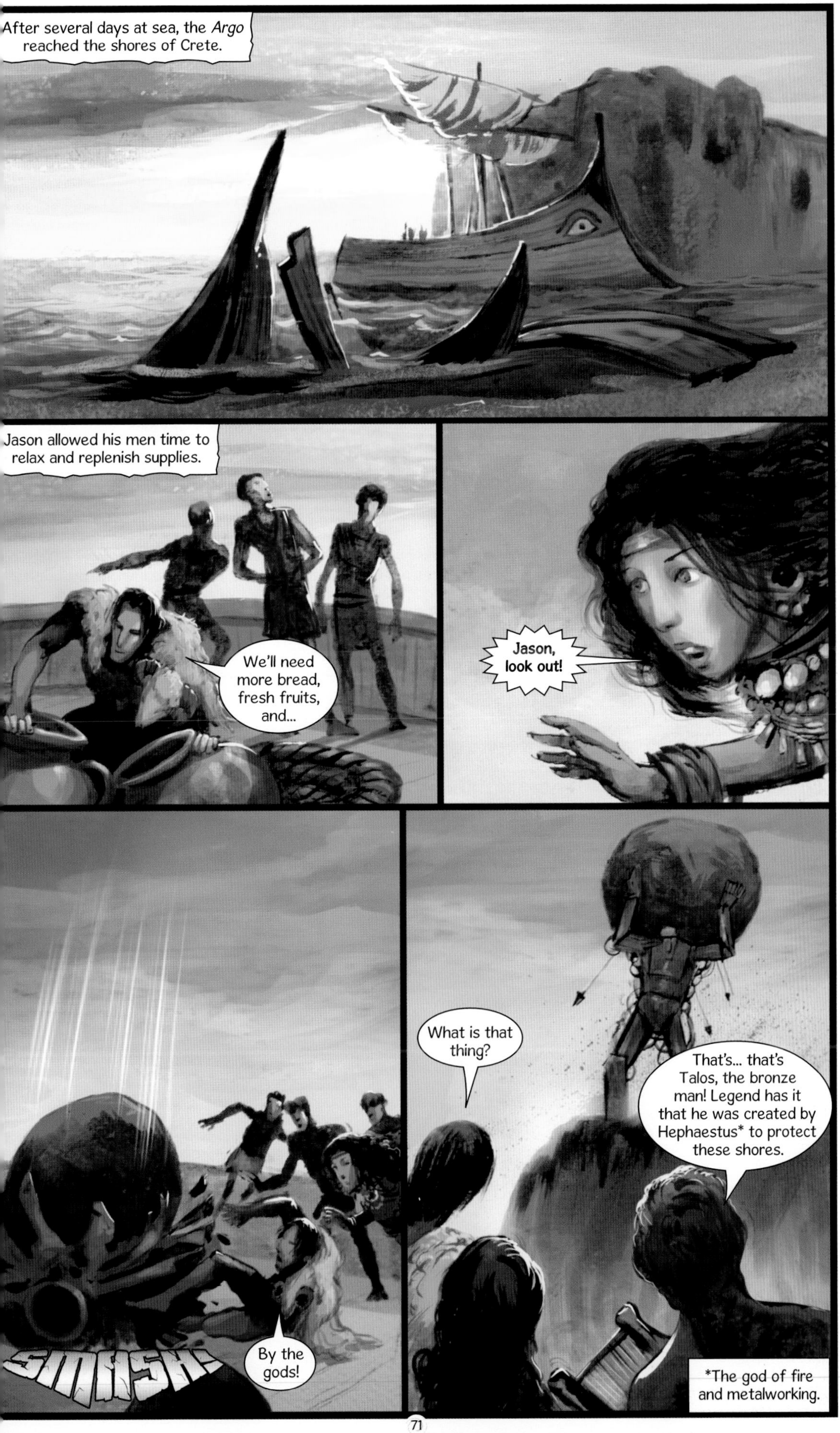
After several days at sea, the *Argo* reached the shores of Crete.
Jason allowed his men time to relax and replenish supplies.
We'll need more bread, fresh fruits, and...
Jason, look out!
SMASH!
By the gods!
What is that thing?
That's... that's Talos, the bronze man! Legend has it that he was created by Hephaestus* to protect these shores.
*The god of fire and metalworking.

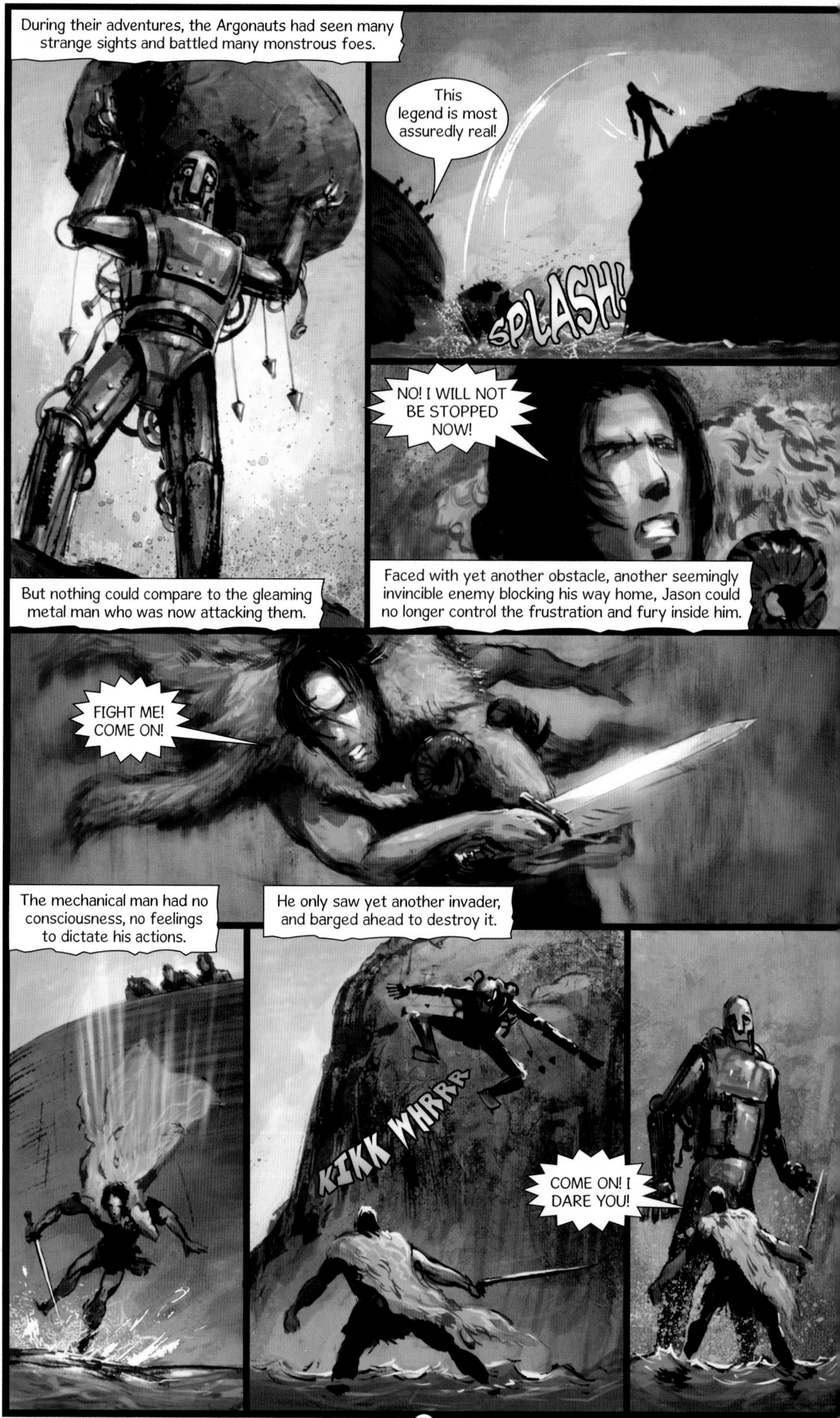
During their adventures, the Argonauts had seen many strange sights and battled many monstrous foes.
This legend is most assuredly real!
SPLASH!
But nothing could compare to the gleaming metal man who was now attacking them.
NO! I WILL NOT BE STOPPED NOW!
Faced with yet another obstacle, another seemingly invincible enemy blocking his way home, Jason could no longer control the frustration and fury inside him.
FIGHT ME! COME ON!
The mechanical man had no consciousness, no feelings to dictate his actions.
He only saw yet another invader, and barged ahead to destroy it.
KIKK WHRRR
COME ON! I DARE YOU!

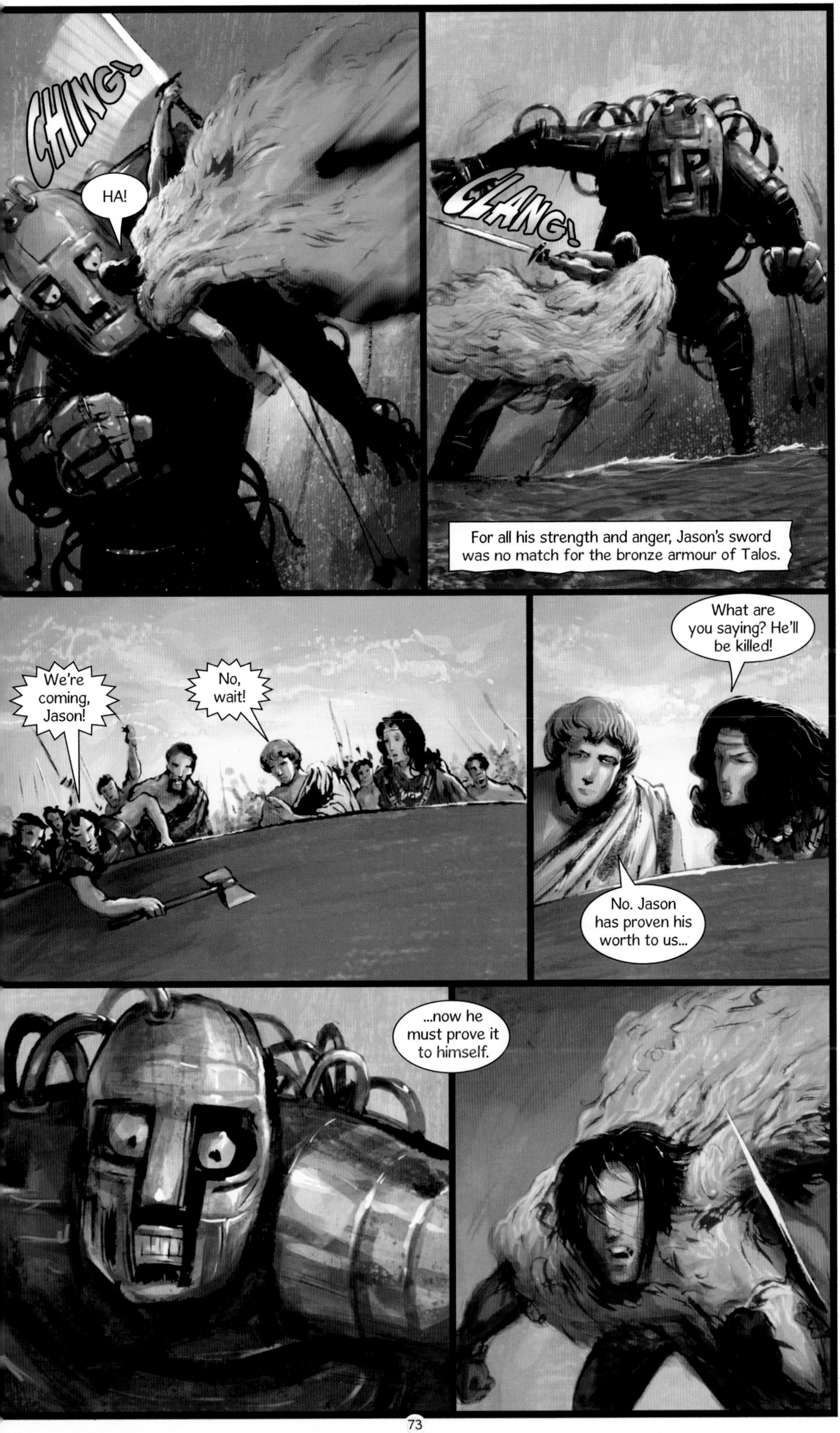
CHING!
HA!
CLANG!
For all his strength and anger, Jason's sword was no match for the bronze armour of Talos.
We're coming, Jason!
No, wait!
What are you saying? He'll be killed!
No. Jason has proven his worth to us...
...now he must prove it to himself.

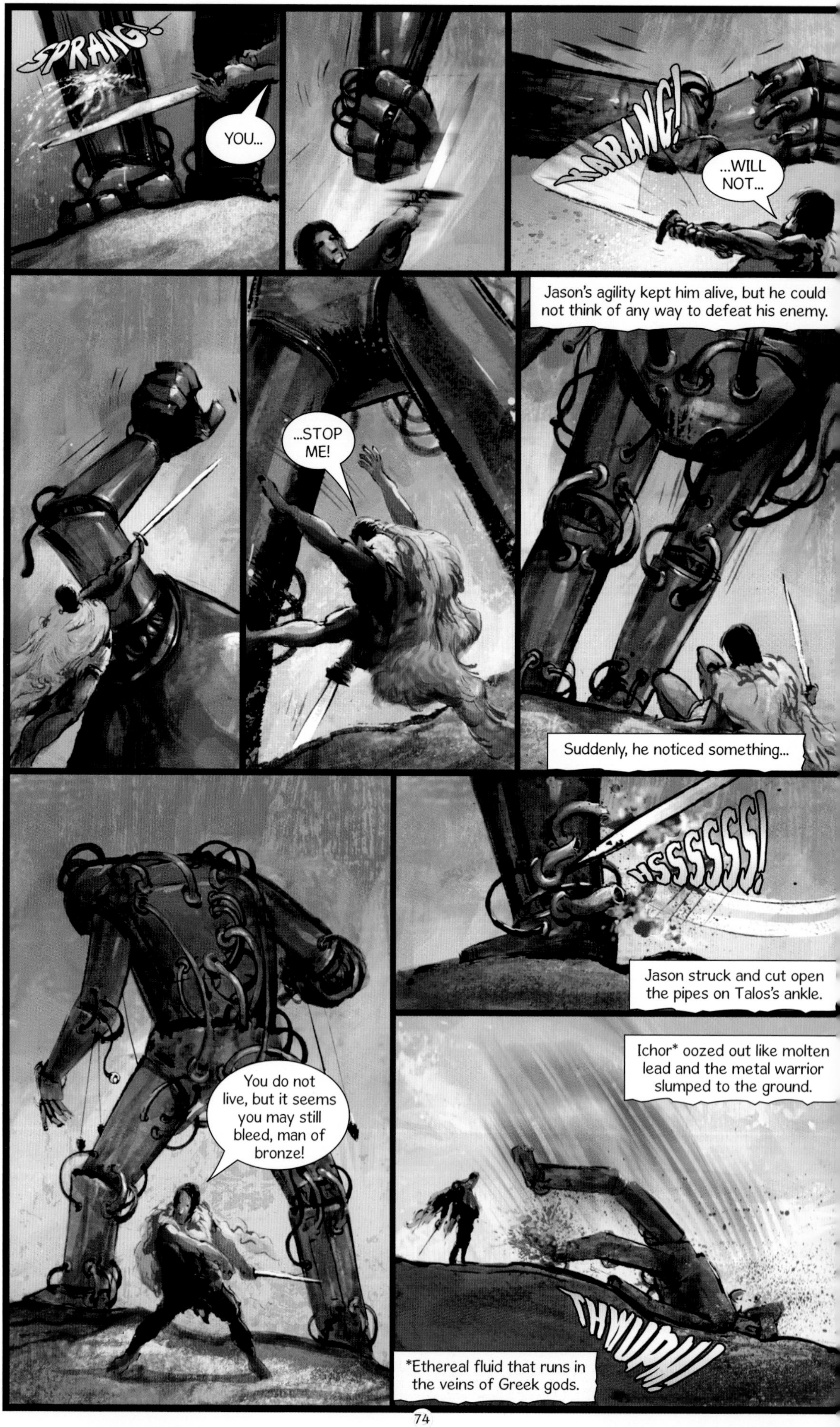
SPRANG!
YOU...
KARANG!
...WILL NOT...
...STOP ME!
Jason's agility kept him alive, but he could not think of any way to defeat his enemy.
Suddenly, he noticed something...
You do not live, but it seems you may still bleed, man of bronze!
HSSSSSS!
Jason struck and cut open the pipes on Talos's ankle.
Ichor* oozed out like molten lead and the metal warrior slumped to the ground.
THWUMP!
*Ethereal fluid that runs in the veins of Greek gods.

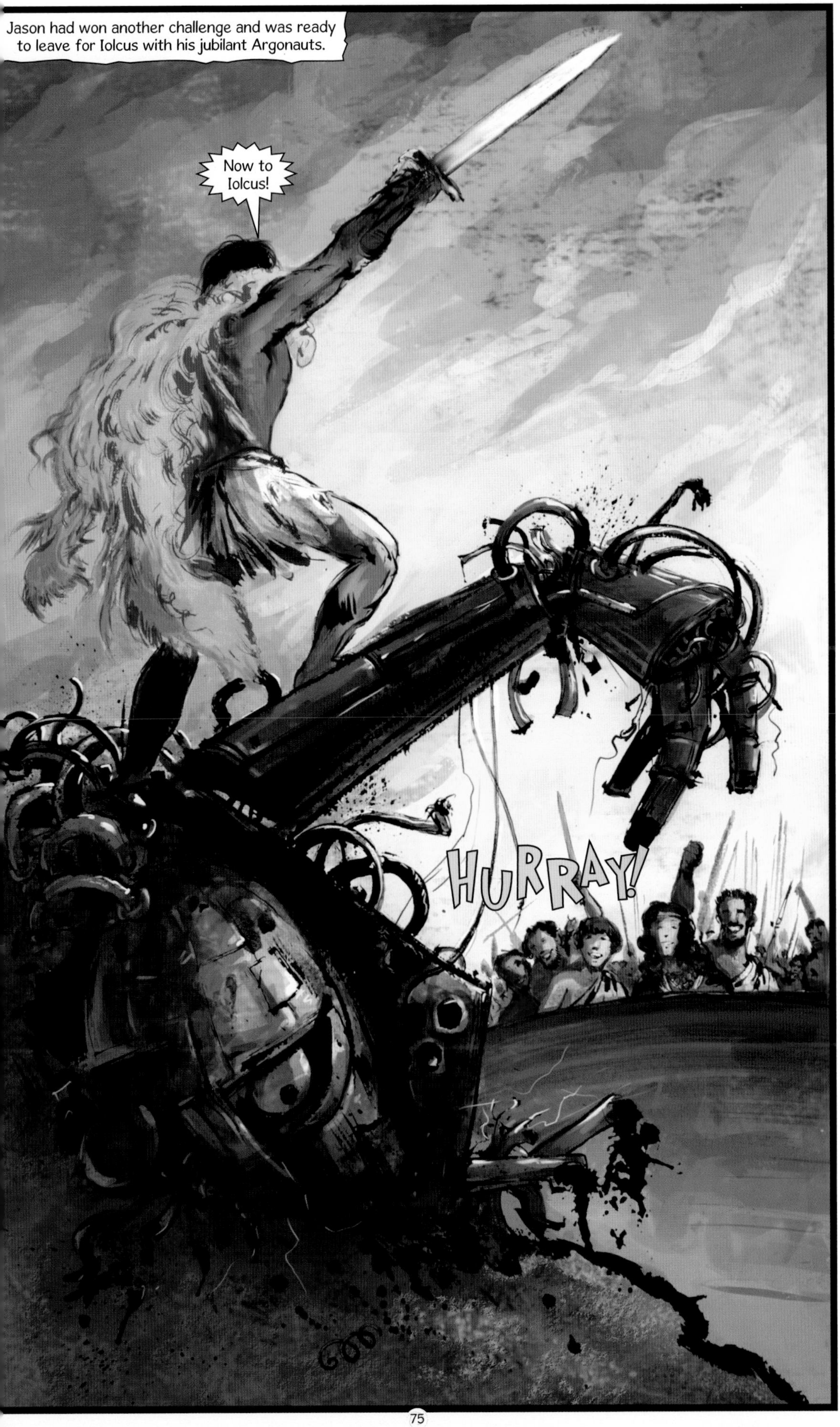

Jason had won another challenge and was ready to leave for Iolcus with his jubilant Argonauts.
Now to Iolcus!
HURRAY!

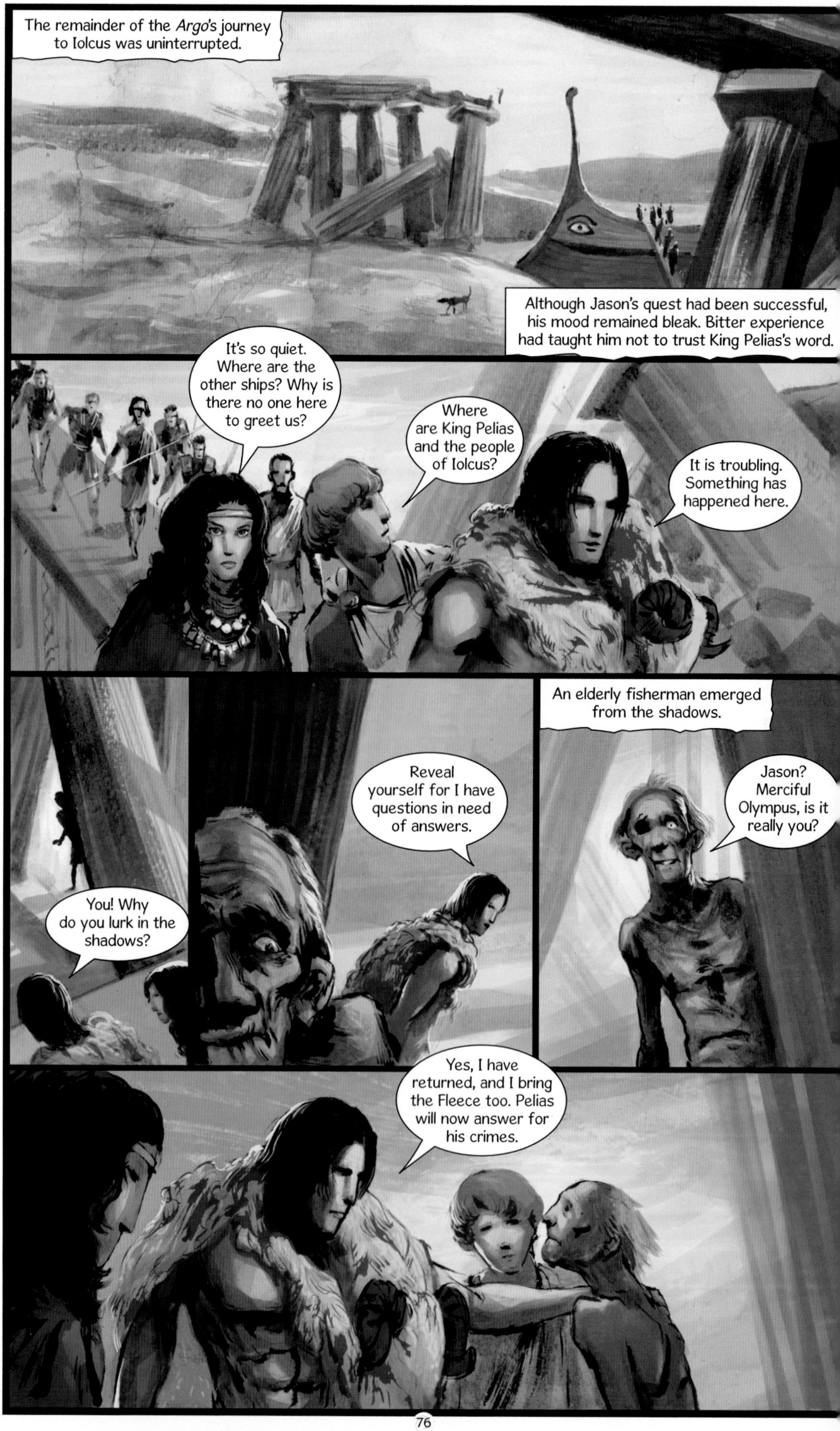
The remainder of the *Argo*'s journey to Iolcus was uninterrupted.
Although Jason's quest had been successful, his mood remained bleak. Bitter experience had taught him not to trust King Pelias's word.
It's so quiet. Where are the other ships? Why is there no one here to greet us?
Where are King Pelias and the people of Iolcus?
It is troubling. Something has happened here.
You! Why do you lurk in the shadows?
Reveal yourself for I have questions in need of answers.
An elderly fisherman emerged from the shadows.
Jason? Merciful Olympus, is it really you?
Yes, I have returned, and I bring the Fleece too. Pelias will now answer for his crimes.

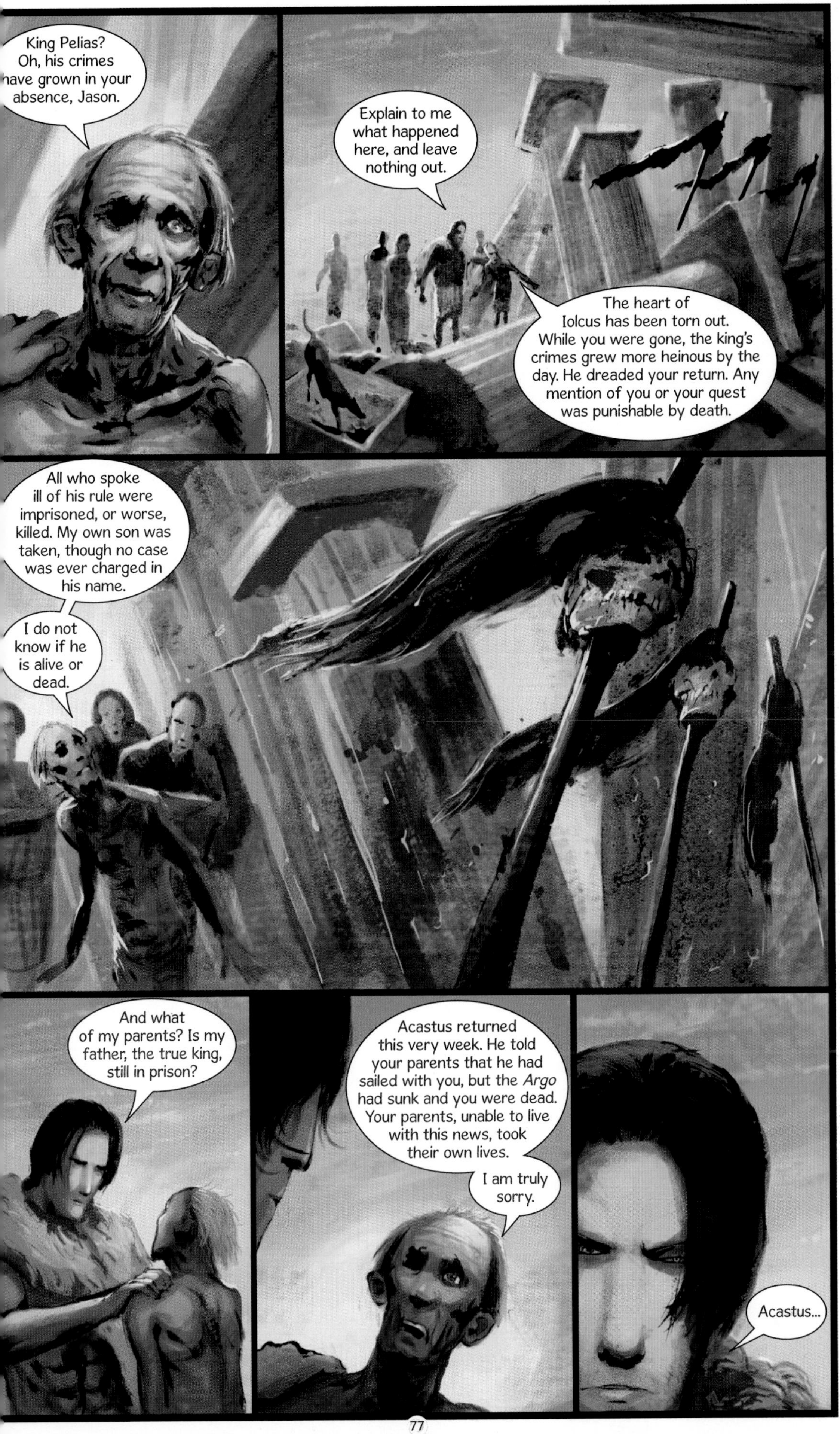

King Pelias? Oh, his crimes have grown in your absence, Jason.
Explain to me what happened here, and leave nothing out.
The heart of Iolcus has been torn out. While you were gone, the king's crimes grew more heinous by the day. He dreaded your return. Any mention of you or your quest was punishable by death.
All who spoke ill of his rule were imprisoned, or worse, killed. My own son was taken, though no case was ever charged in his name.
I do not know if he is alive or dead.
And what of my parents? Is my father, the true king, still in prison?
Acastus returned this very week. He told your parents that he had sailed with you, but the *Argo* had sunk and you were dead. Your parents, unable to live with this news, took their own lives.
I am truly sorry.
Acastus...

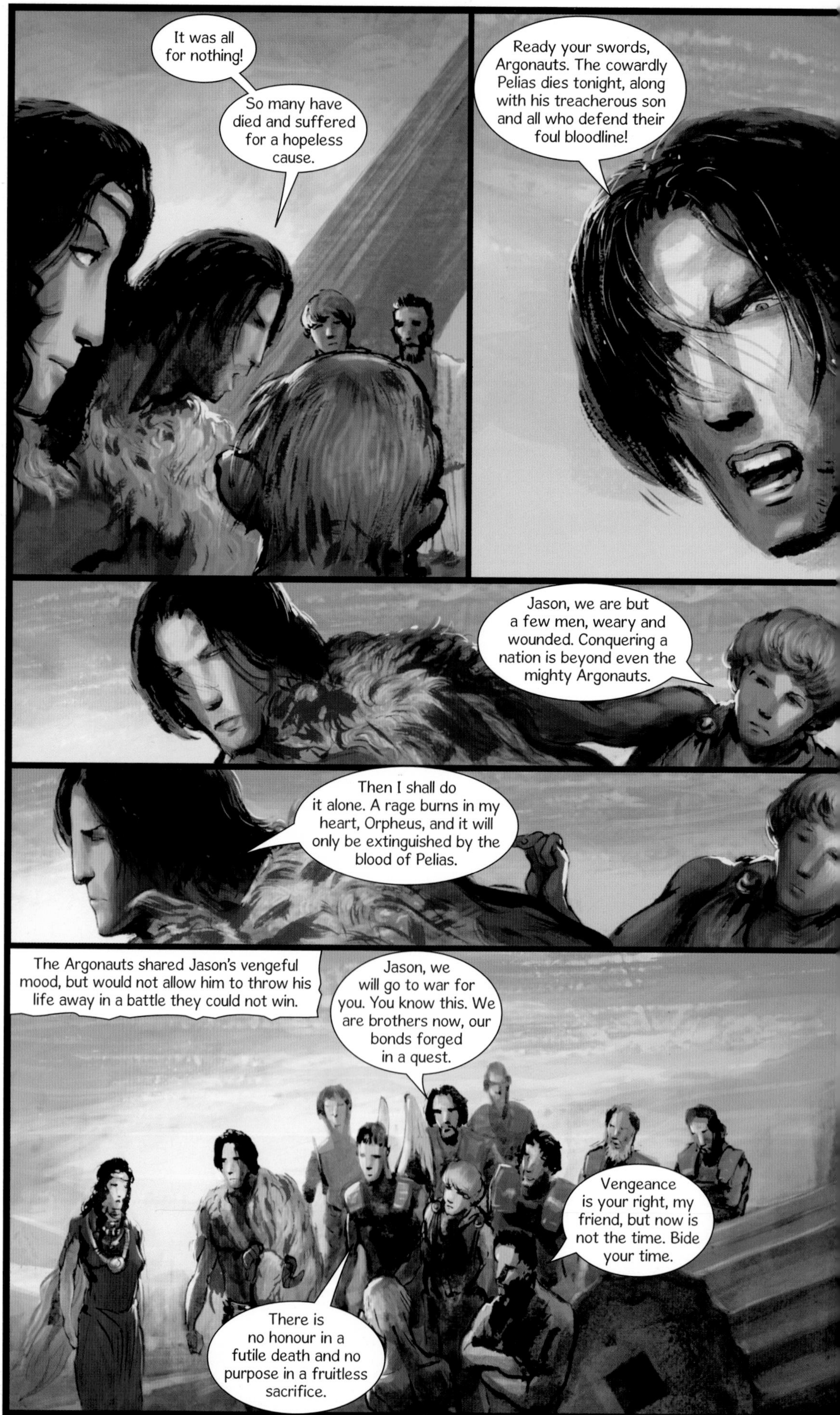
It was all for nothing!
So many have died and suffered for a hopeless cause.
Ready your swords, Argonauts. The cowardly Pelias dies tonight, along with his treacherous son and all who defend their foul bloodline!
Jason, we are but a few men, weary and wounded. Conquering a nation is beyond even the mighty Argonauts.
Then I shall do it alone. A rage burns in my heart, Orpheus, and it will only be extinguished by the blood of Pelias.
The Argonauts shared Jason's vengeful mood, but would not allow him to throw his life away in a battle they could not win.
Jason, we will go to war for you. You know this. We are brothers now, our bonds forged in a quest.
Vengeance is your right, my friend, but now is not the time. Bide your time.
There is no honour in a futile death and no purpose in a fruitless sacrifice.

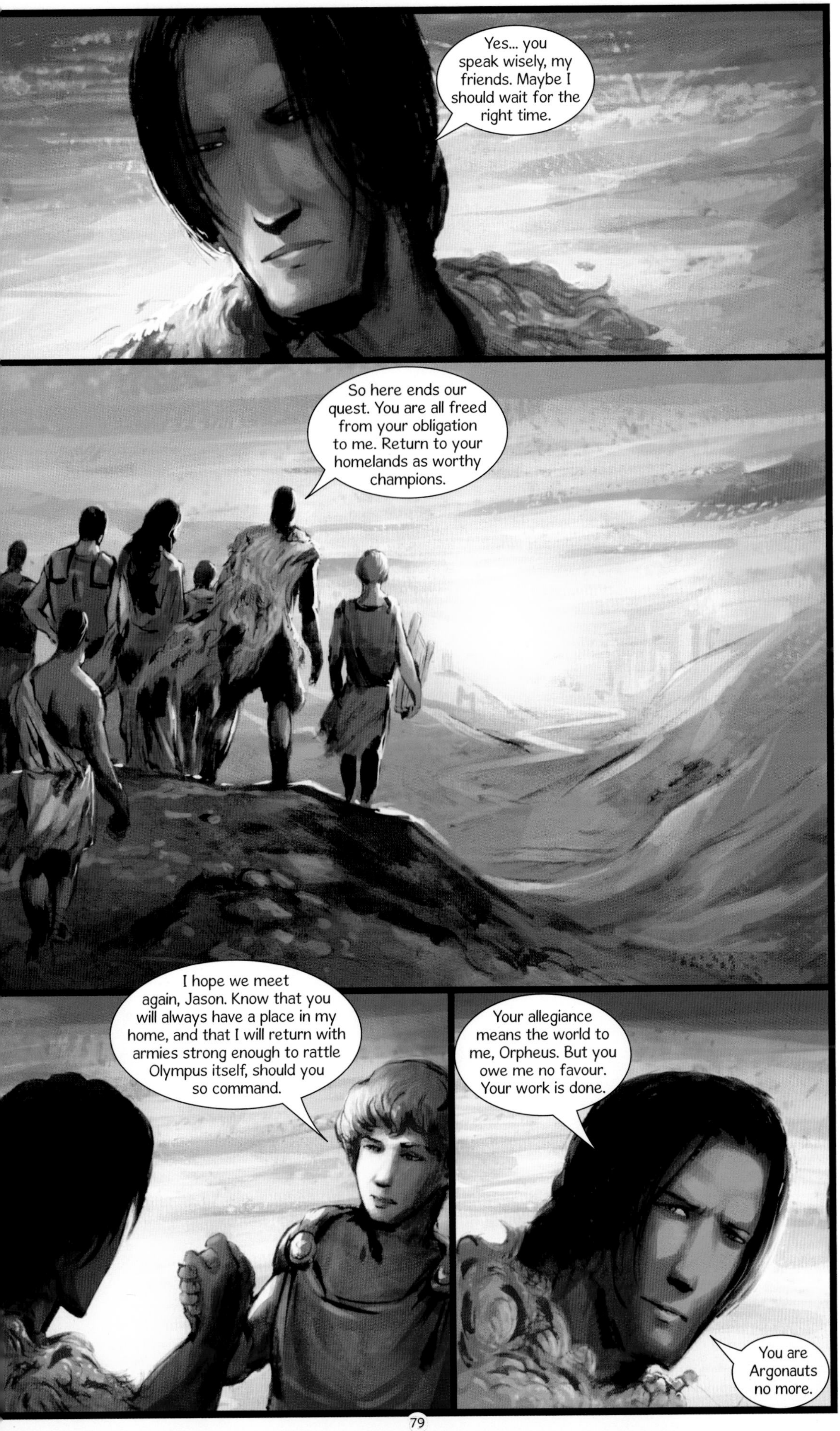
Yes... you speak wisely, my friends. Maybe I should wait for the right time.
So here ends our quest. You are all freed from your obligation to me. Return to your homelands as worthy champions.
I hope we meet again, Jason. Know that you will always have a place in my home, and that I will return with armies strong enough to rattle Olympus itself, should you so command.
Your allegiance means the world to me, Orpheus. But you owe me no favour. Your work is done.
You are Argonauts no more.

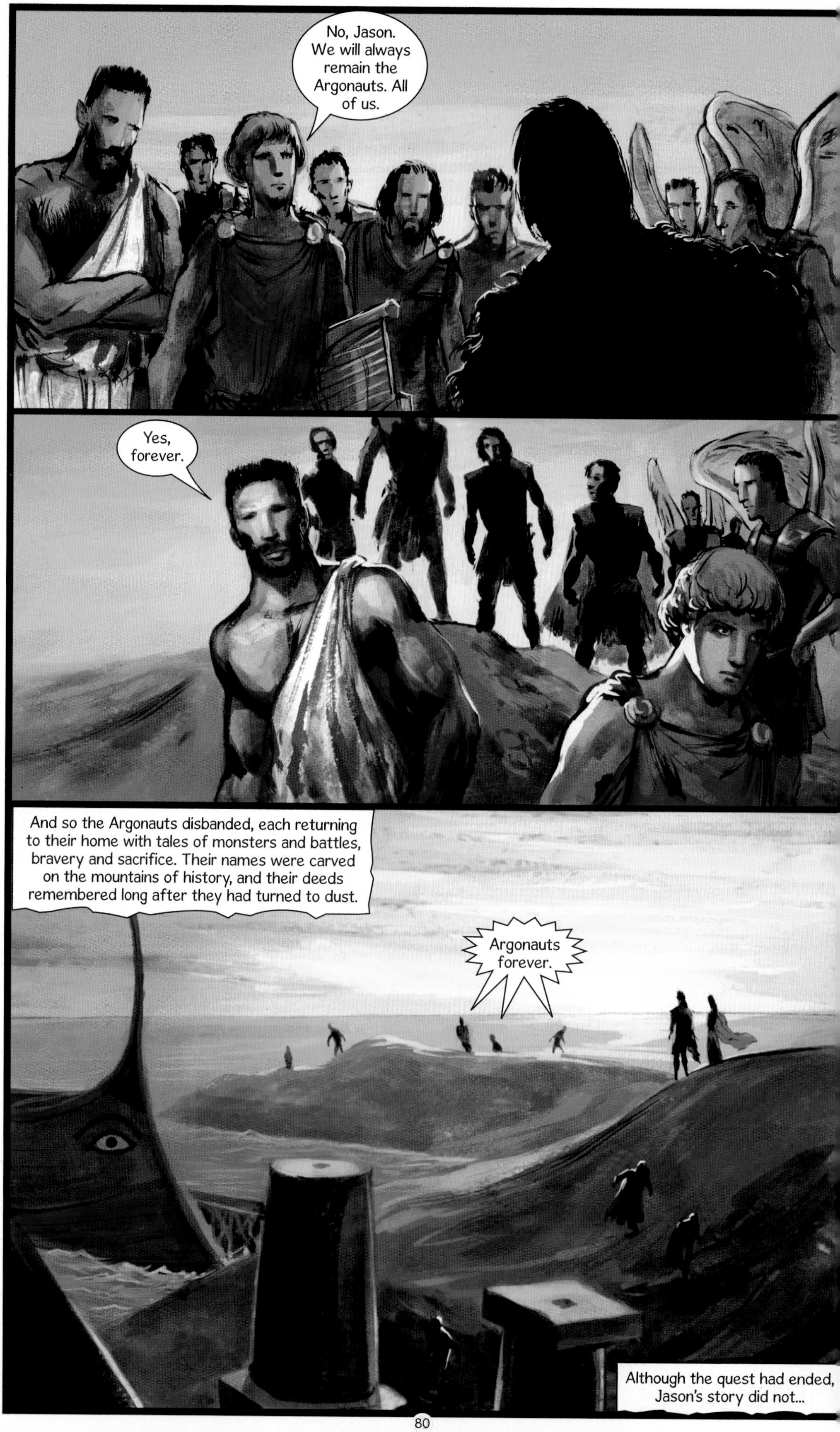
No, Jason. We will always remain the Argonauts. All of us.
Yes, forever.
And so the Argonauts disbanded, each returning to their home with tales of monsters and battles, bravery and sacrifice. Their names were carved on the mountains of history, and their deeds remembered long after they had turned to dust.
Argonauts forever.
Although the quest had ended, Jason's story did not...

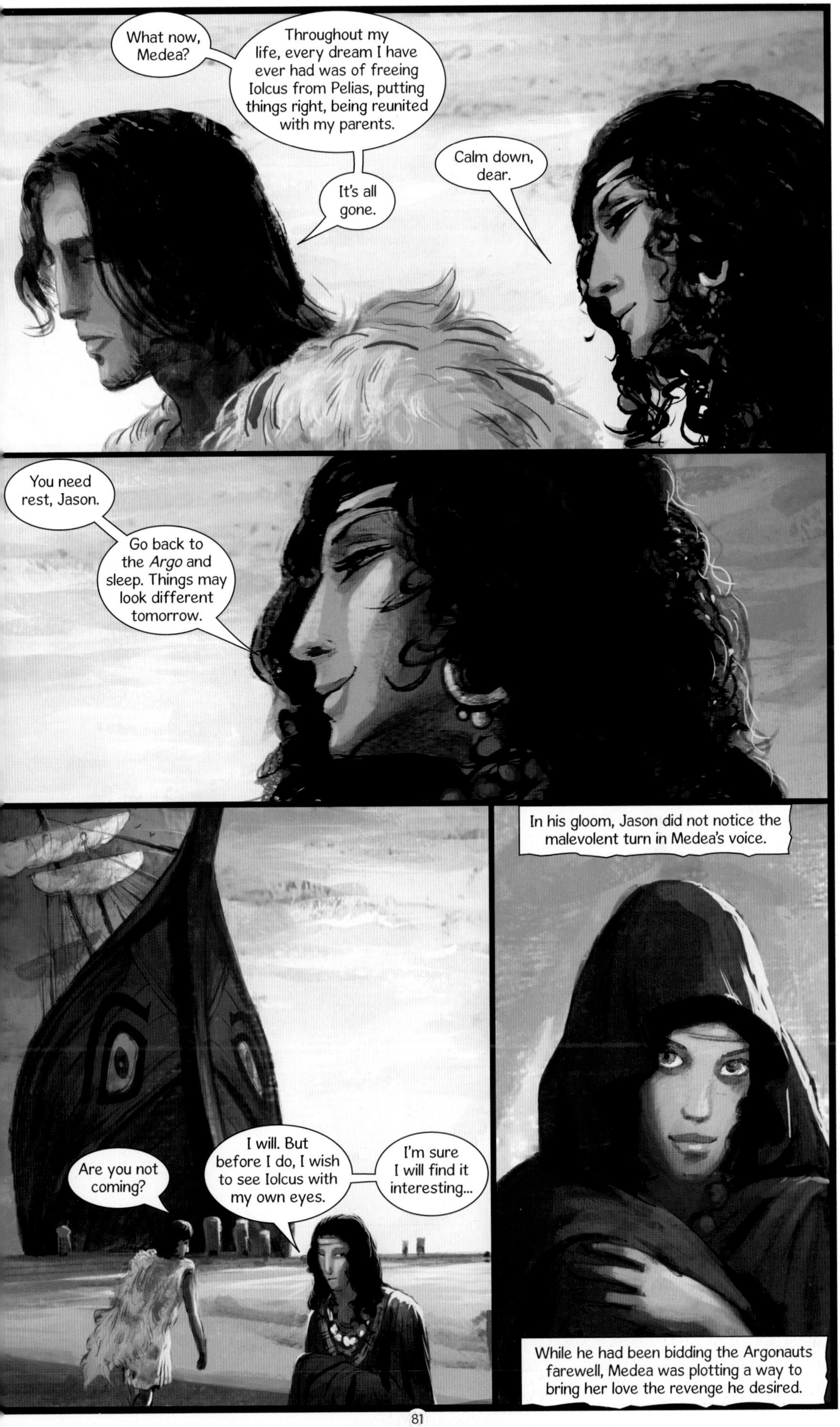
What now, Medea?
Throughout my life, every dream I have ever had was of freeing Iolcus from Pelias, putting things right, being reunited with my parents.
It's all gone.
Calm down, dear.
You need rest, Jason.
Go back to the *Argo* and sleep. Things may look different tomorrow.
Are you not coming?
I will. But before I do, I wish to see Iolcus with my own eyes.
I'm sure I will find it interesting...
In his gloom, Jason did not notice the malevolent turn in Medea's voice.
While he had been bidding the Argonauts farewell, Medea was plotting a way to bring her love the revenge he desired.

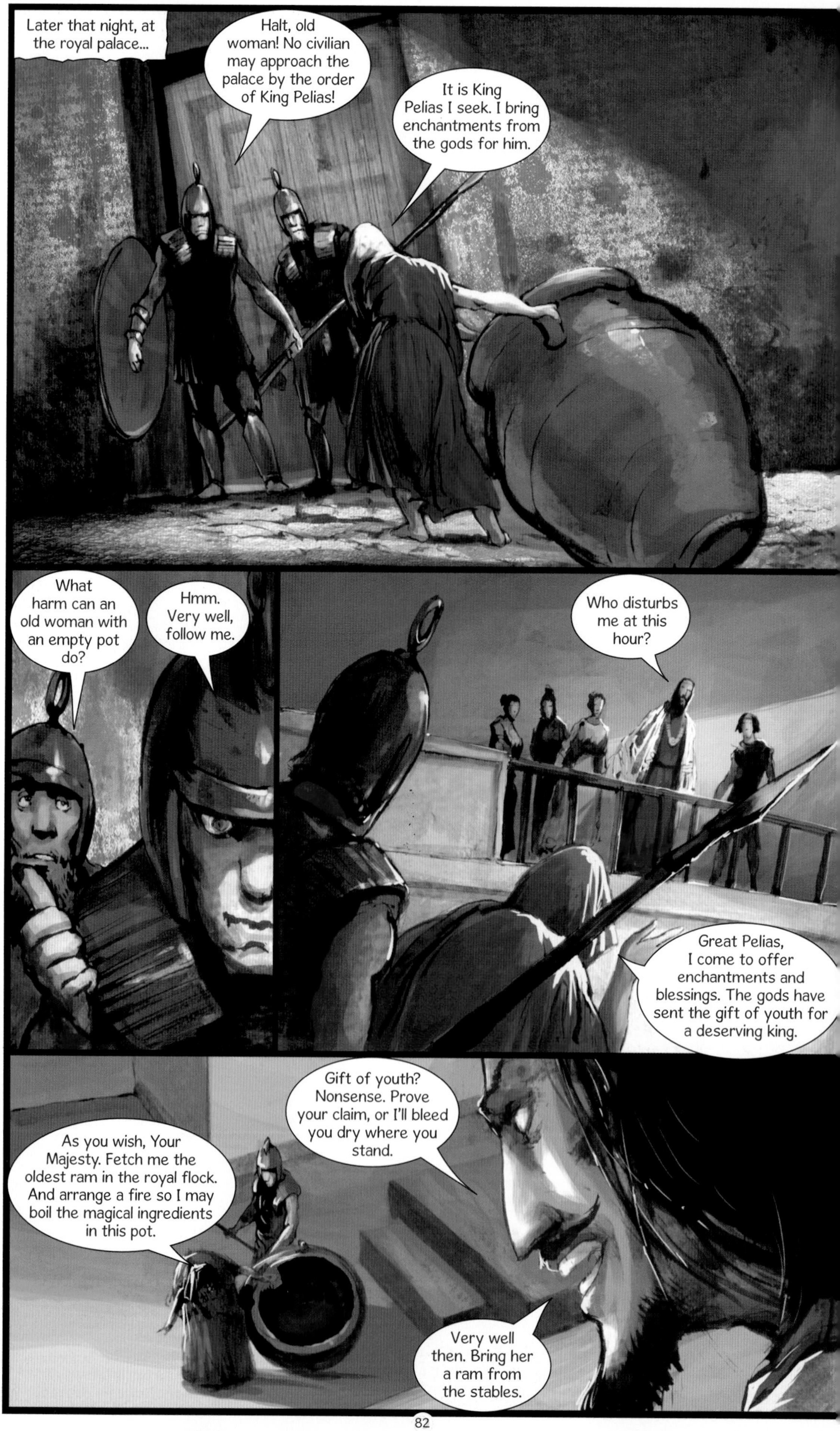
Later that night, at the royal palace...
Halt, old woman! No civilian may approach the palace by the order of King Pelias!
It is King Pelias I seek. I bring enchantments from the gods for him.
What harm can an old woman with an empty pot do?
Hmm. Very well, follow me.
Who disturbs me at this hour?
Great Pelias, I come to offer enchantments and blessings. The gods have sent the gift of youth for a deserving king.
Gift of youth? Nonsense. Prove your claim, or I'll bleed you dry where you stand.
As you wish, Your Majesty. Fetch me the oldest ram in the royal flock. And arrange a fire so I may boil the magical ingredients in this pot.
Very well then. Bring her a ram from the stables.

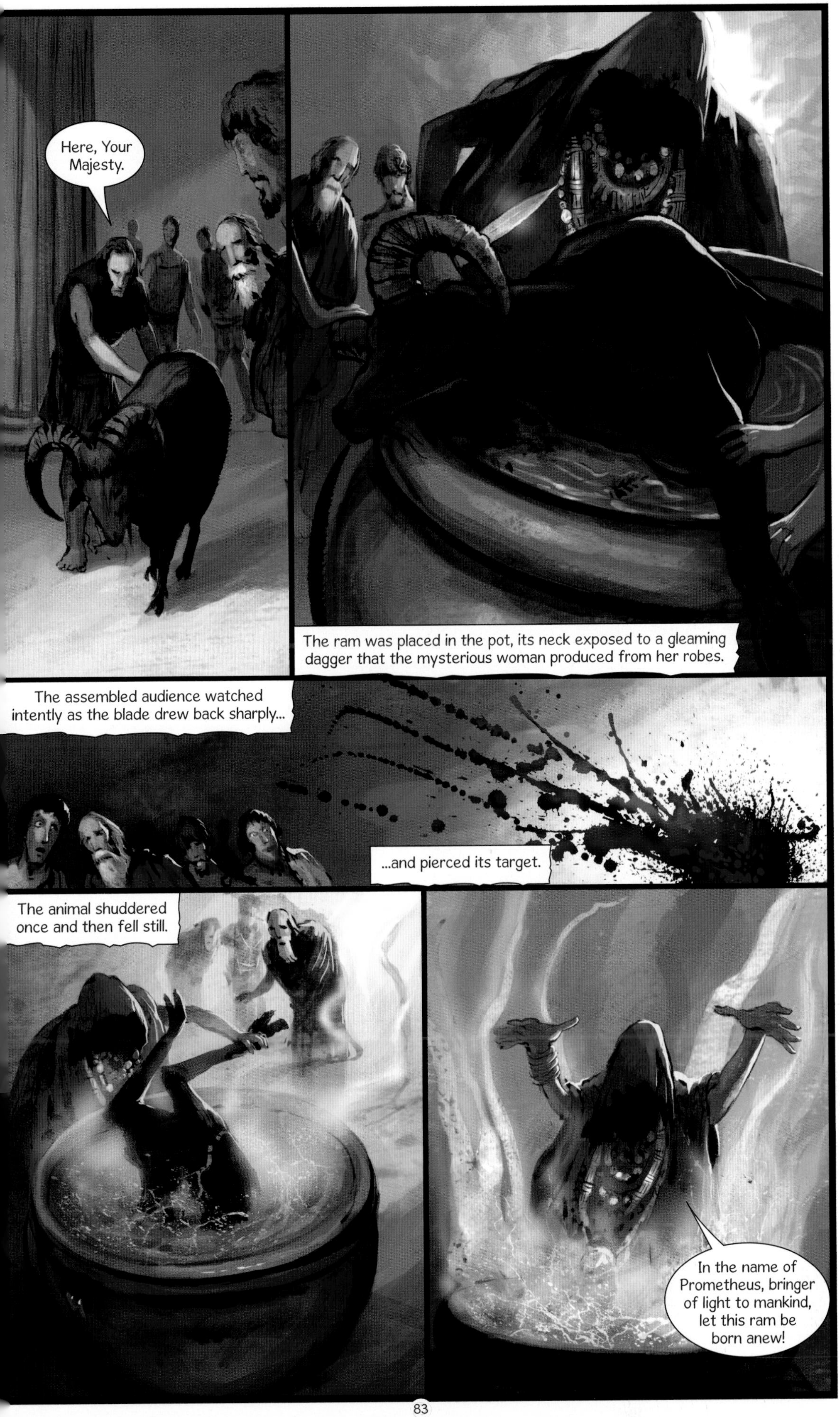
Here, Your Majesty.
The ram was placed in the pot, its neck exposed to a gleaming dagger that the mysterious woman produced from her robes.
The assembled audience watched intently as the blade drew back sharply...
...and pierced its target.
The animal shuddered once and then fell still.
In the name of Prometheus, bringer of light to mankind, let this ram be born anew!

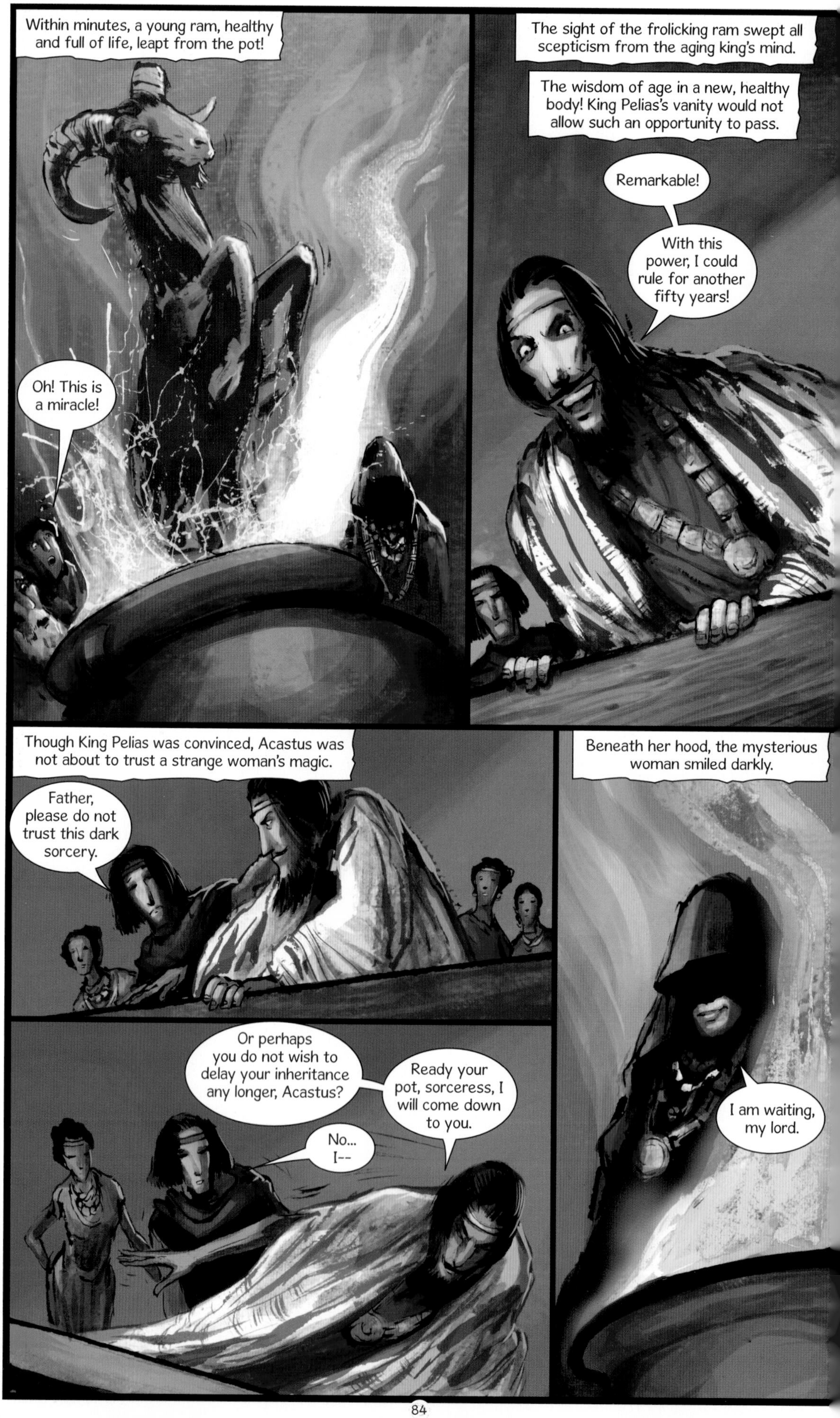
Within minutes, a young ram, healthy and full of life, leapt from the pot!
Oh! This is a miracle!
The sight of the frolicking ram swept all scepticism from the aging king's mind.
The wisdom of age in a new, healthy body! King Pelias's vanity would not allow such an opportunity to pass.
Remarkable!
With this power, I could rule for another fifty years!
Though King Pelias was convinced, Acastus was not about to trust a strange woman's magic.
Father, please do not trust this dark sorcery.
Or perhaps you do not wish to delay your inheritance any longer, Acastus?
No... I--
Ready your pot, sorceress, I will come down to you.
Beneath her hood, the mysterious woman smiled darkly.
I am waiting, my lord.

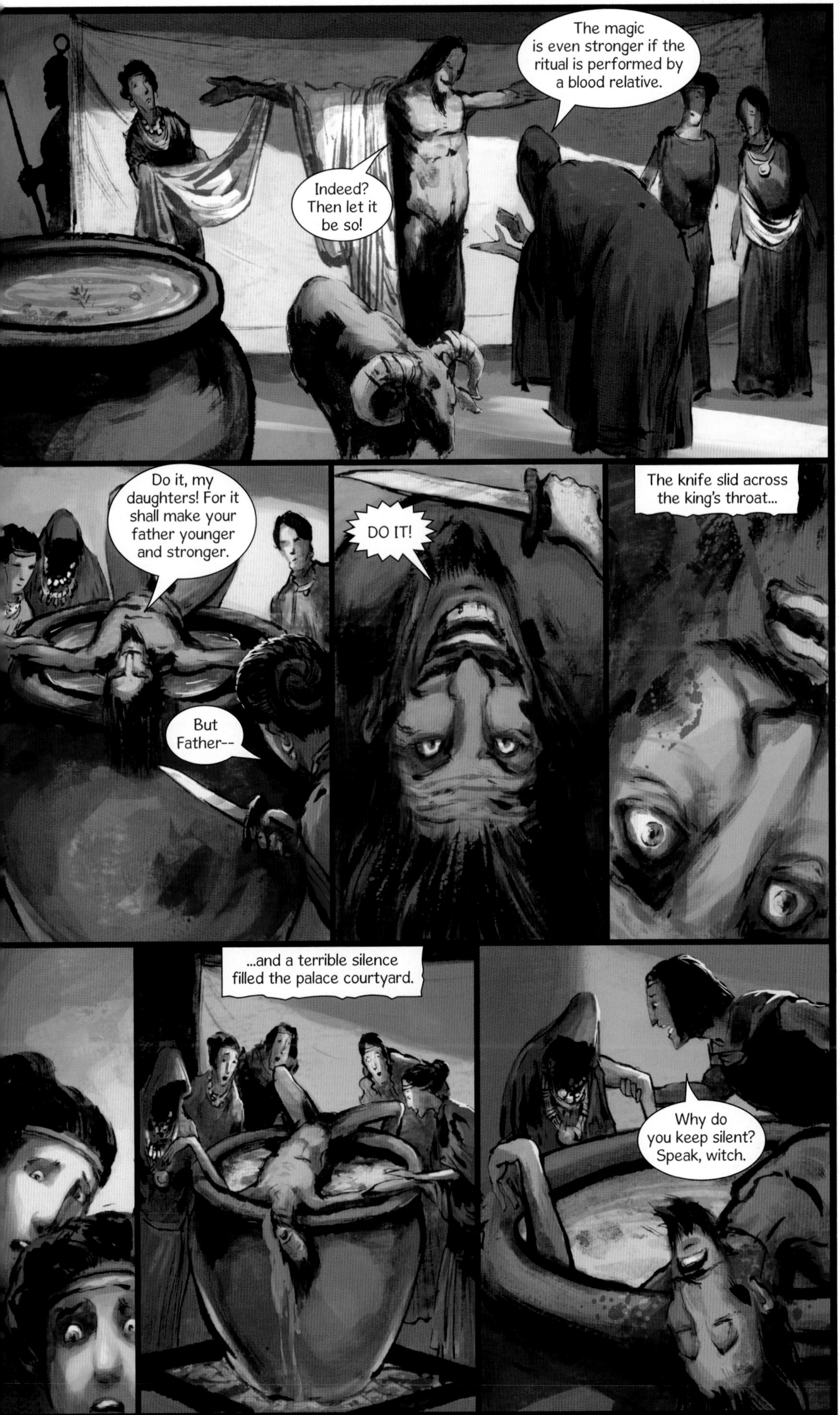

The magic is even stronger if the ritual is performed by a blood relative.
Indeed? Then let it be so!
Do it, my daughters! For it shall make your father younger and stronger.
But Father--
DO IT!
The knife slid across the king's throat...
...and a terrible silence filled the palace courtyard.
Why do you keep silent? Speak, witch.

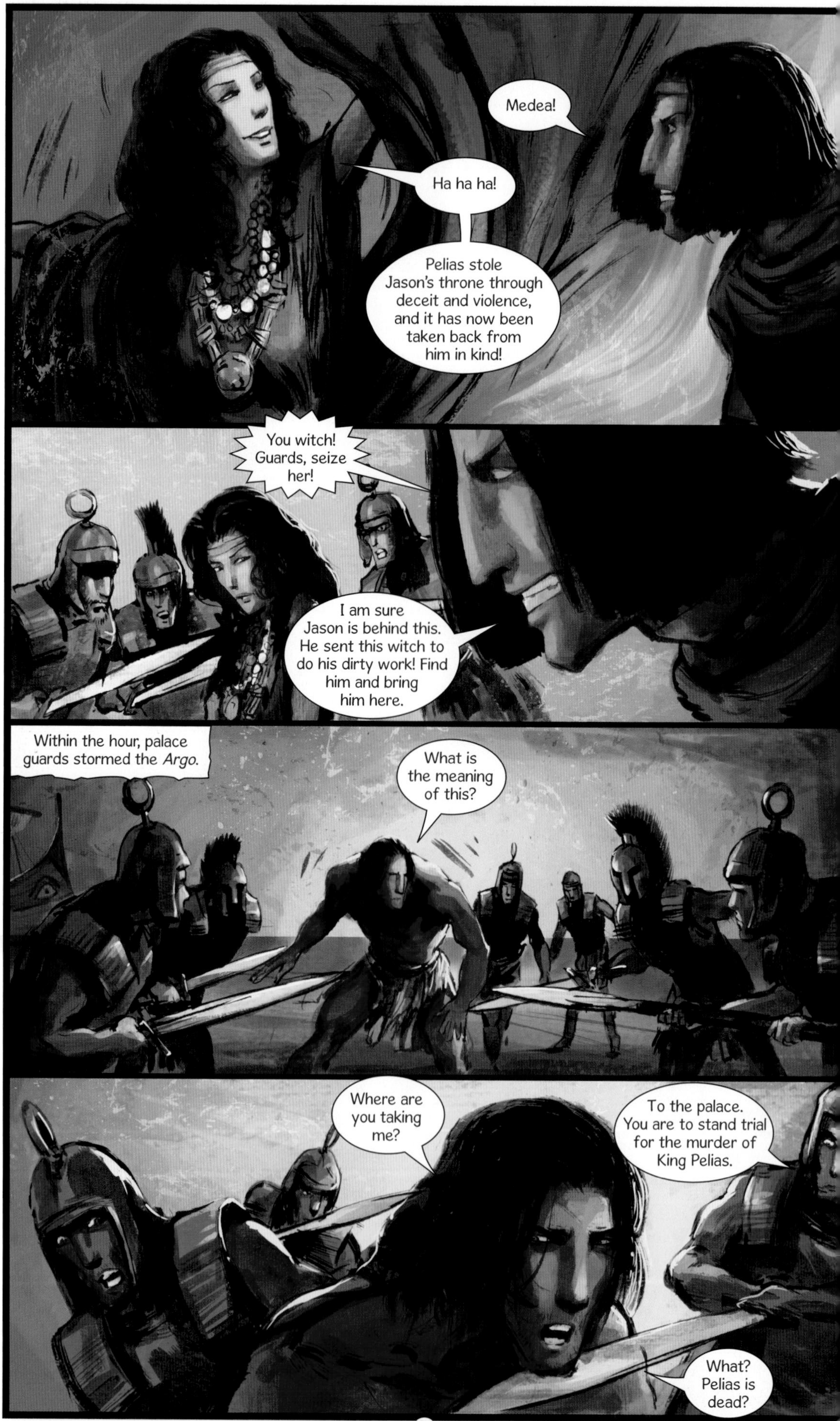
Medea!
Ha ha ha!
Pelias stole Jason's throne through deceit and violence, and it has now been taken back from him in kind!
You witch! Guards, seize her!
I am sure Jason is behind this. He sent this witch to do his dirty work! Find him and bring him here.
Within the hour, palace guards stormed the *Argo*.
What is the meaning of this?
Where are you taking me?
To the palace. You are to stand trial for the murder of King Pelias.
What? Pelias is dead?

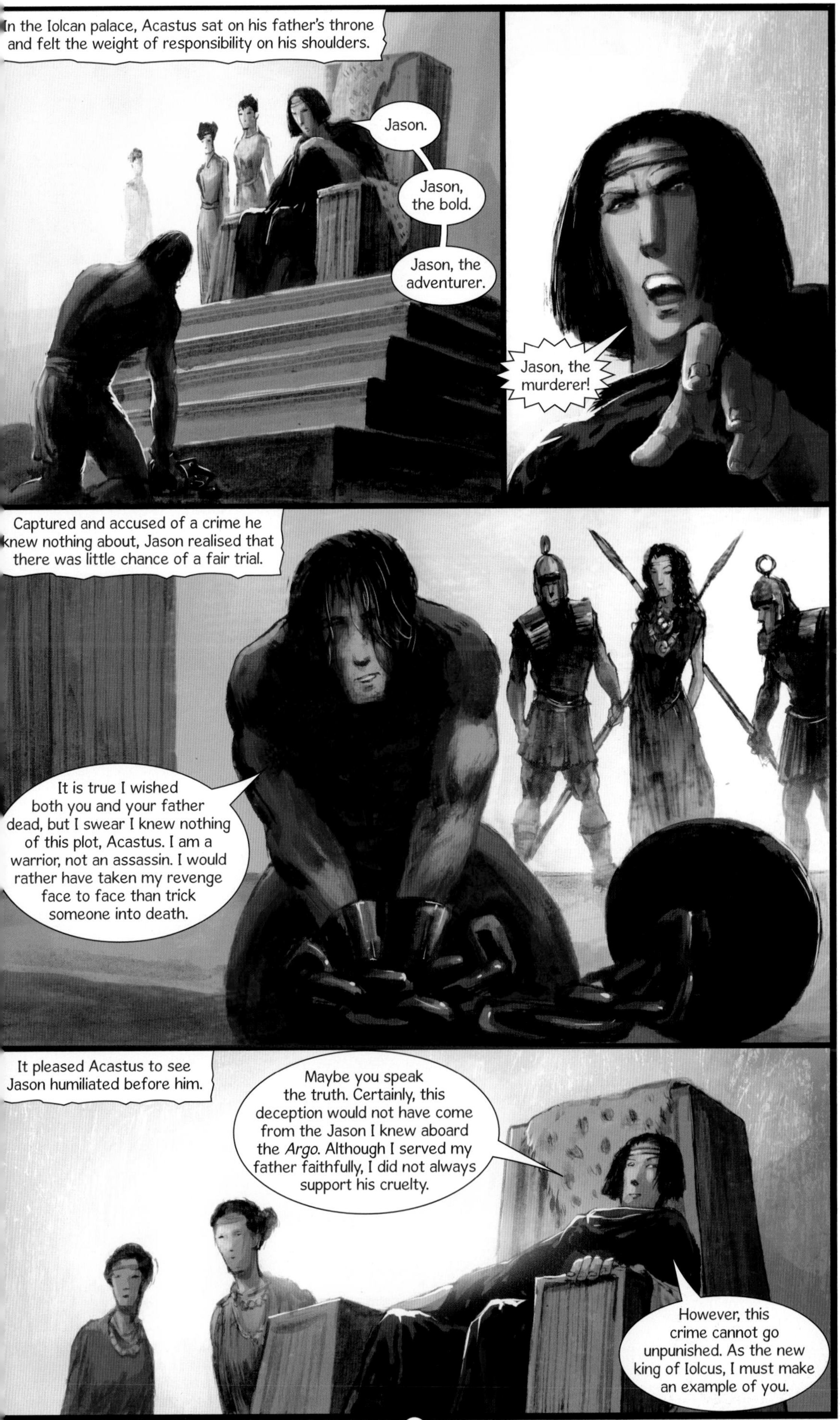

In the Iolcan palace, Acastus sat on his father's throne and felt the weight of responsibility on his shoulders.
Jason.
Jason, the bold.
Jason, the adventurer.
Jason, the murderer!
Captured and accused of a crime he knew nothing about, Jason realised that there was little chance of a fair trial.
It is true I wished both you and your father dead, but I swear I knew nothing of this plot, Acastus. I am a warrior, not an assassin. I would rather have taken my revenge face to face than trick someone into death.
It pleased Acastus to see Jason humiliated before him.
Maybe you speak the truth. Certainly, this deception would not have come from the Jason I knew aboard the *Argo*. Although I served my father faithfully, I did not always support his cruelty.
However, this crime cannot go unpunished. As the new king of Iolcus, I must make an example of you.

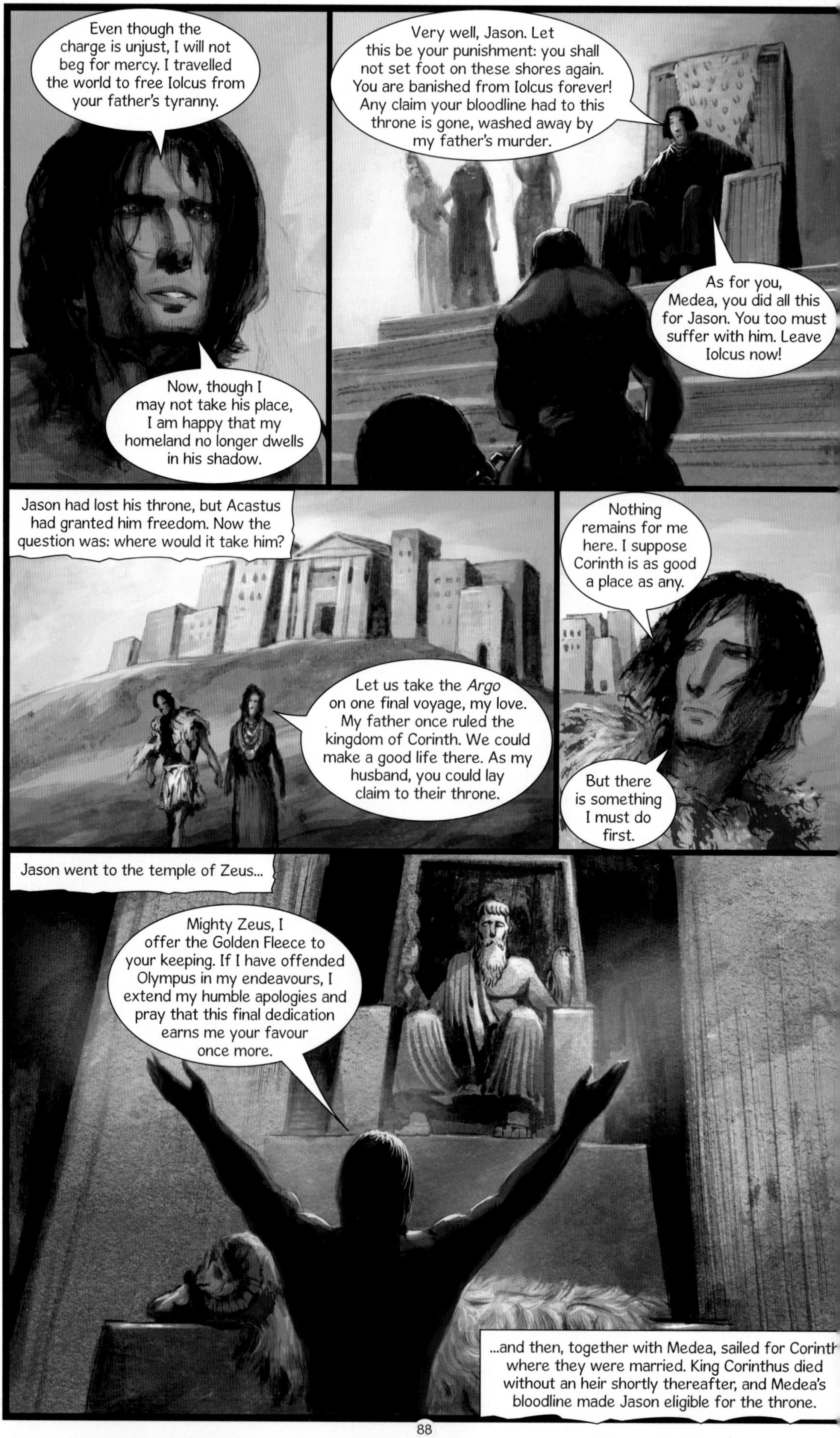
Even though the charge is unjust, I will not beg for mercy. I travelled the world to free Iolcus from your father's tyranny.
Now, though I may not take his place, I am happy that my homeland no longer dwells in his shadow.
Very well, Jason. Let this be your punishment: you shall not set foot on these shores again. You are banished from Iolcus forever! Any claim your bloodline had to this throne is gone, washed away by my father's murder.
As for you, Medea, you did all this for Jason. You too must suffer with him. Leave Iolcus now!
Jason had lost his throne, but Acastus had granted him freedom. Now the question was: where would it take him?
Let us take the *Argo* on one final voyage, my love. My father once ruled the kingdom of Corinth. We could make a good life there. As my husband, you could lay claim to their throne.
Nothing remains for me here. I suppose Corinth is as good a place as any.
But there is something I must do first.
Jason went to the temple of Zeus...
Mighty Zeus, I offer the Golden Fleece to your keeping. If I have offended Olympus in my endeavours, I extend my humble apologies and pray that this final dedication earns me your favour once more.
...and then, together with Medea, sailed for Corinth where they were married. King Corinthus died without an heir shortly thereafter, and Medea's bloodline made Jason eligible for the throne.

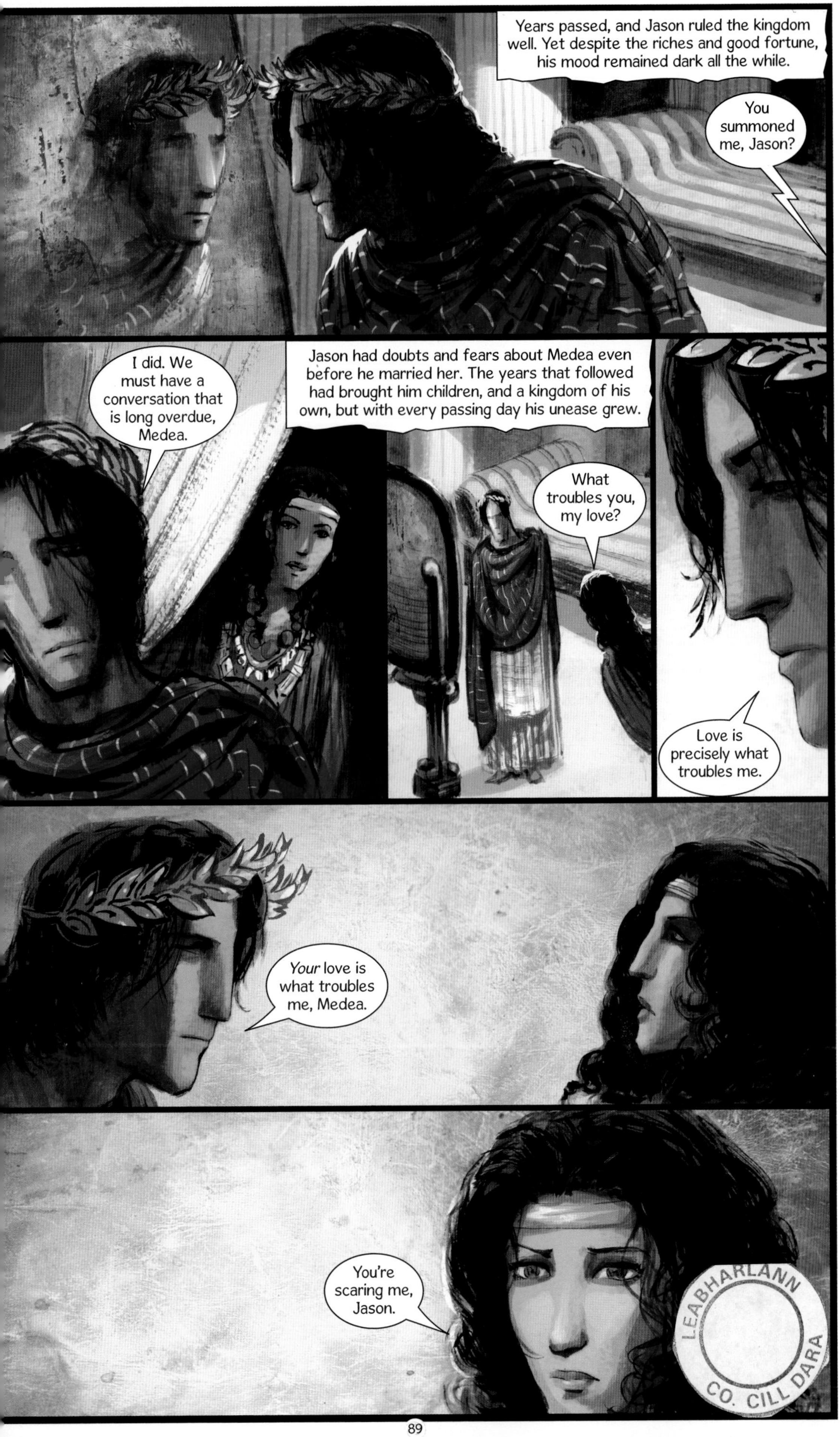

Years passed, and Jason ruled the kingdom well. Yet despite the riches and good fortune, his mood remained dark all the while.
You summoned me, Jason?
I did. We must have a conversation that is long overdue, Medea.
Jason had doubts and fears about Medea even before he married her. The years that followed had brought him children, and a kingdom of his own, but with every passing day his unease grew.
What troubles you, my love?
Love is precisely what troubles me.
Your love is what troubles me, Medea.
You're scaring me, Jason.
LEABHARLANN CO. CILL DARA

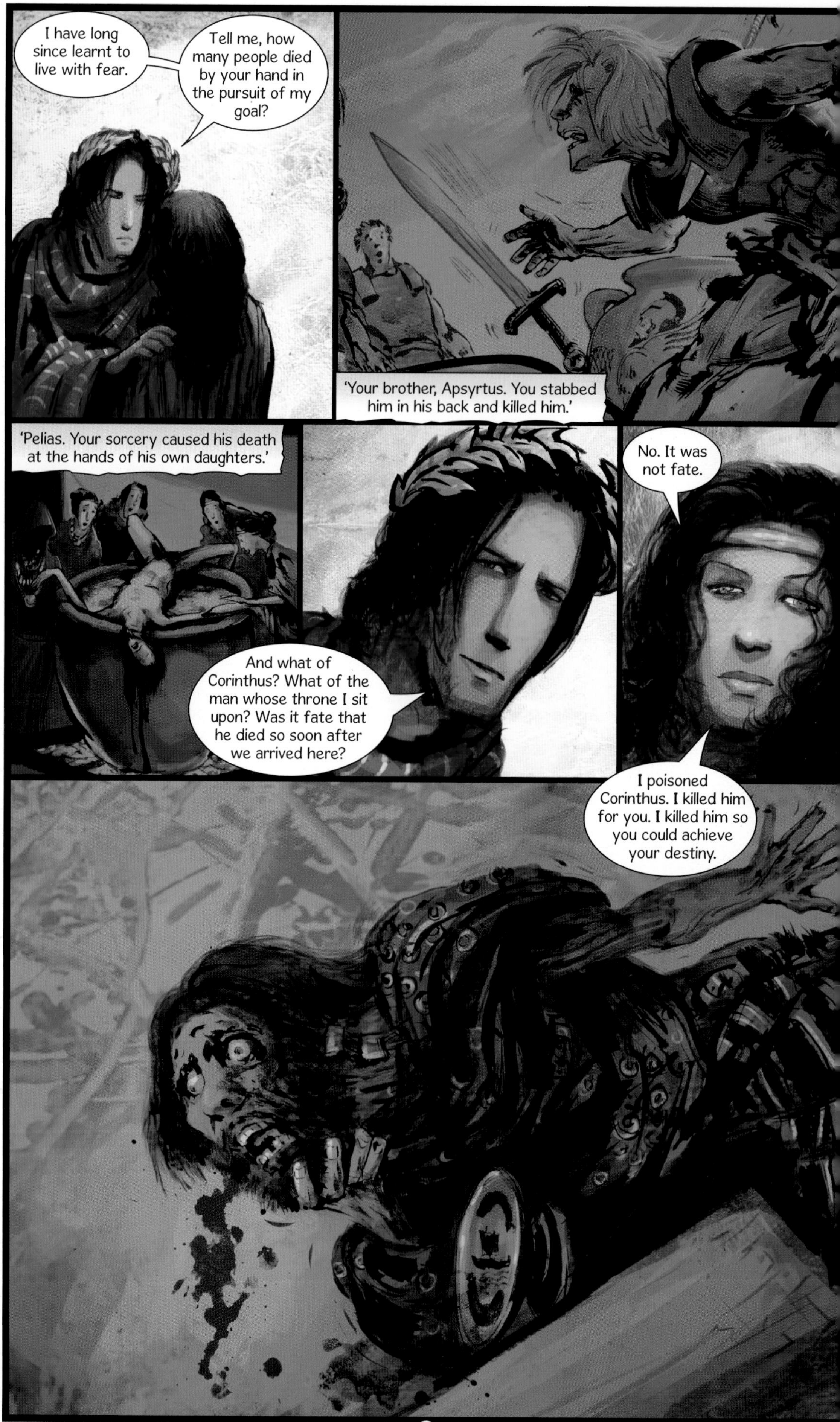
I have long since learnt to live with fear.
Tell me, how many people died by your hand in the pursuit of my goal?
'Your brother, Apsyrtus. You stabbed him in his back and killed him.'
'Pelias. Your sorcery caused his death at the hands of his own daughters.'
And what of Corinthus? What of the man whose throne I sit upon? Was it fate that he died so soon after we arrived here?
No. It was not fate.
I poisoned Corinthus. I killed him for you. I killed him so you could achieve your destiny.

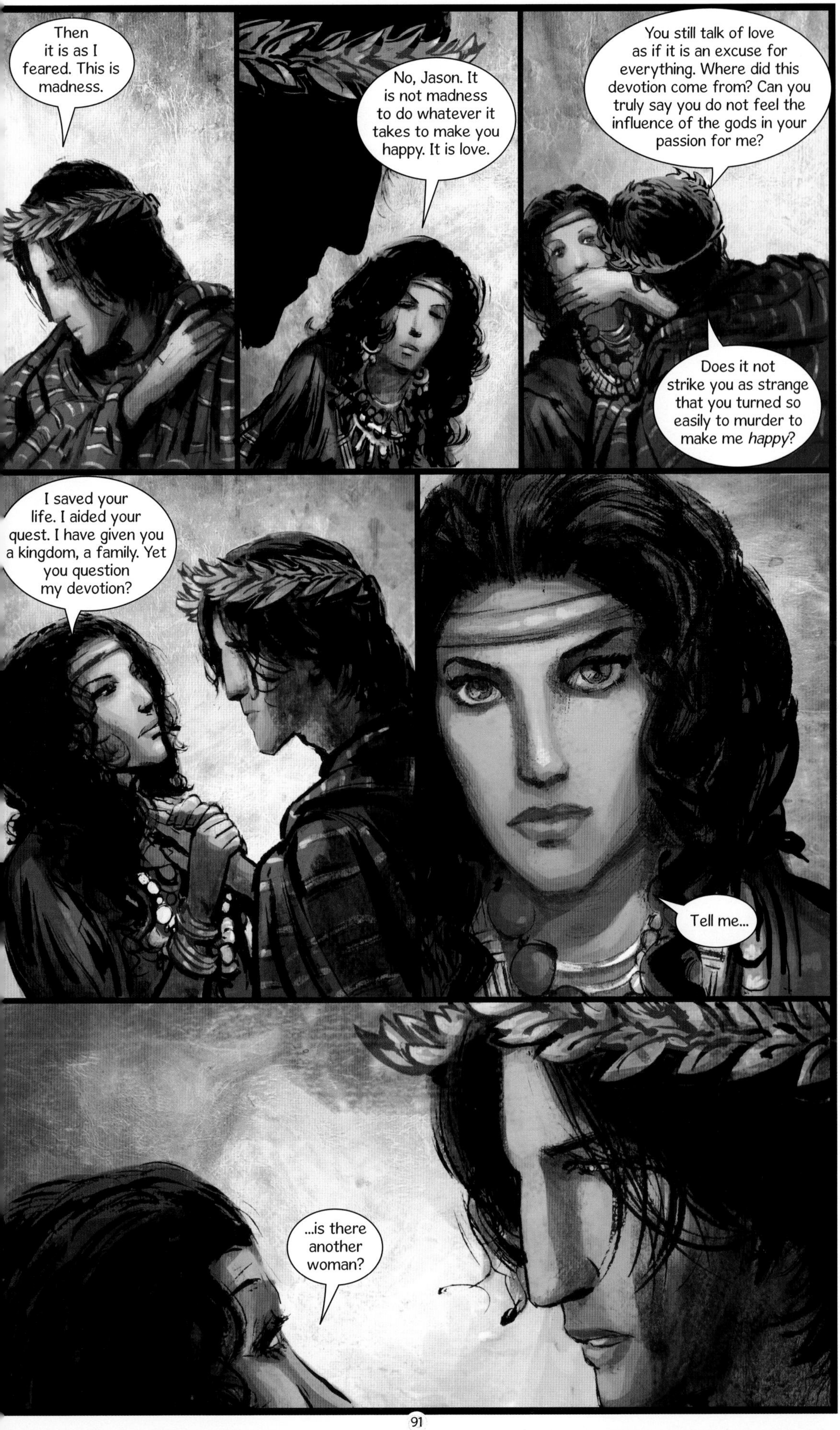
Then it is as I feared. This is madness.
No, Jason. It is not madness to do whatever it takes to make you happy. It is love.
You still talk of love as if it is an excuse for everything. Where did this devotion come from? Can you truly say you do not feel the influence of the gods in your passion for me?
Does it not strike you as strange that you turned so easily to murder to make me *happy*?
I saved your life. I aided your quest. I have given you a kingdom, a family. Yet you question my devotion?
Tell me...
...is there another woman?

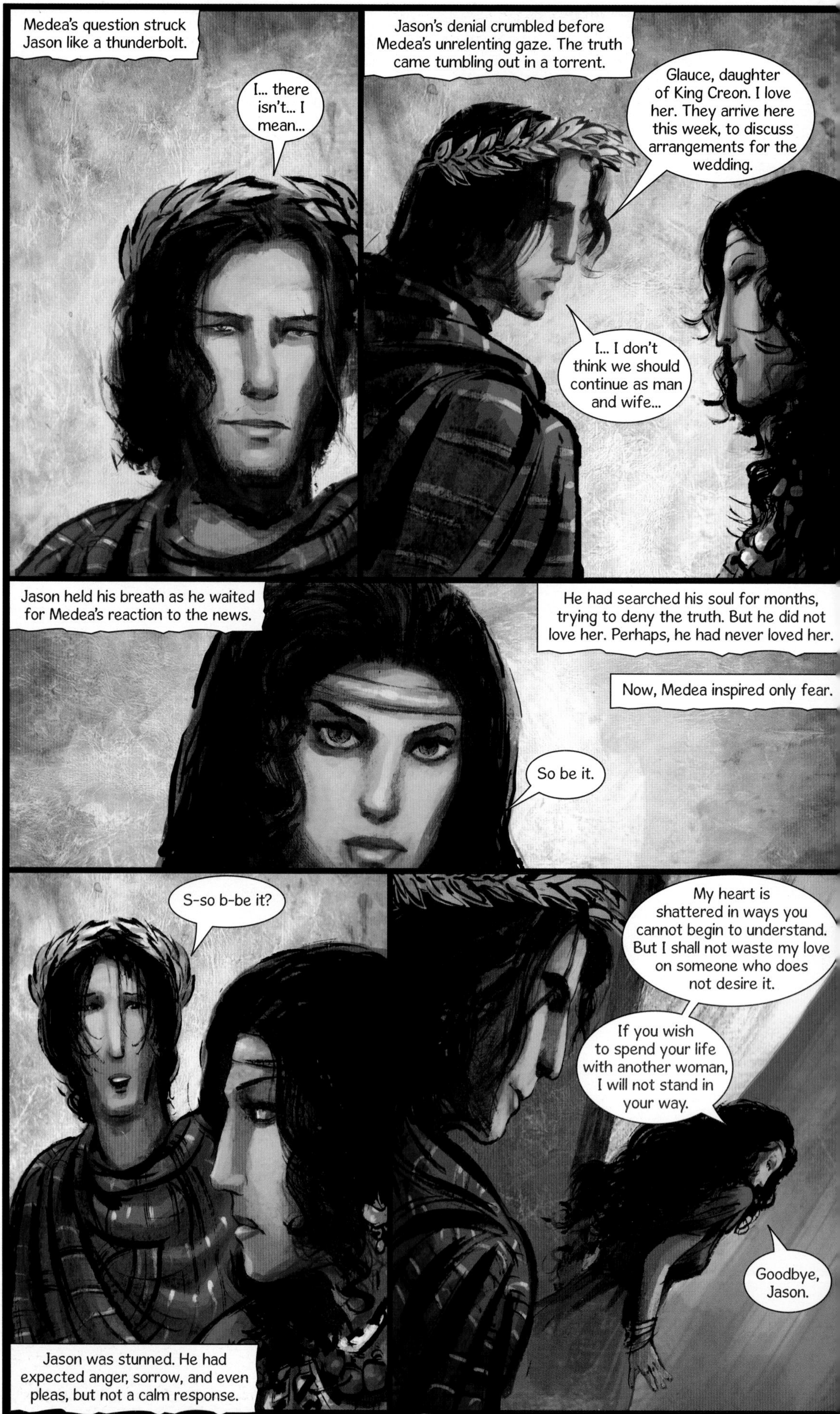
Medea's question struck Jason like a thunderbolt.
I... there isn't... I mean...
Jason's denial crumbled before Medea's unrelenting gaze. The truth came tumbling out in a torrent.
Glauce, daughter of King Creon. I love her. They arrive here this week, to discuss arrangements for the wedding.
I... I don't think we should continue as man and wife...
Jason held his breath as he waited for Medea's reaction to the news.
He had searched his soul for months, trying to deny the truth. But he did not love her. Perhaps, he had never loved her.
Now, Medea inspired only fear.
So be it.
S-so b-be it?
Jason was stunned. He had expected anger, sorrow, and even pleas, but not a calm response.
My heart is shattered in ways you cannot begin to understand. But I shall not waste my love on someone who does not desire it.
If you wish to spend your life with another woman, I will not stand in your way.
Goodbye, Jason.

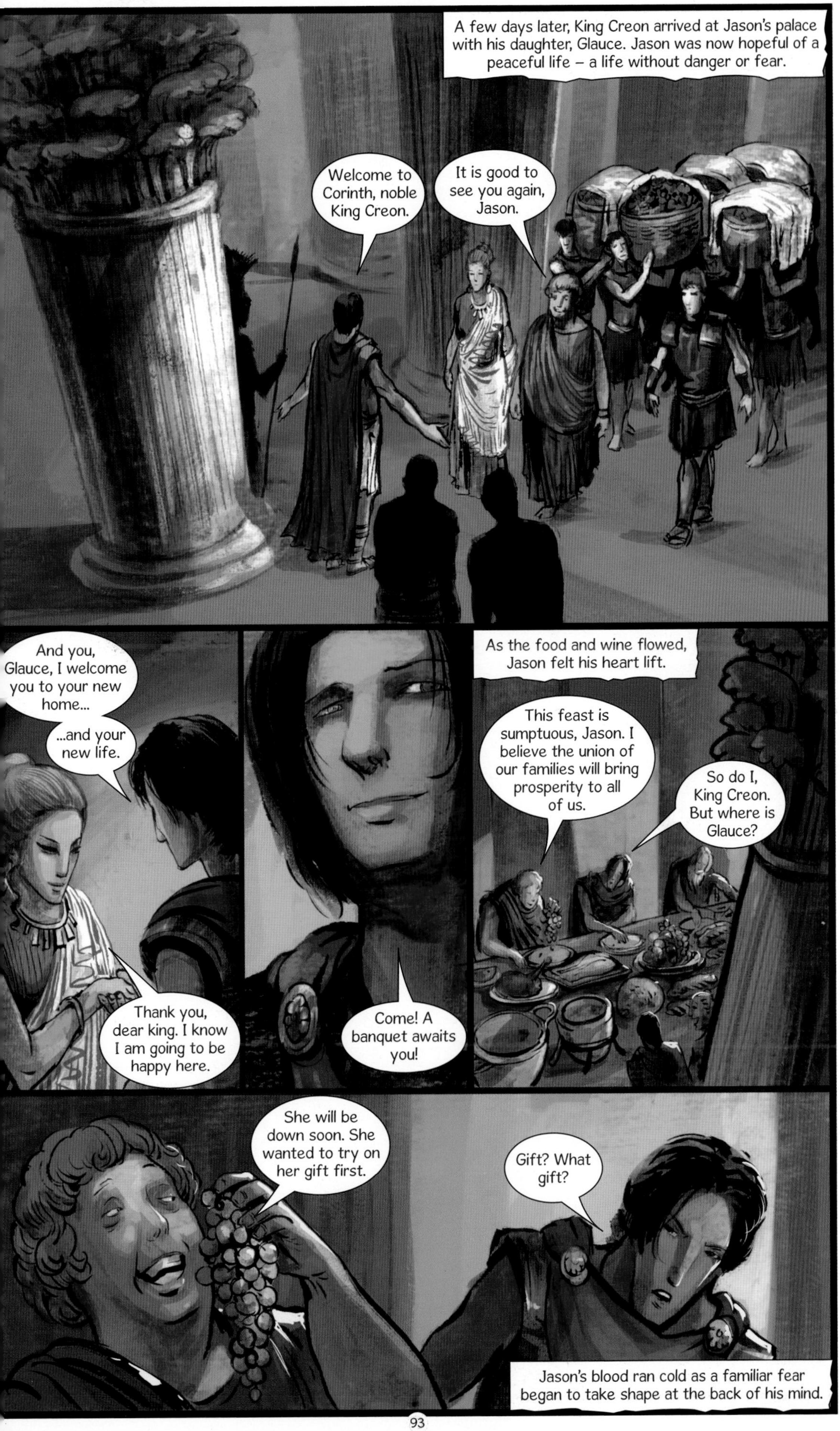
A few days later, King Creon arrived at Jason's palace with his daughter, Glauce. Jason was now hopeful of a peaceful life – a life without danger or fear.
Welcome to Corinth, noble King Creon.
It is good to see you again, Jason.
And you, Glauce, I welcome you to your new home...
...and your new life.
Thank you, dear king. I know I am going to be happy here.
Come! A banquet awaits you!
As the food and wine flowed, Jason felt his heart lift.
This feast is sumptuous, Jason. I believe the union of our families will bring prosperity to all of us.
So do I, King Creon. But where is Glauce?
She will be down soon. She wanted to try on her gift first.
Gift? What gift?
Jason's blood ran cold as a familiar fear began to take shape at the back of his mind.

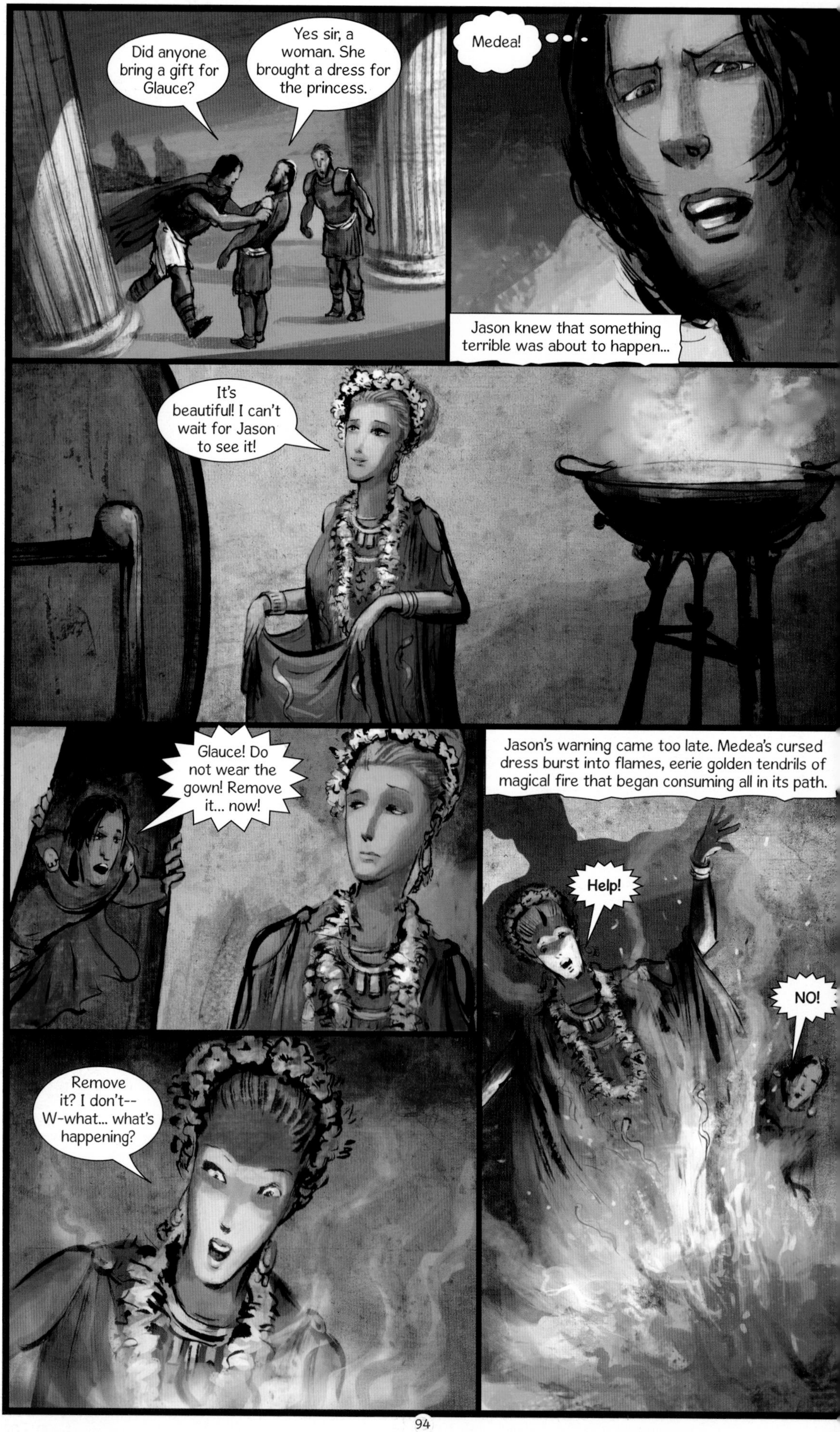

Did anyone bring a gift for Glauce?
Yes sir, a woman. She brought a dress for the princess.
Medea!
Jason knew that something terrible was about to happen...
It's beautiful! I can't wait for Jason to see it!
Glauce! Do not wear the gown! Remove it... now!
Jason's warning came too late. Medea's cursed dress burst into flames, eerie golden tendrils of magical fire that began consuming all in its path.
Help!
NO!
Remove it? I don't-- W-what... what's happening?

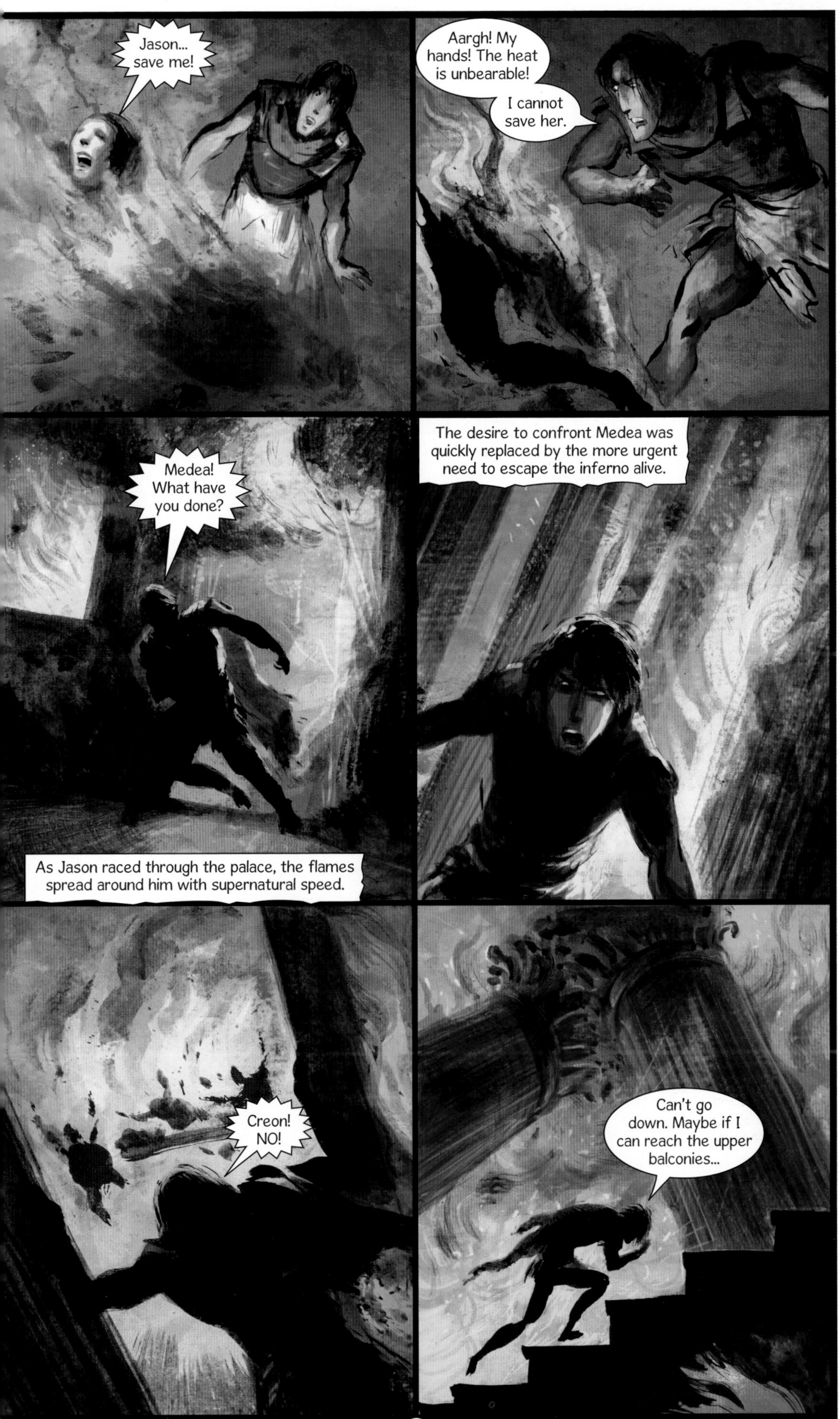
Jason... save me!
Aargh! My hands! The heat is unbearable!
I cannot save her.
Medea! What have you done?
As Jason raced through the palace, the flames spread around him with supernatural speed.
The desire to confront Medea was quickly replaced by the more urgent need to escape the inferno alive.
Creon! NO!
Can't go down. Maybe if I can reach the upper balconies...

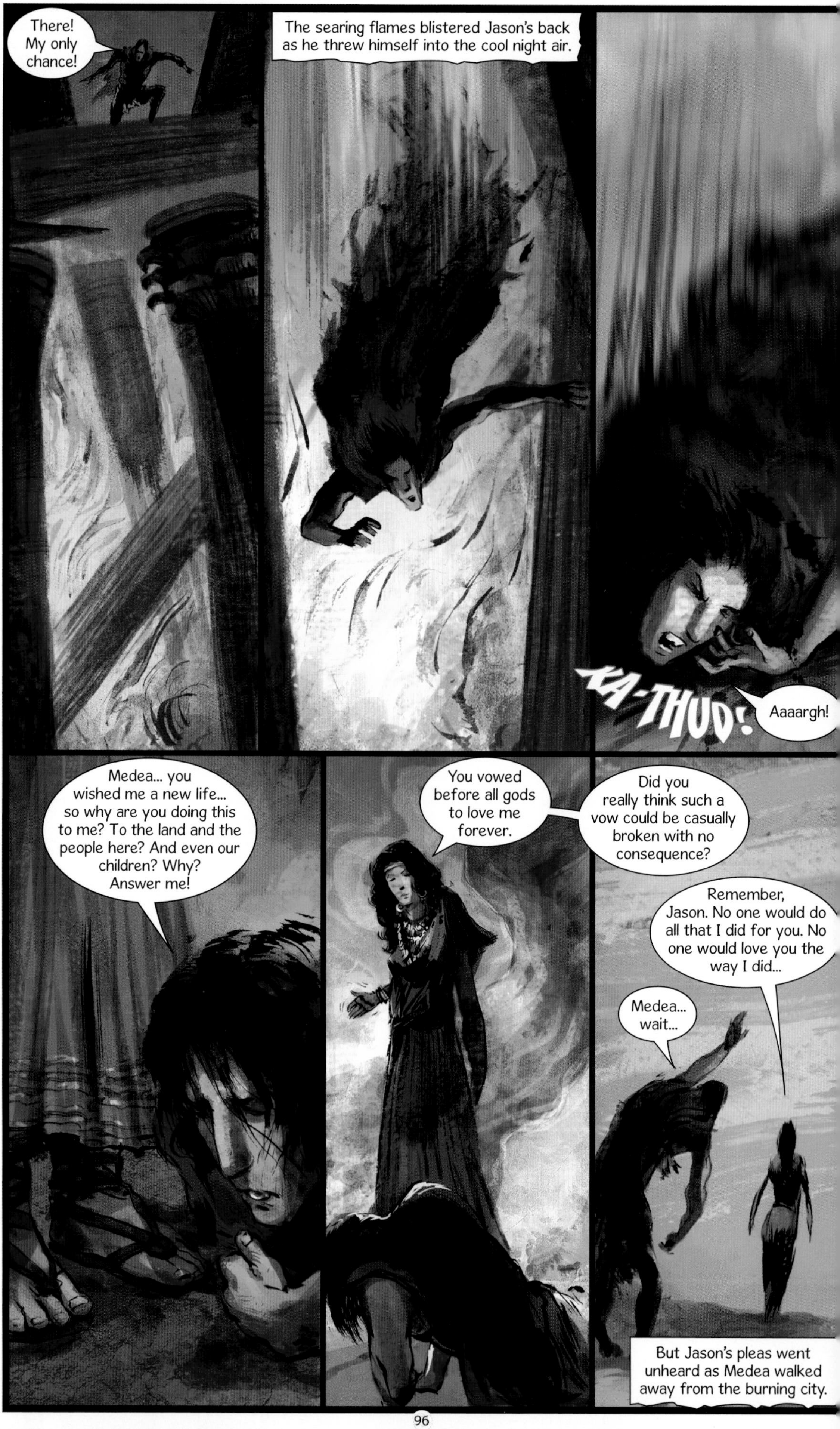
There! My only chance!
The searing flames blistered Jason's back as he threw himself into the cool night air.
KA-THUD!
Aaaargh!
Medea... you wished me a new life... so why are you doing this to me? To the land and the people here? And even our children? Why? Answer me!
You vowed before all gods to love me forever.
Did you really think such a vow could be casually broken with no consequence?
Remember, Jason. No one would do all that I did for you. No one would love you the way I did...
Medea... wait...
But Jason's pleas went unheard as Medea walked away from the burning city.

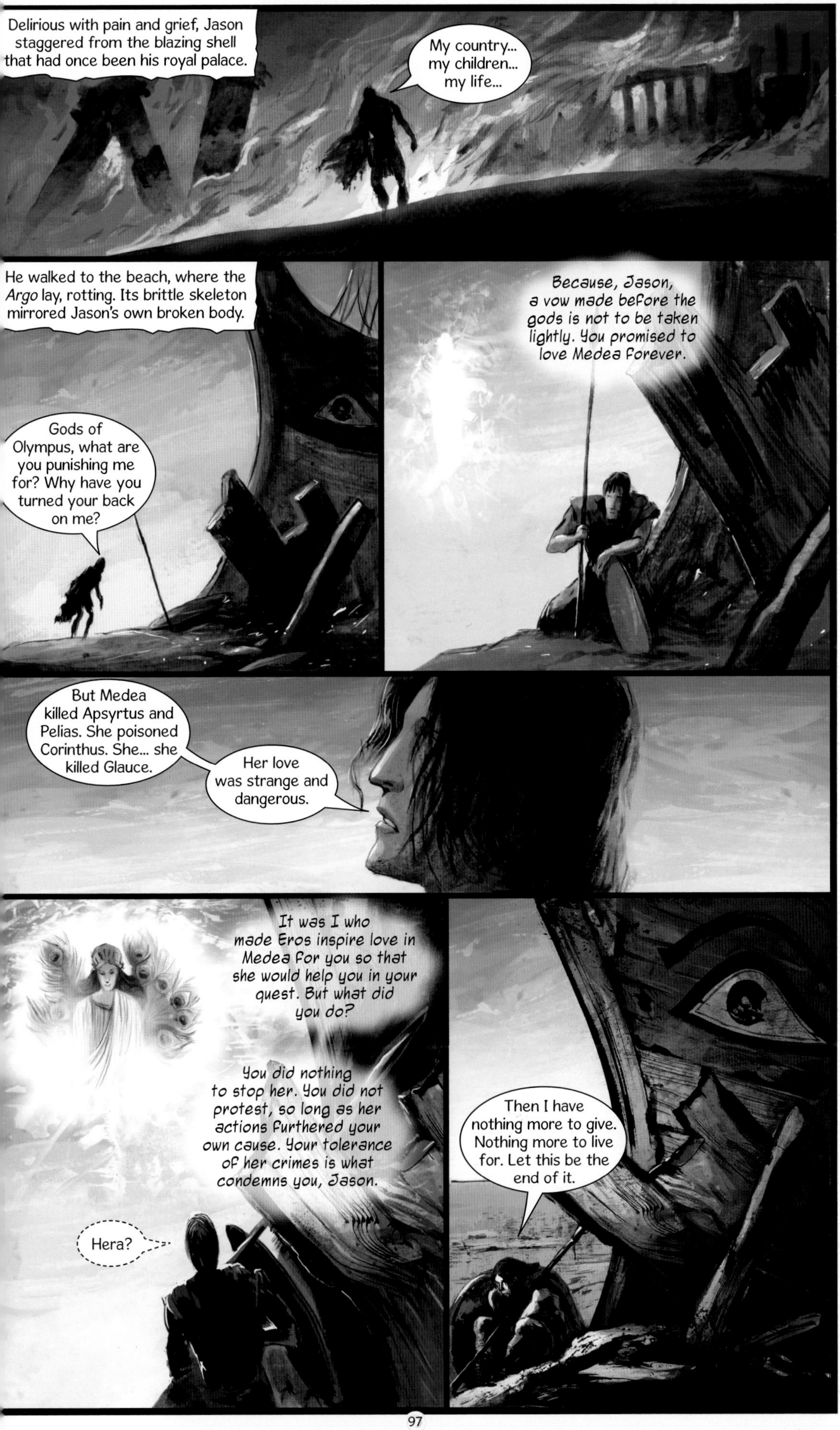
Delirious with pain and grief, Jason staggered from the blazing shell that had once been his royal palace.
My country... my children... my life...
He walked to the beach, where the *Argo* lay, rotting. Its brittle skeleton mirrored Jason's own broken body.
Gods of Olympus, what are you punishing me for? Why have you turned your back on me?
Because, Jason, a vow made before the gods is not to be taken lightly. You promised to love Medea forever.
But Medea killed Apsyrtus and Pelias. She poisoned Corinthus. She... she killed Glauce.
Her love was strange and dangerous.
It was I who made Eros inspire love in Medea for you so that she would help you in your quest. But what did you do?
You did nothing to stop her. You did not protest, so long as her actions furthered your own cause. Your tolerance of her crimes is what condemns you, Jason.
Hera?
Then I have nothing more to give. Nothing more to live for. Let this be the end of it.

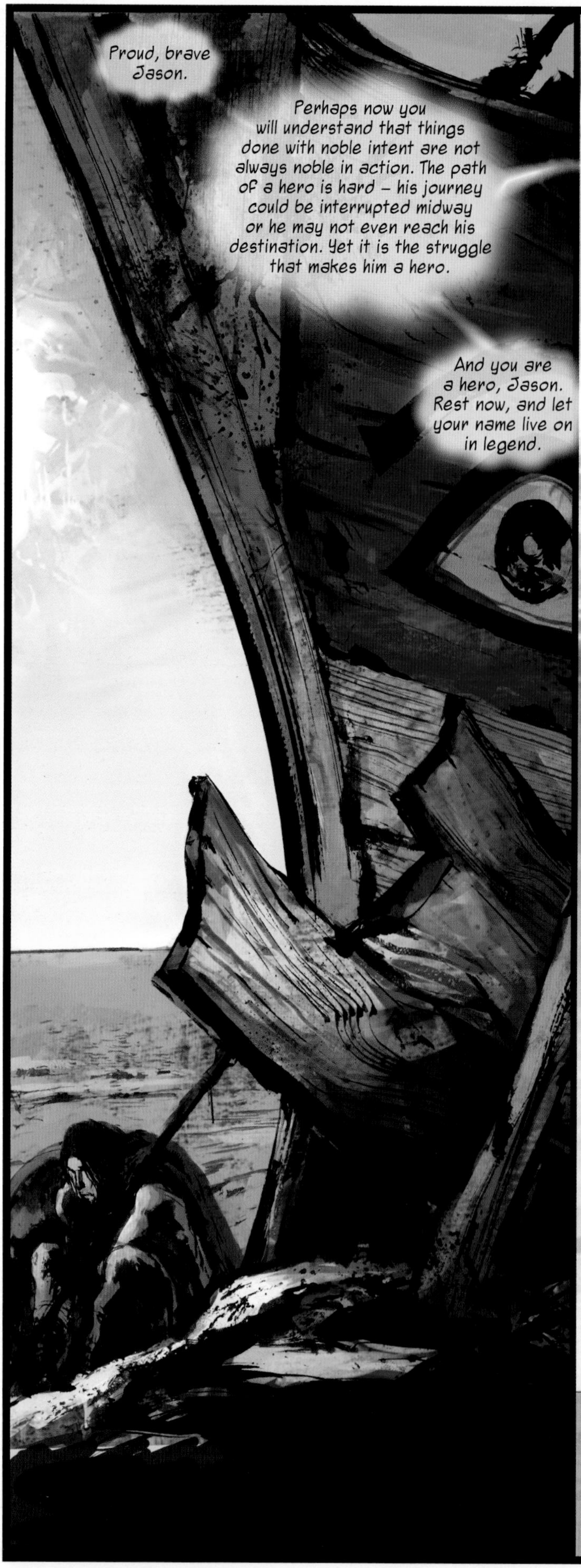
Proud, brave Jason.
Perhaps now you will understand that things done with noble intent are not always noble in action. The path of a hero is hard – his journey could be interrupted midway or he may not even reach his destination. Yet it is the struggle that makes him a hero.
And you are a hero, Jason. Rest now, and let your name live on in legend.

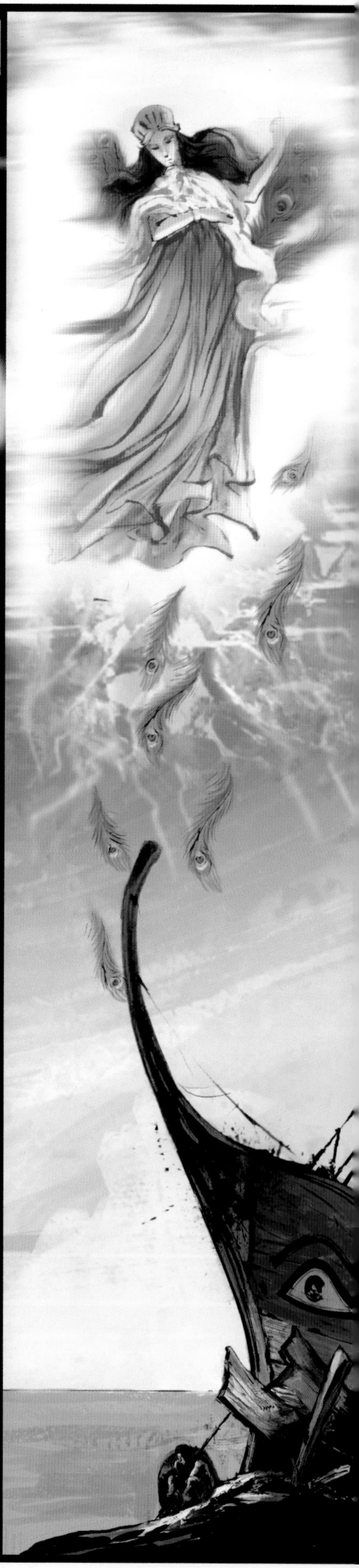

LIMPSES OF THE ARTIST'S SKETCHBOOK

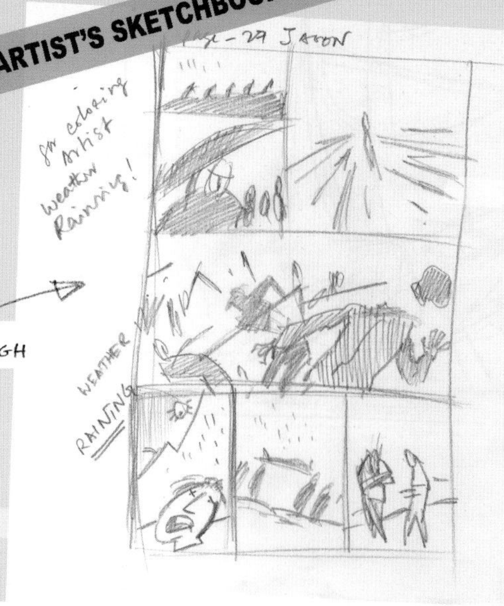

Page-29 Jason
for coloring Artist weather Raining!
WEATHER
RAINING

FIRST ROUGH

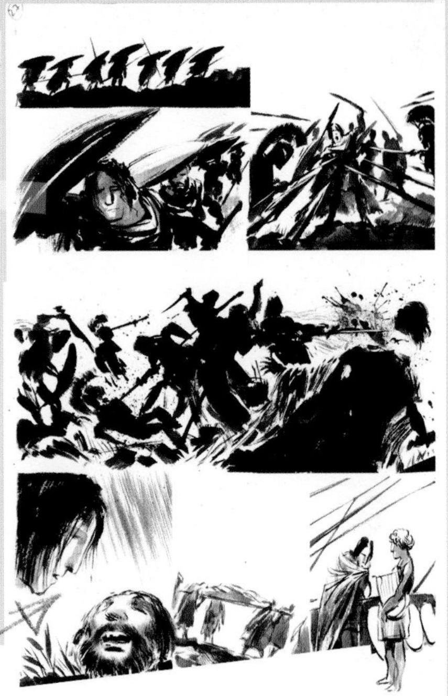

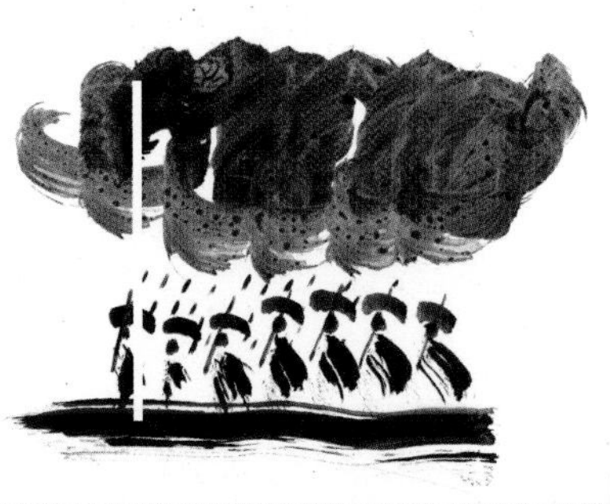

THE FINAL PANEL AND THE FINAL PAGE.

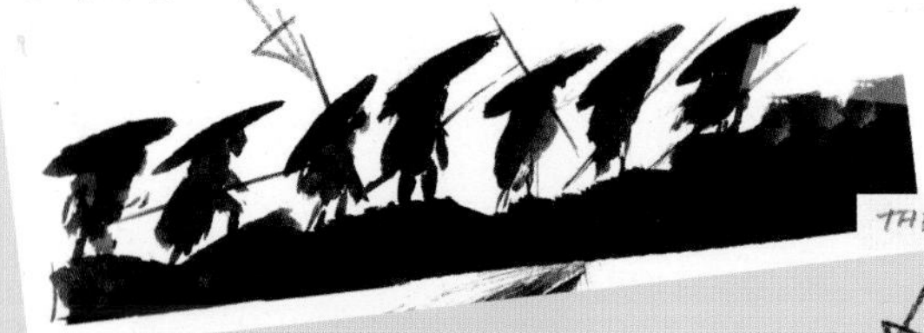

THE SFX

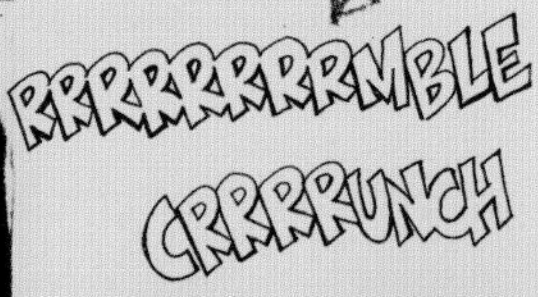

RRRRRRRRMBLE
CRRRRUNCH

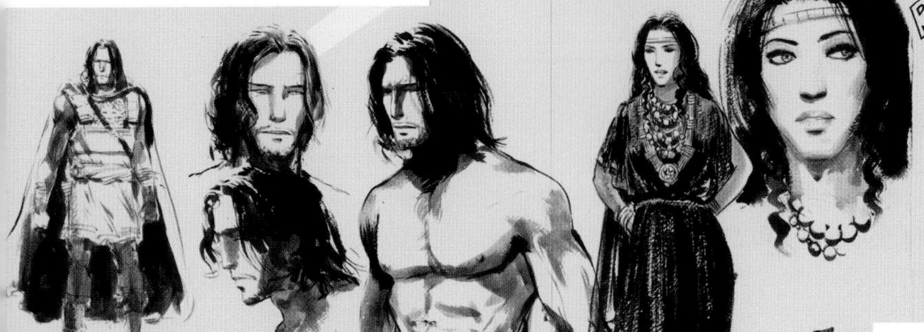

DRAWINGS FOR THE CHARACTERS!

COVERS

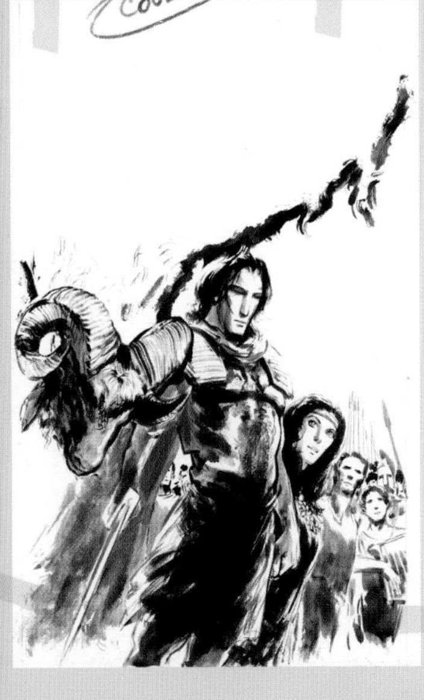

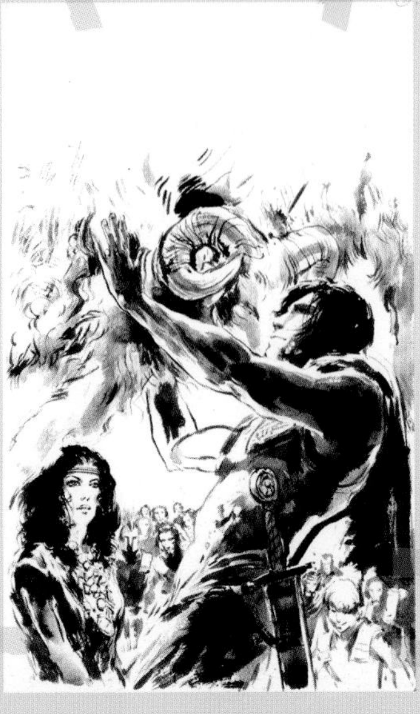

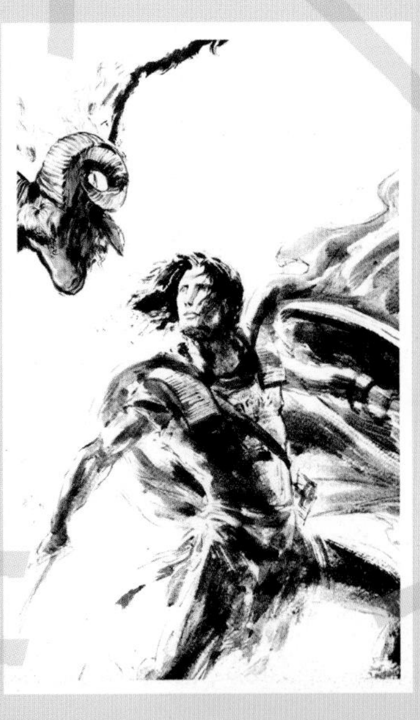

THE TALE LIVES ON...

If you think Jason and the Argonauts are limited to the world of Greek mythology, you are mistaken. Read on to discover some interesting ways in which contemporary culture uses legends and mythical characters...

Playing Jason

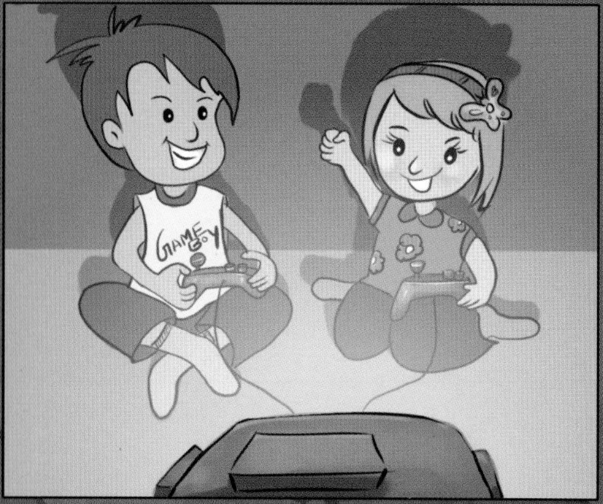
GAME BOY

Do you want to sail the *Argo* and lead the Argonauts? Then grab a CD of the video game that has been adapted from the legend of Jason and the Argonauts. In this game, the player assumes the role of Jason and sets out to seek the Golden Fleece. The aim is to overcome monstrous beasts, and traverse hostile islands and deep forests to bring back the coveted prize. Many of the greatest figures of Greek mythology, such as Heracles, Perseus, and Zeus, have also been brought to life in this medium with fantastic animation and special effects.

Jason in the sky

Jason-1, launched in 2001, is a joint project of the NASA and CNES, the space agencies of the United States and France, respectively. It is a satellite oceanography mission that monitors global ocean circulation. Named after Jason, the project is aimed at increasing our understanding of oceans better by measuring the temperature of the water, the moisture in the air, the movement of the tides, and the changes in sea levels. The results of these tests help us to predict the weather more accurately and forecast the intensity of hurricanes. Jason-1 also provides data to track ocean mammals, like whales, and monitor and route ships on the oceans. Interestingly, there is also an observation system called Argo, which gives data to conduct research on climate, weather, oceanography, and fisheries.

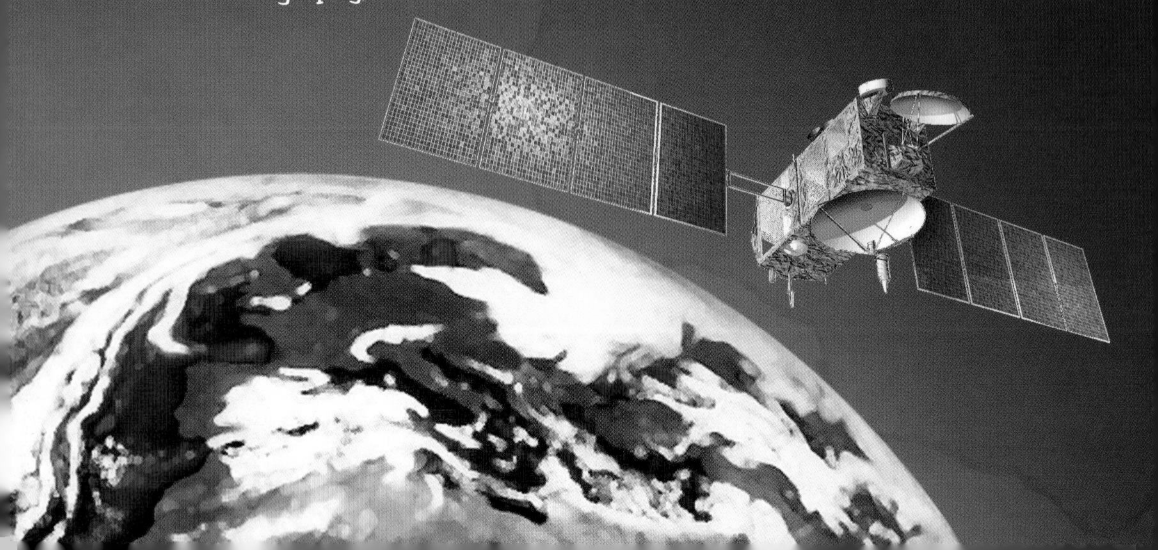

Jason, the founder

Jason is believed to be the mythical founder of Ljubljana, the capital city of Slovenia. According to legend, while sailing back with the Fleece, the Argonauts stopped by a huge lake surrounded by a marsh. It was home to the Ljubljana Dragon, which Jason bravely fought and killed. Ljubljana uses this dragon as its symbol today. The city's flag, as well as its coat of arms, depicts a dragon on top of a castle in remembrance of Jason's heroic adventures.

Jason's *Argo* sets sail

In 2008 a team of shipbuilders built a replica of the *Argo*, modelling it on an ancient Greek warship, the penteconter. It has fifty oars and a ram to attack and sink enemy ships. What is remarkable is that the team built it without any modern machinery. For three years they worked with only iron tools and wood, employing ancient Greek methods. Around 5,000 wooden pegs and wedges, made from the wood of oak and pine trees, were used to hold the ship's frame together. The modern 28-metre ship sailed from Volvos in Greece to Venice in Italy, tracing part of Jason's return journey on its two-month long voyage.

DID YOU KNOW?

The Harpy Eagle is named after the Harpies in the Greek legends. It is one of the world's largest and most powerful eagles, and has talons the size of a grizzly bear's claws! It's mostly found in Central and South America, but its numbers are declining due to deforestation and hunting.

CAMPFIRE
ABHIMANYU SINGH SISODIA
RAVANA
ROAR OF THE DEMON KING
ART BY SACHIN NAGAR

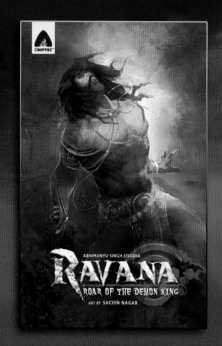

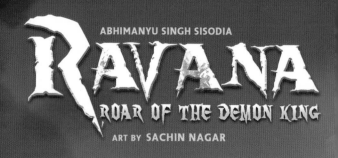

ABHIMANYU SINGH SISODIA

RAVANA

ROAR OF THE DEMON KING

ART BY SACHIN NAGAR

If any character in mythology has as many apologists as it has denouncers, it is Ravana.

Born of a union between Brahmin intelligence and demonic aggression, Ravana rose from the obscurity of life in a hermitage to conquer the world, and beyond. No less than a god to his own people, he is the embodiment of evil to his enemies. This arrogant demon brooks no hindrance to snatching his heart's desire, and his terror seems unstoppable even to the gods. But then he makes the mistake of abducting the wife of Lord Rama, the divine prince of Ayodhya.

Ravana is the story of a demon who dared to challenge the gods, and almost got away with it. So what was it that proved to be the downfall of someone as powerful as Ravana? Was it only the desire for a woman? Or was it something more, rooted in the incidents of his life, in the history of his race?

Culminating in a massive battle at his island fortress, Ravana's tale is one that never fails to inspire awe and fear.

CAMPFIRE™

www.campfire.co.in

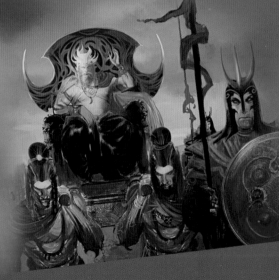

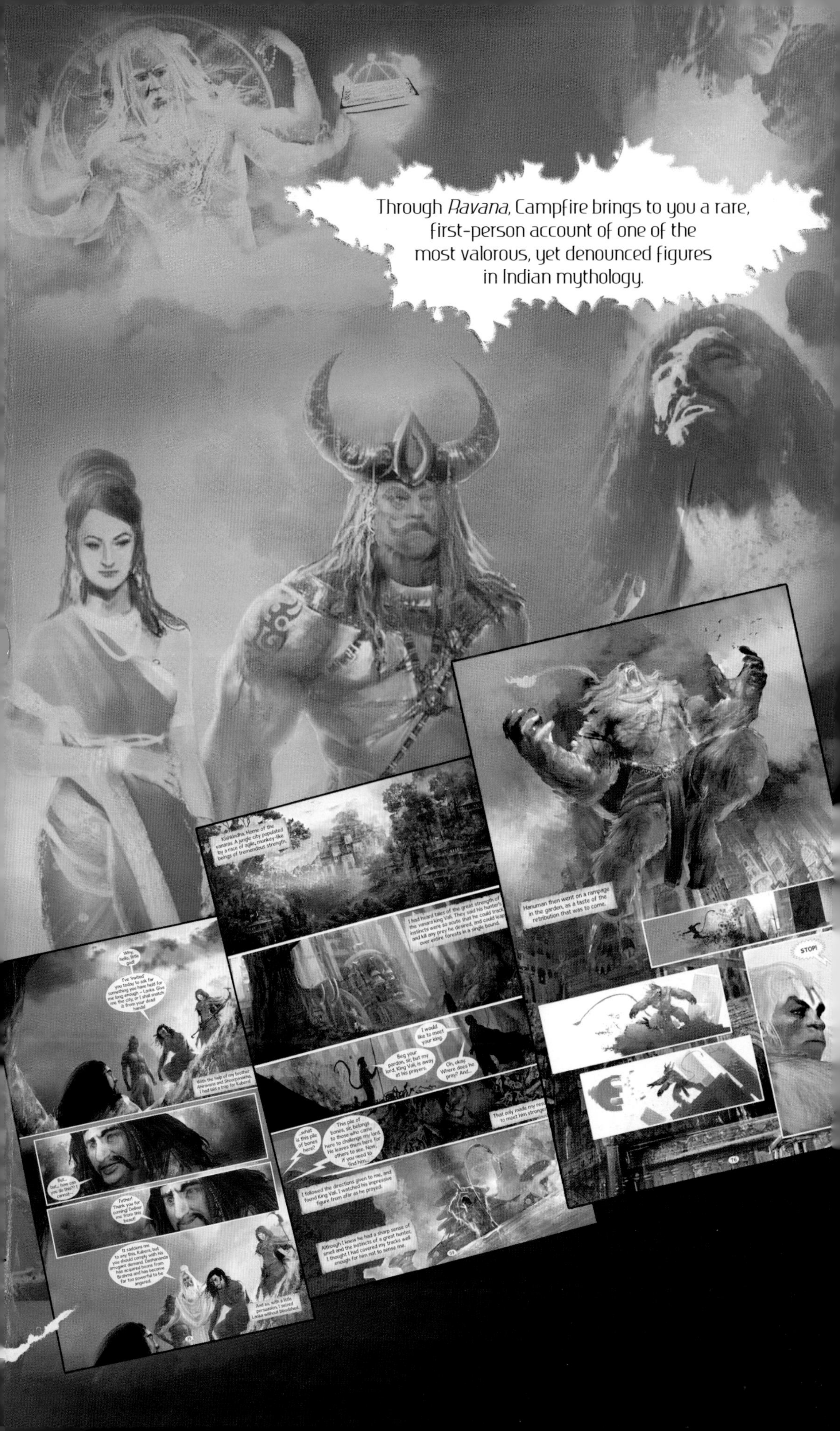
Through *Ravana*, Campfire brings to you a rare, first-person account of one of the most valorous, yet denounced figures in Indian mythology.
Why, hello, little god!
I've 'invited' you today to ask for something you have held for me long enough – Lanka. Give me the city, or I shall snatch it from your dead hands!
With the help of my brother Ahiravana and Shoorpanakha, I had laid a trap for Kubera!
But... but... how can you do this?? I cannot--
Father! Thank you for coming! Deliver me from this beast!
It saddens me to say this, Kubera, but you should comply with his arrogant demand. Dashananda has acquired boons from Brahma and has become far too powerful to be angered.
And so, with a little persuasion, I seized Lanka without bloodshed.
25
Kishkindha. Home of the vanaras. A jungle city populated by a race of agile, monkey-like beings of tremendous strength.
I had heard tales of the great strength of the vanara king Vali. They said his hunter's instincts were so acute that he could track and kill any prey he desired, and could leap over entire forests in a single bound.
I would like to meet your king.
Beg your pardon, sir, but my lord, King Vali, is away at his prayers.
Oh, okay. Where does he pray? And...
...what is this pile of bones here?
This pile of bones, sir, belongs to those who came here to challenge my lord. He leaves them here for others to see. Now, if you need to find him...
I followed the directions given to me, and found King Vali. I watched his impressive figure from afar as he prayed.
Although I knew he had a sharp sense of smell and the instincts of a great hunter, I thought I had covered my tracks well enough for him not to sense me.
59
Hanuman then went on a rampage in the garden, as a taste of the retribution that was to come.
STOP!
76

You may also like to read other titles from our **MYTHOLOGY SERIES**

RYAN FOLEY'S
LEGEND
THE LABOURS OF HERACLES
ILLUSTRATED BY
SANKHA BANERJEE

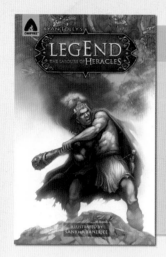

LEGEND THE LABOURS OF HERACLES

Heracles has it all: a beautiful home, a loving family, and a reputation as a great soldier who would stop at nothing to defend his homeland. As a result of a viscious plot, he is hypnotised into committing the worst crime of all. He finally finds solace in the fact that he can atone for his sins by completing ten impossible tasks. Where other men would give up and accept defeat, Heracles is undeterred in his mission. Will he succeed? Or has destiny other plans for him?

STOLEN HEARTS THE LOVE OF EROS AND PSYCHE

Aphrodite, the Greek goddess of beauty grows jealous of the praise being heaped upon a young mortal girl named Psyche. Under her instructions, her son, Eros, the god of love, performs a nasty trick that backfires when he falls in love with Psyche. But then Psyche is tempted into doing the forbidden, and is spurned by Eros. Nevertheless, she sets out against impossible odds to regain the trust of her one true love. A wonderful story of love, penance, and redemption.

STOLEN
HEARTS
The love of Eros and Psyche
Ryan Foley
Illustrated by Sankha Banerjee

Saraswati Nagpal
Sita
Daughter of the Earth
Illustrated by Manikandan

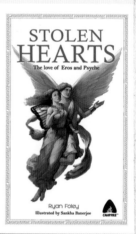

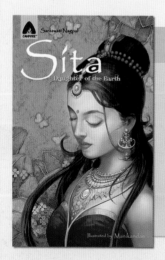

SITA DAUGHTER OF THE EARTH

Sita is the kind-hearted and intelligent princess of Videha. Married to Rama, Prince of Ayodhya, her journey in life takes her from exhilaration to anguish. Ensnared in the evil plans of the wicked demon-king Ravana, Sita is abducted and hidden away. Will Rama muster up a strong army to rescue Sita from the demon's clutches? Will Sita return to Ayodhya to become queen of the land? Adapted from the ancient Indian epic, the *Ramayana*, this is a touching tale of love, honour, and sacrifice in an unforgiving world.